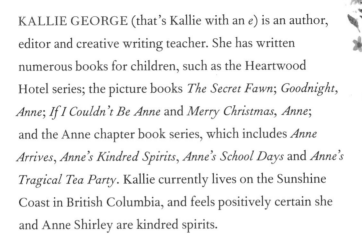

KALLIE GEORGE (that's Kallie with an *e*) is an author, editor and creative writing teacher. She has written numerous books for children, such as the Heartwood Hotel series; the picture books *The Secret Fawn*; *Goodnight, Anne*; *If I Couldn't Be Anne* and *Merry Christmas, Anne*; and the Anne chapter book series, which includes *Anne Arrives*, *Anne's Kindred Spirits*, *Anne's School Days* and *Anne's Tragical Tea Party*. Kallie currently lives on the Sunshine Coast in British Columbia, and feels positively certain she and Anne Shirley are kindred spirits.

ABIGAIL HALPIN is an illustrator living in southern Maine, a few miles from the sea. Her illustrations are a blend of traditional and digital media, and she has illustrated many beautiful children's books, including *Mama's Belly*, *Finding Wild* and the Anne chapter book series. Her parents gave her a copy of *Anne of Green Gables* for her eighth birthday, which still sits on a bookcase in her studio, and her work for *Anne's School Days* was influenced by her teen memories of Prince Edward Island as one of the most beautiful, magical spots on the planet.

To my Gilbert —K.G.

For Aunt Polly and Uncle Richard —A.H.

With undying gratitude to L.M. Montgomery for creating the classic story on which this book is based.

Paperback edition published by Tundra Books, 2022

Text copyright © 2021 by Kallie George
Illustrations copyright © 2021 by Abigail Halpin

Tundra Books, an imprint of Penguin Random House Canada Young Readers, a division of Penguin Random House of Canada Limited

Library and Archives Canada Cataloguing in Publication

Title: Anne's school days / adapted by Kallie George ; pictures by Abigail Halpin.
Names: George, K. (Kallie), 1983- author. | Halpin, Abigail, illustrator.
Series: George, K. (Kallie), 1983- Anne chapter book ; 3.
Description: Series statement: An Anne chapter book ; 3 | Inspired by Anne of Green Gables. | Previously published: 2021.
Identifiers: Canadiana 2021015375X | ISBN 9780735267343 (softcover)
Subjects: LCSH: Shirley, Anne (Fictitious character)—Juvenile fiction.
Classification: LCC PS8563.E6257 A83 2022 | DDC jC813/.6—dc23

Published simultaneously in the United States of America by Tundra Books of Northern New York, an imprint of Penguin Random House Canada Young Readers, a division of Penguin Random House of Canada Limited

Library of Congress Control Number: 2020936939

Acquired by Tara Walker
Edited by Peter Phillips
Designed by Emma Dolan
The artwork in this book was rendered in graphite, watercolor and colored pencil, and completed digitally.
The text was set in Fournier.

Printed in China

www.penguinrandomhouse.ca

1 2 3 4 5   26 25 24 23 22

Penguin
Random House
TUNDRA BOOKS

INSPIRED BY ANNE OF GREEN GABLES

Anne's
SCHOOL DAYS

ADAPTED BY
KALLIE GEORGE

PICTURES BY
ABIGAIL HALPIN

tundra

CHAPTER 1

Everyone loved autumn in Avonlea.
Especially Anne of Green Gables.

"What a splendid day," said Anne to
Diana Barry as they walked to school.
"Isn't it good to be alive on a day like this?"

Three weeks of school had gone by and,
so far, Anne loved it.

She loved walking to school through Lover's Lane.

She loved all the new friends she had made. Prissy Andrews even said Anne had a pretty nose. Anne was very sensitive about her looks (*especially* her red hair).

Most of all, Anne loved sharing these moments with her best friend — her bosom friend — Diana.

Today, Diana had news.

"Did you hear?" said Diana. "Gilbert Blythe is coming to school. He was away visiting cousins, but he's back now."

"Gilbert Blythe?" asked Anne.

"He's very handsome, Anne," said Diana. "He's smart, too. Just like you."

Anne didn't care that he was handsome. But she was glad that he was smart.

"Good," said Anne. She was top of their class. Though she *would* like a little challenge.

CHAPTER 2

The Avonlea schoolhouse was a white building, with one big room. The desks had lids that opened and shut. Behind the school, there was a silvery stream where all the students put their milk to keep it cool and sweet until lunch.

Anne sat with Diana.
Gilbert sat nearby.

"What do you think of him, Anne?" whispered Diana.

Anne looked at Gilbert. He had curly brown hair and hazel eyes that twinkled with trouble. He was busy pinning Ruby Gillis's braid to the back of her seat. When he saw Anne looking at him, he winked.

"He *is* handsome," Anne whispered back to Diana. "But he's *very* bold. It isn't good manners to wink at a strange girl. Or pin a girl's braid."

Anne turned away and quickly forgot about
Gilbert. Instead, she gazed off and started
imagining. Anne loved imagining. This
time, she dreamed she was a fancy lady with
puffed sleeves and glossy black hair.

All of a sudden, she was tugged out of her
daydream.

It was Gilbert.

He had slid over and now he was pulling *her* braid!

"Carrots," he whispered.

Anne's eyes went wide. Anne's red hair was her lifelong sorrow. That was the worst name Gilbert could call her. The worst name *anyone* could call her.

CHAPTER 3

"*Carrots!*" Gilbert teased louder.

"How dare you!" Anne cried. "You mean boy!"

Anne jumped up, holding her writing slate.

In the blink of an eye, she was behind
Gilbert and . . .

CRACK!

She hit him over the head with the slate.

"Oh!" everyone gasped.

Gilbert gasped the loudest. He wasn't hurt,
but he *was* surprised.

Anne froze.

Their teacher, Mr. Phillips, was furious.

"It was my fault," said Gilbert quickly.
"I teased her."

Mr. Phillips did not listen to Gilbert. He made Anne stand in front of the class. Then he wrote on the board, "Ann Shirley has a very bad temper." And he forgot the *e*. It was horrible.

But Anne did not cry. She did not hang her head. She was too angry. Her heart was hurt to its core.

After school, Anne marched home with Diana. Gilbert caught up to them.

"I'm sorry I made fun of your hair," he said. "Honest, I am." But his smile still teased.

Anne swept silently past him. Diana followed.

"Gilbert makes fun of all the girls," Diana whispered to Anne. "But I've never heard him apologize before. You should forgive him."

Anne shook her head. "My feelings have been hurt — *excruciatingly*. I will never forgive him. Never!"

CHAPTER 4

Anne didn't think things could get worse with Gilbert.

But they did.

The next day, at lunch, all the students were playing in the spruce grove near the school.

The boys climbed trees. The girls played below. Anne was daydreaming as usual.

She put lilies in her hair and made up poems as she wandered through the woods.

When the bell rang, Anne was late, along with the boys.

Mr. Phillips didn't want to punish everyone. Instead, he decided to punish only Anne. After all, she had caused trouble the day before.

"Anne, since you are so fond of the boys' company, you will have to share a desk with one," he said. "Go sit next to Gilbert."

Anne went pale.

"Did you hear me, Anne?" asked Mr. Phillips.

"Yes, but I didn't think you really meant it," said Anne.

"I did," said Mr. Phillips sternly. "That is your new seat for the rest of the year."

It was so unfair. The boys had been late, too. And to have to sit with Gilbert Blythe. Anne could not bear it. She flopped her head on the desk. She didn't even want to look at Gilbert.

What could Anne do?

When school was over, Anne took her books and her pen and ink and piled them on her broken slate.

"What are you doing?" asked Diana.

"I am not coming back to school," declared Anne.

Diana gasped. "What will I do without you?"

Anne didn't know. She would miss Diana, too. But her mind was made up.

At Green Gables, Anne made the same announcement.

"Nonsense," said Marilla. Marilla and her brother, Matthew, had adopted Anne not so long ago. Matthew was shy and understanding, while Marilla was stern.

"It isn't nonsense," said Anne stubbornly. "I will do my lessons here and be a good girl. But I am *not* going back. I was insulted."

"Insulted, fiddlesticks!" exclaimed Marilla.

But when Marilla heard the whole story, she took Anne's side. It wasn't fair what Mr. Phillips had done. Matthew thought so, too.

So Marilla decided Anne could stay at home — at least for a little while.

"Sooner or later, Anne will want to go back," thought Marilla.

CHAPTER 6

Marilla was right. As much as Anne disliked Gilbert, she loved Diana. She just couldn't be apart from her. Eventually, Anne went back to school.

She did not talk to Gilbert.

Many months passed. Mr. Phillips left for a new job, and Miss Stacy took his place. Right away, Anne felt she was a kindred spirit. When the new teacher said Anne's name, Anne just knew she was saying it with an *e*.

Still, Anne did not talk to Gilbert. She did not even look at him.

Until one day.

It was hot, and Anne, Diana and two other
schoolmates, Jane and Ruby, were standing at
the bank of the pond. They were playacting a
poem about a beautiful maiden, Elaine, who
lived in the lilies. She was called the Lily Maid.

In the poem, Elaine floated down a river in a
boat. It was *so* romantic. Anne and her friends
didn't have a river or a boat. But they *did* have
a wooden raft and the pond.

"You should be Elaine, Anne," said Diana.

"I'd love to," said Anne. "But Elaine didn't have red hair."

"Your hair is ever so much darker than before," said Diana. "It's practically auburn."

"Really?" Anne blushed with delight. She climbed on the raft.

She lay down, just the way she imagined Elaine would lie down, with her hands clasped on her chest.

The other girls pushed the raft into the water.

For a few moments, Anne drifted across the pond. She was enjoying how romantic it was.

Then something happened that *wasn't* romantic.

The raft began to leak!

CHAPTER 7

Elaine — *Anne* — sat up in a hurry. She gazed blankly at the big crack.

Where were the oars? Left behind!

What was she going to do? She would sink before she made it to shore. There was one chance. Just one. The bridge was near.

When the raft floated under the bridge, Anne jumped onto one of the bridge's posts. She clung on to the post and watched as her wooden raft sank.

Diana, Jane and Ruby saw the raft disappear. But they didn't see Anne. They shrieked and ran for help.

Meanwhile, Anne clung to the post for dear life. Why didn't someone come? How long could she hang on?

CHAPTER 8

At first, Anne thought she imagined Gilbert. But he was really there, rowing under the bridge in a boat.

"Anne Shirley, how on earth did you get there?" he exclaimed.

Gilbert didn't wait for an answer. He put out his hand. Anne had no choice. She reached for it and scrambled into the boat.

"What happened?" he asked, taking up the oars.

Anne explained. To her surprise, Gilbert didn't make fun of her.

Instead, when they landed on shore, he said,
"Look here, Anne. Can't we be friends?
I'm so sorry I made fun of your hair that
one time. Please don't stay mad."

For once, he didn't look like he was teasing.
Anne paused. Maybe Gilbert did deserve
a second chance. She had made lots of
mistakes before, too.

She wasn't sure what to say.

"I have to go, Gilbert," she answered at last. "Everyone will be worried about me."

"Okay." Gilbert waved as she left.

And Anne waved back.

As Anne ran to her friends, she knew something had changed. She might not ever be able to fully forgive Gilbert. After all, he *had* called her Carrots. But she wasn't mad anymore.

Back at Green Gables, Anne told everyone what had happened.

"Thank goodness you are all right," Marilla clucked.

"How romantic," gushed Diana.

Anne did not think so. Still, she smiled. As much as she wasn't sure about Gilbert, she was sure of one thing. She loved her kindred spirits and Green Gables very much. But she didn't say it aloud like she usually did.

Instead, she kept the dear, pretty thought in her heart, like a treasure. Maybe Anne had changed, just a little. But she'd always be Anne, with an *e*.

IRREDEEMABLY ... ROMANTIC?

"Shall I threaten to fall upon my nonexistent sword if you don't marry me right away or will following you about with puppy-like adoration suffice?"

Cleo could not help but giggle again. "Oh, falling on your sword would be far more entertaining."

"Bloodthirsty wretch," he quipped. "So, what exactly do you plan? And how can I help?"

Cleo purposely looked out at the dancers. Leslie was as game as he'd always been, but she could not shake the feeling that the playmate of her youth was gone. She could not remember admiring the feel of muscle under his coat as she did now. Nor imagine how it might feel to rest her head against his chest and feel his arms around her.

"Cleo?" He pulled on her arm so that she must face him. "You do have a plan, don't you?"

His dark eyes were narrowed with obvious confusion. His head was cocked as he watched her, and she could see that the sophistication he put on was little more than a mask. Deep down, he was still the same Leslie from her childhood. He'd ridden and hunted and fished with her. They had shared scrapes and scraps together. Surely he would understand.

"Yes, Leslie," she admitted. "I have a plan. And it is not so far from what you jokingly suggested. I think we should pretend to fall madly in love with each other and behave so reprehensibly that our families have no choice but to leave us alone, once and for all."

The Irredeemable Miss Renfield

Regina Scott

ZEBRA BOOKS
Kensington Publishing Corp.
http://www.kensingtonbooks.com

ZEBRA BOOKS are published by

Kensington Publishing Corp.
850 Third Avenue
New York, NY 10022

All Kensington titles, imprints, and distributed lines are
available at special quantity discounts for bulk purchases for
sales promotion, premiums, fund-raising, educational or in-
stitutional use.

Special book excerpts or customized printings can also be
created to fit specific needs. For details, write or phone the
office of the Kensington Special Sales Manager: Kensington
Publishing Corp., 850 Third Avenue, New York, NY 10022.
Attn. Special Sales Department. Phone: 1-800-221-2647.

Pinnacle and the P logo Reg. U.S. Pat. & TM Off.

First Printing: December 2001
10 9 8 7 6 5 4 3 2 1

Printed in the United States of America

To Joan Hepperlen and Kristin Manke,
who always wanted Leslie to get his own story.

One

Leslie Petersborough, the recently vested Marquis of Hastings, was used to being summarily summoned. He hadn't spent five years shadowing London's favorite scandalmaker, Chas Prestwick, for nothing. He'd received requests to abduct opera dancers and purchase prize horseflesh. He'd even been coerced into helping steal a stained sofa, just so the high stickler to whom it belonged would not know of Prestwick's mischief in her home. Of course, those requests had halted abruptly last year when his friend had married the unflappable Anne Fairchild. To make matters worse, he'd gone and inherited a title, of all things. Because of the two events, Chas had determined that he must live the life of depressingly sedate respectability, leaving Leslie alone on the stage.

But there was always his father. Leslie was also quite used to receiving odd requests from the former Marquis of Hastings. Once he'd had to rescue a wagonload of smuggled French liquor. Another time he'd hidden a Prussian prince from assassins. When one was the son of the man who ran England's elite spy ring, one had to be prepared for anything. On the other hand, he was more often summoned into his father's presence to receive a dressing down for his latest escapade. His father had had distinct ideas on the role and conduct of a gentleman, and he and Leslie had been known to disagree. Still, the old bird had been a constant source of encouragement, companionship, and admonishment. Who would have thought his courageous father could have been carried off by something as simple as a sudden bout of influenza? Now, six months later, Leslie still wasn't fully recovered from the loss. He felt as if a part of himself had gone missing.

But it was most unfair of his godmother, Lady Agnes DeGuis, to take advantage of his moment of weakness to step into the role of guardian. He glanced again at the note she had written him, pausing in his stroll up Baker Street.

"You promised me to marry after you completed mourning," she had written in sharp, black lines. "I understand you have recently put off the black. You may call on me at three in the afternoon on Tuesday next to discuss your choice of bride."

Leslie snorted, pocketing the note. His choice of bride? If he knew Lady Agnes, she didn't intend to give him a choice. Not that it appeared to matter. Each year's crop of debutantes seemed more vacuous and cloying than the last. He'd have sooner married his godmother. Not one female of his acquaintance possessed her unique blend of insight and plainspeaking. Of course, that was probably all to the good. If every female in London refused to talk unless she could fight, the Season would be a decidedly difficult feat.

It would, however, be a blasted sight more entertaining. As the Marquis of Hastings, he was expected to attend one tedious ball after another. If he had something better to do, he might have been able to come up with a plausible excuse to ignore his godmother's summons.

He continued up the street, looking for the rented house in which his godmother was staying for the Season. He couldn't help noticing that the houses here were a cut below those in more fashionable Mayfair. What was Lady Agnes doing in one of them? She had her own inheritance, he knew, and even if she hadn't, her nephew, Lord Thomas DeGuis, would have seen the old bird set up in fine style. By all that was holy, Leslie would have been happy to support her himself. She hardly needed to pinch pennies at her age. But then, he could imagine what she'd say if he proposed to make her a kept woman.

His smile tilted up at one corner as he considered the other woman he hoped to keep in such a fashion. Miss Lolly Dupray was one of the most delectable opera dancers to perform at Covent Garden in years. Warm, willing, and wondrously built, Miss Dupray already had three titled gentlemen angling for the honor of paying all her bills. Leslie fully intended to be the winner.

But first he had to fend off his godmother. That, he knew from experience, would be no easy matter. Lady Agnes had been a part of his life for as long as he could remember. She held the singular honor of being the only person besides himself who could actually make his father angry. When his mother had been alive, Lady Agnes had visited often. He couldn't remember an early birthday without her smiling face at the table. But once he went to Eton, her involvement had dwindled to a regular supply of outrageously witty letters, which he had been sadly neglectful in answering, and an annual month-long sojourn at her country house near Castle Combe. He supposed, however, that with his father gone, she was all the family he had left. The fact made him predisposed to do her bidding.

Except in a choice of bride.

He located the place, a drab stucco town house crowded close to the street. Climbing the steps, which were mercifully clean, he banged the shiny brass door knocker and grinned at the dour-faced butler who answered.

"Good afternoon, Mr. Cowls," he said. "I believe my godmother is expecting me?"

The tall, spare butler readjusted his white-powdered wig on his narrow head before answering, making Leslie step back to keep the dust from salting his navy superfine coat and gray trousers. "Lord Petersborough, is it?" he wheezed, peering at Leslie and wrinkling his long nose as if he could smell a falsehood.

Leslie knew he should correct the fellow's use of the title. With his father's passing, he was now Lord Hastings. But he had yet to feel comfortable with the title and merely nodded as Cowls opened the red-enameled door with a creak that could have come from either the barrier or the butler.

Glancing about, Leslie was relieved to see that the interior of the house appeared to be in better order, if somewhat eclectic taste. The mirror on the wall opposite him had a Baroque frame and the reflection in the amber-tinted glass made his dark hair and eyes look slightly faded. The half-moon table near the front door was a complicated black enamel with gold fittings. Reminiscent of the Egyptian furnishings that had been all the rage a few years earlier, it clashed badly with the simple style of the oak-framed landscape above it.

"Your hat, my lord?" Cowls stood stiffly, swaying slightly. As Leslie handed him his top hat, he caught a whiff of camphor and beeswax. The man not only resembled an Egyptian mummy, he smelled like one as well. But then, he had been old when Leslie had been in his teens. He had served Lady Agnes at her country house and had obviously been brought to London to serve her here as well. Again he wondered whether his godmother was in financial difficulty that she would resort to bringing the old boy out of what must have been a well-deserved retirement.

"How have you been, Mr. Cowls?" he asked politely.

The butler swung his head to peer at him through rheumy blue eyes. "I have been better, Lord Petersborough."

Leslie could well imagine that, but he decided it was safer not to say so as Cowls led him down the long marble-tiled hall and up the narrow, polished wooden stairs to the drawing room.

His first impression when he entered the room was that his godmother had somehow shrunk. He knew he was considerably taller at six feet than he had been in his youth, but she had always seemed so powerful in his mind that he was shocked to find that she only came to the top of his rib cage. Her navy dress seemed to swallow her in its voluminous folds. It did not help that the sofa beside her had massive ball-and-claw feet with an ornate back that reached nearly to her shoulders, even with her standing. Though her hair was the same iron gray he remembered from childhood, she looked frail. Certainly the rather sickly sea green paint of the lower walls of the room only made her papery skin appear more blue-veined.

In fact, the only thing in the room that looked healthy was Hector, the bright green parrot Lady Margaret DeGuis had given her a few years earlier. The fellow regarded him with a wicked black eye from his gilded cage, but, as seemed typical with the bird, he said nothing. Leslie wasn't sure he could talk; however, with the acerbic Lady Agnes as company, the bird might very wisely have decided not to compete.

The fire in his godmother's blue-gray eyes was not diminished as he stepped forward to bring her hand to his lips. That, and the strength in her slender fingers reassured him that she intended to torment him for a good many years to come. The thought was strangely reassuring.

"You are too thin," Lady Agnes declared as Leslie released her hand. "Has your cook forgotten her skills with your father gone?"

"Good afternoon to you too, Godmother," he replied with a smile. "I generally take dinner away from home, and so did Father. Cook just serves to keep that army of other servants I inherited fed."

She shook her head at such ramshackle living as she perched upon the massive sofa. Leslie sank onto the scroll-armed chair opposite her. "You will take ill that way, you wait and see," she said. "I am quite glad I chose you a wife. You obviously need one."

Leslie kept his smile in place with difficulty. "Very thoughtful of you, to be sure. But I must insist on my ability to take care of myself, and to choose my own bride, when I am ready."

She frowned. "Why would you want to choose your own bride?"

Leslie blinked. "I have needs, preferences, if you will. Marriage is a serious matter, madam, and one that takes intimate knowledge and understanding."

He was rather pleased at how mature he sounded. His godmother snorted.

"You cannot even get yourself dinner," she pointed out. "Besides, what you need is objectivity. To pick the proper mate, you need a certain distance and worldly understanding, neither of which you can claim to have."

He couldn't help but smile at her audacity. He leaned back and crossed his legs, prepared to thoroughly enjoy himself. "And you can make that claim? May I remind you, madam, respectfully, that you are a spinster, and that you have never been outside the country?"

"Precisely! I have learned by watching others, young man, countless others over the decades, making countless mistakes. I find myself in a unique position to assess marriages. In addition, I know you as well as your father did."

Leslie's smile widened. "I shall grant you that you know me better than most."

She grinned at him as well. "By the by, how is Miss Dupray these days? Has she accepted the duke's protection?"

"He offered! Blast the fellow! I could have countered anything but his title." Her grin widened, and he realized he was discussing his potential mistress with his godmother of all people. His face burned. "How the devil did you know about Miss Dupray?"

"Why do you think I brought up Mr. Cowls from the country?" Lady Agnes replied, chortling. "He has the best ear in twelve counties. I understand she is an empty-headed widgeon, by the way. From Dublin. She cannot even spell her fancy French name. I am shocked you did not see through that atrocious accent. And those red curls come from a bottle. They shall all fall out soon enough. You are well off without her."

Leslie knew his mouth was opening and shutting wordlessly and rather thought he looked a bit like Hector, green coloring and all. He shook his head. "Madam," he managed, "you astound me."

"Good," she declared, shaking out her skirts. "Now perhaps you will listen to me. It is high time you married, and I have just the girl."

"And can I assume she is without artifice?" Leslie asked with upraised brow.

"Quite," his godmother assured him. "In fact, she is already known to you. Cleopatra Renfield."

"Cleo?" Leslie blinked. His mind readily conjured up a picture of a stringy preadolescent young lady, twigs sticking out of her long dark braid, expensive gown frayed at the hem, her entire being smelling like leather and horse sweat. "Cleo Renfield? She's a child!"

"She will soon be nineteen," Lady Agnes said. "I am her chaperone for the Season. She has already been presented at court and developed no little following."

He felt as trapped as the bright-eyed parrot in his gilded cage. Leslie put a hand to his head. "But she's like a little sister to me. I cannot imagine her as a wife."

"You cannot imagine her in your bed," Lady Agnes countered, bringing the blood to his cheeks once again. Confound the woman! He hadn't blushed since Chas Prestwick had introduced him to his first opera dancer. He squared his shoulders.

"Now see here, my good woman," he told her. "That is quite enough from you about my private life. I am perfectly capable of taking care of my own affairs." She snickered, and he hurriedly amended himself. "My own life, I should say. Good God, the revered peers in Parliament saw fit to give me the titles and responsibilities of the Marquis of Hastings. I will admit I have yet to earn the right, but I certainly should be able to pick my own wife."

She narrowed her eyes. "Are you reneging on your promise, then?"

"Promise?" He cocked his head. "I don't remember making you a promise."

She wrinkled her nose impatiently. "Can you be so quick to forget your father's funeral?"

"I will never forget my father's funeral," Leslie informed her with a frown. "And, yes, I vaguely remember speaking with you then. You made some remark about continuing the line, just the sort of sentiment one often utters at funerals, comforting and encouraging and somewhat lacking in substance."

"Precisely. You replied that you would consider marrying when your mourning was complete. And you promised to let me pick the bride."

Leslie surged to his feet. "I never did!"

She raised a silver-feathered brow. "Are you calling me a liar?"

He ran a hand back through his hair. How had he gotten himself into such a situation? He knew he had to start behaving like a marquis. Indeed, there were times when he was certain he could hear his father's voice telling him just how lacking his behavior was. However, even his father would not have insisted that he honor Lady Agnes's wishes. He hated to hurt the old dear, but the last thing he needed was to be shackled to some fresh-from-the-schoolroom miss who preferred her pony to him.

"Certainly I would never wish to offend you, madam," he replied with care. "Might you, in fact, be mistaken?"

"Certainly not." She sniffed, raising her chin. "I know exactly what you said to me. And I am appalled that you would go back on your word to your own godmother. What manner of man have you become, sir?"

A rather desperate one, he thought. He sank back onto the chair and reached out to take her hands. "Lady Agnes, please. I don't remember promising to let you pick my bride. I cannot think why I would make such a statement. Perhaps I was deranged by grief. In your goodness, you cannot hold me to it."

She scowled at him for a moment more; then her gaze, usually so stern, softened. "No, I certainly cannot."

Leslie let out his breath in glorious relief.

"However," she continued, gaze once more implacable, "I can insist that you at least meet the girl. I am her godmother as well, you know, and I want her to be happy. That is more than I can say for the rest of her family."

Leslie frowned, releasing her hands and leaning back once more. "What do you mean? I thought her parents doted on her. They let her get away with almost anything when we were younger."

"Her parents have been dead for the last five years," Lady Agnes replied. "It is her sisters that concern me."

Leslie tried to dredge up a picture of them as well and only managed to form a shadowy memory of height, weight, and arrogance. "They were a great deal older than Cleo, if I recall. Have they not been happily married for some time?"

"Happiness is a relative word," his godmother said. "They are determined that she marry to advantage, even to the loss of her own happiness. She has no one to stand up for her but me; even her friends seem more focused on catching a husband than supporting her. Besides, the girl appears to have attracted that fortune-hunting Cutter fellow, who shows equally uneducated taste in Miss Dupray, if rumors serve."

"Rumors serve," Leslie replied, thinking that the

dashing major was also out of luck if Lolly accepted the duke's protection. "But Major Cutter's not such a bad chap. Cleo could do worse."

"And she could do a great deal better," she scolded him. "She is much too fine for your Major Cutter. She is lovely, intelligent, and principled."

And likely completely over her head in society, Leslie thought. If he knew Cleo, she was probably clumping about drawing rooms in her fishing boots. Still, when he was younger, her unorthodox ways had taken the edge off the summer days away from the excitement of London and studies of Eton and Oxford. For that, he owed her his continued goodwill. Besides, his father would have said it was his duty as a gentleman to assist. Perhaps helping Cleo would help him learn to be a marquis.

"I suppose it would do no harm for the girl to be seen with me," he said. "But I refuse to court her simply to please you."

"Just meet with her," Lady Agnes urged. "I think you will like what you see. I understand you have been invited to Lady Prestwick's ball at Almack's?"

Leslie nodded. "Purely as an onlooker, you understand. Every woman there will be out to snare Viscount Breckonridge. Anne told me as much."

"Widgeons," Lady Agnes replied with a shake of her head. "As if Breckonridge would choose a dewy-eyed bride. He will want a woman with intelligence and breeding, you mark my words."

"Then of course you will not take Cleo," Leslie said blandly.

He had hoped to nettle her, which she so enjoyed, and was pleased when she bristled immediately, eyes bright with challenge. "I most certainly will. She must be seen in all the right circles if she is to catch someone better than that fancy-jacketed major. But you are right that she would be wasted on Breckon-ridge."

Leslie rather thought she might. He had nothing against Breckonridge, but Lady Agnes was right that he'd surely want a wife with better social connections than a horse-mad orphan from Castle Combe.

"So, you will dance with her at the ball?" Lady Agnes pressed. "Get reacquainted?"

"Very well," Leslie replied with a sigh. "I promise to be a gentleman and meet her. I will even help her find her way in society. But I will not allow you to dictate my choice of bride, and there is nothing you or Cleopatra Renfield can do about it."

Two

Cleopatra Renfield stood stiffly along the satin-draped wall at Almack's. No one looking at her would have seen anything but a docile young debutante, she was sure. Her modest gown was of white silk with gold lamé trimming and glass bead spangles. Her long brown hair was done up in a thick bun at the nape of her neck, effectively hiding its red highlights that hinted of a fire within. She was quiet and unassuming. She hadn't spoken above four words to any gentleman all evening. She hadn't favored any of them with a second dance, no matter how hard she was begged. No one would be able to find fault in her behavior. No one would know that a rebellious heart beat in her breast.

Certainly Electra on her right and Andromeda on her left did not appear to notice anything more objectionable than usual in her. Both her half sisters stood equally stiff, though far less demure, their ostrich plume fans waving condescendingly before their dark silk ball gowns. Anyone seeing them would know them for what they were—comfortable society matrons. Never mind that Ellie had been the belle of the Season once. The tarnished blond hair in its tight bun had flowed in golden waves down her back and her amply padded girth had been a nicely curved bundle. Cleo remembered that much from her childhood. Annie had always been the plainer of the two, with her soft brown hair and perennially plump body. But even then they had known how to act in unison to thwart her.

The very fact that they had taken up residence at her side since her arrival at the assembly rooms galled her. They had insisted on chaperoning her tonight alongside Lady Agnes, as if Cleo could not be trusted to keep her word. She had agreed to meet Leslie Petersborough. There was no need for them to keep watch over her as if she were some kind of prisoner.

Yet the feeling of being on the gallows persisted as she watched others waltzing across the ballroom floor. She had not yet been given permission to waltz, despite the fact that in the four years since its introduction the dance had been embraced by most everyone in London society. Why even the Prince danced it! However, if her sisters had their way, she would never be given the opportunity to ask one of the famed lady patronesses for permission.

Indeed, it was only through Lady Agnes's connections that she had gotten vouchers for Almack's regular assemblies. Neither Ellie nor Annie were particularly well looked upon by the haughty patronesses. Ellie had married into trade, though Cleo suspected she had calculatingly chosen her wealthy husband, George Carlisle the banker. His funds had allowed Annie a better dowry, and she had married an impoverished baron. Unfortunately, the fact that Lord Stephenson gambled heavily and flirted with other men's wives kept many from receiving Annie.

But however unhappy her sisters might be, she did not think that gave them the right to make her equally wretched. She could not understand why they would begrudge her even such a little bit of fun as the waltz, but begrudge her they did. They watched the dancers now with the looks of cats who had sipped sour cream. And Cleo could do no more than stand between them and fight with herself to keep from dashing away to freedom.

She waited impatiently for any sign of her godmother. Lady Agnes had claimed to have seen Leslie arrive just as the waltz had begun and had gone off to fetch him. Unfortunately, Cleo's diminutive stature prevented her from seeing beyond the couples immediately in front of her, offering only glimpses of the rest of the attendees as the dance parted before her.

It was a tremendous crush. Lady Prestwick must have been pleased to see her first ball so well attended. Of course, Cleo had no intention of attracting the famous Lord Breckonridge. Why would she want to marry a fellow nearly old enough to be her father? But by the number of young ladies swirling past in the dance or promenading by her, she was the only unmarried female to feel that way. She could only imagine the thicker clump of bodies on the far side of the room must have been surrounding the great man himself.

"Look, it's that Compton chit," Ellie said over her head to Annie.

Annie tsked. "They swarm to her like bees to clover," she complained. "I wish she would leave a few for the rest of us."

Cleo longed to stand on tiptoe and crane her neck to see how accurate her sister's comments might be. She'd heard similar jealous comments from others concerning Miss Persephone Compton, the reigning Incomparable. But she knew her sisters would be mortified by such unladylike behavior. A lady did not call undue attention to herself. Of course, they would soon be far more than mortified if Leslie Petersborough agreed to the plan she had concocted. The problem was, she wasn't sure she could convince him to help.

She hadn't seen Leslie since the summer before her parents had died, six years ago. He had spent part of every summer near their country home, visiting the godmother they shared. Eight years her senior, he had nonetheless been ready to ride with her and fish with her and hunt with her. At least, at first. That last summer, he'd been far more interested in setting up a flirtation with the buxom barmaid at the local inn than in anything she might suggest. He'd even refused to smuggle her into the bare-knuckles brawl between the county champion and a gentleman from London.

At thirteen, she had not been particularly interested in the way a gentleman looked. Perhaps he had been handsome, but he had seemed just as gangly as she was then, all long arms and legs. He certainly didn't have the dash of one Major Anthony Cutter. But then, she didn't have the dash of one Persephone Compton. If she had the courage to proceed with her plan, she would never wear Miss Compton's Incomparable label. She rather thought the term applied to her would be Irredeemable. But none of that mattered as long as she was allowed to make her own choices.

"Miss Compton will catch Breckonridge as well," Annie predicted. "You wait and see, Mrs. Carlisle."

"I'm sure you are correct, Lady Stephenson," Ellie replied with a regretful shake of her head. "His dancing this waltz with her chaperone no doubt only serves to convince her of his devotion to every aspect of her life. A sad display."

The crowds parted for a moment, and Cleo was treated to a picture of a mature couple swirling in the dance. He was tall, his features dark and rugged, his demeanor smacking of a man used to power. She was blond, calm, composed. But the thing that struck Cleo most was the intense way they gazed into each other's eyes. Oh, to have a man gaze at her so!

She allowed a sigh to escape her and felt each of her sisters take a step closer, hemming her in as if expecting her to bolt on them. She would have liked nothing better, but she knew she had nowhere to go.

It had been that way since her parents had died. Her sisters hadn't even waited for the funeral to end before telling her that her days of pleasure were over.

"I am certain you must wonder what we plan for you," Ellie had intoned as they were walking in the funeral procession. At thirteen, Cleo hadn't wondered anything more than why God, who she had always been taught was a merciful, loving fellow, would want to take her mother and father from her. "You must grow up, Cleo."

"Father cozened you terribly," Annie added, as if that explained everything.

"And I do not approve of cozening children," Ellie had continued, as if from great experience, even though she had not been blessed with any children of her own. "As soon as things are settled here, you will be going off to school to learn to be a proper lady. No more of this wildness, miss."

She hadn't been certain exactly what wildness she was supposed to stop but soon learned it seemed to have something to do with everything she found enjoyable. She had loved their little manor house near Castle Combe. She had to vacate it for the distant male relative who had inherited it. She loved her books and childhood toys given to her by her parents and godmother. She was forced to choose only a few personal belongings that would fit in a trunk for school and watch the others given away to charity. Above all, she loved her precious horse Pegasus, spending hours each day in the saddle or combing and currying the lovely bay mare. She had sobbed as their neighbor, Mr. Matthews, had led the horse away for his odious son Kirby. That was when she discovered she did not know how to be a lady.

Ellie and Annie knew all about being ladies. Their mother, it seemed, had been one, while Cleo's had not. They had any number of rules to prove they were ladies. Ladies did not ride astride. Ladies did not fish or hunt. Ladies didn't do anything even remotely smacking of fun, that she could tell.

She had hoped the school they chose for her might be easier, but if anything it was worse. There, ladies did nothing but paint with watercolors, carry on conversations about the weather, and bat their insipid eyes until some fellow took pity and married them. Between her sisters and the Barnsley School for Young Ladies, she had been given a very thorough grounding in what it took to be a lady.

She still wasn't sure she wanted to be one.

The waltz ended. The couples parted, and several applauded Lord Breckonridge and Miss Compton's chaperone, who was her cousin Miss Sarah Compton, if memory served. Cleo rather hoped the elder Miss Compton had won the man's heart. He had certainly looked besotted.

As her view widened, she spotted several of her former classmates across the room, all now debutantes like herself. Her friend Marlys Rutherford raised a hand in greeting. The others quickly hid behind their fans, causing her to pale and lower her hand. Marlys didn't flaunt the rules; she had a tyrannical mother and a healthy fear of censure. Cleo liked her all the better for her show of bravery.

The fans were set once more in motion as another of their classmates glided by. Eloise Watkin had been the year ahead of her in school and quite the envy of her classmates. The well-curved beauty had dressed in a modestly cut gown of pale peach, designed to draw attention to her considerable assets. Most of the men present were noticing, pausing in their conversations as she approached, raising their quizzing glasses as she passed. Even Major Cutter, the most interesting man of Cleo's acquaintance, had shown a marked preference for her company.

"She is as cruel as Miss Compton in keeping the gentlemen's attention," Marlys had complained only yesterday. "Why, when Major Cutter favored her with two dances at the Badgerly ball last week, I was possessed of an unladylike desire to spill punch all down the front of her expensive gown."

"It would only have made it cling all the more," Cleo had pointed out with a commiserating smile.

Marlys might envy Eloise, but Cleo had other feelings entirely. In the five years she'd known the girl, Eloise had always craved attention. She had won the best marks; excelled at voice, pianoforte, and harp; and mastered her seat on a horse. Only Cleo and the head mistress of the Barnsley School knew just how far she'd go to get the attention she so prized.

And Cleo had promised never to tell.

"Here comes Lady Agnes," Ellie said sharply, interrupting her thoughts. "Smile, Cleo!"

"Remember your manners," Annie added, stiffening. "Do nothing to make him take you in dislike."

Cleo stiffened as well, but even that did not give her a view of her godmother. Then, suddenly, the people in front of her moved aside, and she gasped.

Leslie Petersborough was little like what she remembered. He had grown into his long legs and large hands. Indeed, he filled the shoulders and chest of the well-cut black evening coat as well as the spotless white satin breeches with a lithe body that moved gracefully and confidently. She didn't think the glossy shine in his short, straight black hair was from a cosmetic jar, or the spring in his step from endless hours over a gaming table. Eyes that were once as friendly as hot chocolate now percolated with something far warmer and more potent.

The only thing about him that hadn't changed was his self-deprecating half smile. Even as he approached, one side of his mouth tilted up in wry appreciation. She wasn't sure what he found so very amusing, but it did her composure little good. How could she possibly propose her plan to such a paragon?

"I feared we would not get here alive," Lady Agnes complained, fanning herself with her hand. "What a crush. My dear Leslie, you remember Lady John Stephenson and Mrs. George Carlisle. And, of course, my goddaughter, Miss Cleopatra Renfield. Annie, Ellie, Cleo, Lord Hastings."

Annie and Ellie dropped deep curtsies. Cleo almost followed suit, but Leslie's hand shot forward to clasp one of hers. Her fingers were dwarfed in his grip.

"My dear Miss Renfield," he intoned, "how you have grown."

Cleo stared at him. His voice was as warm as a fur-trimmed cloak and just as enveloping. Her heart started beating unaccountably fast. He inclined his head, slowly bringing her hand to his lips. The scent of leather and mint washed over her. He pressed a kiss against her knuckles, and she caught her breath. Then, under cover of his kiss, he pressed his thumb more deeply into her fingers in a quick caress. Goose bumps pimpled her arms.

Annie elbowed her in the side, and she remembered that ladies were supposed to respond to a gentleman's advances. "Lord Hastings," she murmured, "you are much changed as well."

She managed to drop a curtsey at last, hoping that would force him to release her hand. Instead, he merely used her movement as an excuse to hold her hand even longer, ostensively to raise her back up. Again his thumb caressed her fingers.

"Not at all," he assured her, as if discussing the weather. "Would you do me the honor of a promenade? We have a number of years to catch up on."

If he was anyone else, she would have turned him down. Her emotions skittered from annoyance to fascination and back again. Leslie Petersborough had never flirted with her before. She wasn't entirely sure Leslie Petersborough knew how to flirt, the barmaid at the Castle Combe Inn notwithstanding. Who was this man pretending to be her childhood friend?

She peered up at him, confused, and for the first time saw the twinkle of glee in those dark brown eyes. He was laughing at the entire situation, playing their game the same way she was. She nearly grinned in relief but remembered herself in time.

"It would be my pleasure, my lord," she assured him, allowing him to thread her hand through his arm.

"With your gracious permission, ladies?" he inquired of her sisters.

"Certainly, Lord Hastings," Ellie purred. "Take as long as you like."

"I am certain she's in good hands with you," Annie agreed.

"Have her back in time to partner Nathan Witherall in the quadrille," Lady Agnes commanded.

Leslie made a noise that must have sounded agreeable to Lady Agnes, for all it sounded noncommittal to Cleo, and they were free. As they stepped away from her sisters, she saw them exchange triumphant glances. Only Lady Agnes looked unenthusiastic, her feathery brows drawn together over her long nose in a frown.

Cleo thought perhaps he would revert to the Leslie she remembered right away, but as they began their stroll around the dance floor, he maintained his sophisticated veneer.

"Lovely weather for this time of year, don't you think, Miss Renfield?" he asked, moving slowly through the crush of the crowd.

She could not be so serious. "Oh, most certainly, Lord Hastings," she murmured, batting her eyes vacuously. "And may I be so bold as to inquire the name of the fold of your cravat? I vow I have never seen one so elegantly tied."

He lifted his head as if to better display the rather ordinary white silk. "It's the Incomparable, if you must know. Invented it myself."

She stifled a giggle, and he cast her a quick grin before schooling his face to studied boredom once more. "Of course," he continued with a familiar glint in his eyes, "I very nearly named it the Incompetent, as it is a deuced pain to tie."

She laughed out loud, and the group of women they were passing whispered behind their fans. Leslie's narrowed-eye stare made them suck in their breaths. He turned Cleo away from them and steered her toward an empty spot near a bust of Diana.

"So, Sprout," he said when they were as alone as they could be in the crowded room. She grinned to hear his childhood nickname for her. "How are you coming on? I was sorry to hear about your parents."

"As sorry as I was to hear about your father, I'm

sure," she replied. "But I have had some time to get used to my loss. Are you all right?"

He shrugged, but she could see the flash of pain in his eyes. "Some days are better than others." He seemed to collect himself with difficulty. "But enough of the maudlin. I came here tonight with the express purpose of rescuing you."

Cleo stared at him. "You did?"

He nodded. "I am attempting to live up to my new role as the Marquis of Hastings. Care for the widows and orphans, that sort of thing. But you don't look as if you need my help. I would guess you are the belle of the Season."

"I was enjoying myself," Cleo confessed. "Until my sisters took it upon themselves to find me a husband."

"A great deal of that matchmaking going around. Are they giving you grief?"

Cleo sighed. "Extraordinary amounts. Make no mistake, Les. We're in the suds this time."

He raised a dark brow. "We?"

"As you are my intended victim, I had hoped we were in this together."

She watched as his grin quirked. "I made Lady Agnes no promises. But I feel I can tell you, Cleo, as one old friend to another. That is not the kind of rescue I envisioned. I have no interest in marrying—you or anyone else."

Cleo waited for the expected rush of relief and was surprised when it didn't come. "Nor have I any interest in marrying," she hastened to assure him all the same. "At least, not to anyone my sisters drop in my lap. And so I have told them, repeatedly. My wishes, it appears, have nothing to say in the matter. I am merely told I require a strong hand."

He muttered something under his breath, and she

was delighted to hear that it was completely derogatory of her sisters' intelligence. She giggled again, and he grinned at her.

"Baggage," he said in mock censure. He raised his head then, to gaze at the people passing them, and Cleo was forced to remember her surroundings as well. She couldn't see around the room to where her sisters and Lady Agnes waited, but the couples passing her were casting them curious gazes. She wondered whether Leslie felt as if he were on display as well, and was about to ask when she noticed his gaze was moving. Following it, she saw that he had taken particular notice of one of the young ladies at the ball, a young lady whose exquisite green eyes widened in expressive interest as she strolled past on the arm of her heavyset chaperone.

Eloise Watkin.

It was quite one thing to commiserate with Marlys over Major Cutter's interest, and another to find Leslie's attention wandering. Cleo tugged on his arm. "You *must* have developed other interests since Castle Combe."

He cocked a lazy grin, leaning back against the wall. "Since when did you notice I had an interest in women?"

Since I became one, she wanted to say, but that wasn't exactly ladylike, and somehow she wasn't comfortable saying it to Leslie at the moment. "I knew what you were doing down at the inn that last summer," she explained instead. "Every boy in the neighborhood was after that barmaid. Only think what your poor father would have said had you actually brought her home."

"Oh, never fear there," he replied with a chuckle. "I learned a long time ago that there are ladies one brings home and women one does not."

She felt a blush heating her cheeks. This was one of those conversations ladies were not supposed to have. "Well, I assure you, Eloise Watkin belongs to the 'bring home' camp."

Leslie's grin reappeared. "Eloise Watkin, is it? Are you certain? She is rather flashy. I take it you refuse to introduce me?"

"Absolutely," Cleo declared. "I am supposed to be attaching your regard for myself."

"And a tremendous job you are doing too," he replied. "Shall I threaten to fall upon my nonexistent sword if you don't marry me right away, or will following you about with puppylike adoration suffice?"

She could not help but giggle again. "Oh, falling on your sword would be far more entertaining."

"Bloodthirsty wretch," he quipped. "So, what exactly do you plan? And how can I help?"

She purposely looked out at the dancers. He was as game as he'd always been, but she could not shake the feeling that the playmate of her youth was gone. She could not remember admiring the feel of muscle under his coat as she did with this man. She could not remember being so acutely aware of how tall he was, and how tiny she felt beside him with her head near his chest. Nor imagine how it might feel to rest her head against his chest and feel his arms around her. She shook her head again.

"Cleo?" He pulled on her arm so that she must face him. "You do have a plan?"

His dark eyes were narrowed with obvious confusion. His head was cocked as he watched her, and she could see that the sophistication he put on was little more than a mask. Deep down, he was still the same old Leslie from her childhood. He knew her better than most people, surely better than her sisters. He'd ridden and hunted and fished with her. They had shared scrapes and scraps together. Surely he would understand.

"Yes, Leslie," she admitted. "I have a plan. And it is not so far from what you jokingly suggested. I think we should pretend to fall madly in love with each other and behave so reprehensibly that they have no choice but to leave us alone, once and for all."

Three

Leslie stared at her. Who *was* this woman? She couldn't possibly be the spirited little hoyden he had ridden with in Castle Combe. Someone was having him on.

Of course, he'd doubted her identity from the first moment he'd spotted her across the room. The last time he'd seen her, she'd been a scrawny thirteen-year-old intent on convincing him to smuggle her into a bare-knuckles brawl. How could such a sorry little seed have blossomed into this curvaceous young lady with doelike eyes?

She certainly didn't act like Cleo, crazed plan notwithstanding. Cleo Renfield had the rough-and-ready manners of a stable boy; this woman smiled sweetly and dimpled at his compliments. Moreover, Cleo Renfield had skin made up of several shades of brown, with one part being mud from the nearest creek bottom. This enticing lady had skin like cream, with the slightest sprinkling of cinnamon freckles across the bridge of her button nose, like spice on a frosted cake. Then there was the way she looked at him. Cleo Renfield would look at him straight on, with eyes nearly as dark as his own. This temptress had a way of slanting a look at him out of the corner of her raisin-colored eyes that made him want to beg for seconds, or howl at the moon. Only the light in those dark eyes told him that his childhood scamp still existed underneath all the window dressing. But even Cleo Renfield wouldn't have proposed such an audacious plan.

She made a face at him, her pixie nose wrinkling, those kissable rosebud lips pursing. "I've shocked you, haven't I?" she asked. "Sorry, Les. But I do believe such drastic measures are necessary. My sisters are determined."

He glanced back at the two women, spotting them easily over the top of the crowd. They were staring at him, as they'd been staring since he'd been introduced. He rather thought vultures stared like that as they waited for a calf to die in the desert, gaze full of hunger and calculation. He could almost feel their claws digging into him, searching for the choicest morsel. He suppressed a shudder, turning to Cleo.

"I can believe you feel trapped," he commiserated. "But I assure you, I will not be a willing party to this coercion."

"I wish you would," she replied petulantly. Leslie blinked, and she hurried on. "Better the devil you know than the devil you don't. Can't you see, Les? If it isn't you, they may set their sights on someone far worse!"

That was a lowering thought. Of course, he wasn't sure which was the worst of the matter—that this delightfully confusing creature might be wed to someone terrible or that she considered marriage to him to be a fairly poor deal. He felt her sisters' eyes drilling into his back and determined to move away. Taking Cleo's hand and setting it once more on his arm, he started off on a brisk trot around the room. She did not resist. Indeed, he had a feeling that if he had simply continued out the door and down the stairs to the street, Cleo would not have protested. When he was satisfied that the crowd once more blocked them from her sisters' view, he pulled her up short.

"Do you really believe they'd marry you to someone abhorrent?" he demanded.

"Completely," she assured him. "You have only to look at the men my sisters agreed to marry to know they will have no mercy."

He knew both George Carlisle and Lord Stephenson. The banker was a dour man who showed neither emotions nor mercy in his business dealings. If he were even half as cold in his personal life, Cleo's oldest sister could not have an easy time of it. On the other hand, the baron cared only for cards and other men's wives, neither of which held much promise for a happy life for his wife. The idea of Cleo, either the Cleo who had been his little playmate or this beautiful woman who claimed to be her, being wed to anyone like them turned his stomach.

"But surely your sisters wish to see you happy," he protested. "I was never blessed with siblings, but I always wished for a brother or sister to care for. I know I'd take particular pains to see someone in my family happily settled."

She lowered her gaze. "I suppose Ellie and Annie think they are doing what is right. They seem convinced they're working in my best interests. At fourteen and thirteen years my senior, they believe they have the right to make all my decisions. I won't have it, Les. I do not see the world the way they do. I prefer to follow my mother's example. At least she married for love."

He tried to remember her mother and only succeeded in bringing up a pretty round face with a pleasant smile. Her father was more easily remem-

bered—he'd had the heavy jowls her sister Electra
had inherited, coupled with a towering height and a
merry laugh. Even in his youth he had wondered at
the pair. "Your mother was devoted to your father, I
take it," he replied, trying not to sound skeptical.

He must not have succeeded, for her response was
heated. "Absolutely devoted," she assured him. "She
was a poor orphan, raised by the parish through a
gift from Lady Agnes. Nobody even knew who her
parents were. But she had several offers of marriage—one from a viscount, no less—before she accepted my father. He was only a widowed country
squire, quite a bit older than she, and not too plump
in the pocket. Position and wealth certainly made no
difference to her. It is only Electra and Andromeda
who insist that one needs more than love in a marriage. Indeed, I'm not certain they think love is the
least necessary."

Until that moment, he hadn't really considered the
matter. His mother had died when he was young,
but he vaguely remembered her exchanging fond
glances with his father. Certainly the old man had
never seen fit to replace her. And he would have
had to be blind not to see the love glowing from
Chas Prestwick's eyes every time he looked at his
Anne. "I don't think much of your sisters' notion,"
he decided aloud. "It seems the height of injustice,
now that I think on it."

"I quite agree with you," she replied. "And this is
only one instance in which my sisters try to run my
life. So you see why I must fight against them."

He actually didn't see that fighting was the logical
conclusion, at least not the way she proposed. Behaving in a shocking manner would do her reputation
no good. "But surely there's some fellow who would

satisfy both their need for security and your need for happiness," he protested.

She sighed. "If there is, we have yet to find him. My sisters seemed determined that only someone old, stern, and rich as Midas, preferably with a title, will do for me."

He felt his jaw tighten. "Thank you very much for the compliment. I had no idea I was ready to stick my spoon in the wall so soon."

She had the audacity to giggle. "Not you, silly. You're not so very old and decrepit."

"Your praise quite turns my head, madam," he quipped. "If you are this generous with all your beaus, I am amazed you have not received more offers."

She raised a brow. "Will you bridle up on me? I tell you, I do not put you in the abhorrent category. Simply the ineligible."

Now what on earth did she mean by that? He peered at her, watching with fascination as she tilted her head to look up at him from under her thick lashes. The minx was flirting! He shook his head again. "You cannot have it both ways, Cleo," he warned her. "Either your sisters are foul creatures and I am not worth your wiles, or they are exemplary judges of character and I am a candidate for your hand."

Her coy smile widened. "Or you are a wonderful friend and they are ghouls for suggesting I consider you in any other light."

There was logic in that statement, he was sure of it. But for some reason it escaped him. "Very well, since I am as opposed to leg-shackling as you are, I am a wonderful friend. As your friend, I must tell you, I fail to see how shocking your ghoulish sisters will bring them around to your point of view."

She squeezed his arm. "It isn't so very shocking,

actually. I won't do anything truly wicked, I promise. I know there is a line that must not be crossed. I simply want to come close enough to that line that they will leave us both alone. I am right that Lady Agnes attempted to coerce you into marrying me?"

He nodded. "She tried. But, as I said, I am not concerned about my ability to extract myself, if needed."

She raised her head as if he had challenged her. "Oh? And now is it my turn to wonder when I became so abhorrent?"

He felt his own grin widening. "Now, now, Cleo. I thought we had agreed I was a dear friend. As such, my intentions toward you must be purely platonic. Are we agreed?"

She slanted him that look again, and he was very tempted to tell her to forget everything he'd said for the last few minutes. He'd have to be a plaster saint to keep his feelings platonic around this vixen. He reminded himself yet again that this was little Cleo Renfield he was talking with, an innocent. He was used to dealing with far more experienced women. He did not wait for her to answer him but slipped her hand off his arm and held it between his.

"Cleo, as your friend, I am sworn to help you in any way I can. But this plan of yours concerns me. I don't want to see any harm come to you."

He pressed her hand to his lips and admired the way the rose crept over her high-boned cheeks. "Thank you, my lord," she murmured, dropping her gaze.

He still could not find his Cleo under this veneer of sophistication. He tried again.

" 'My lord,' " he said disparagingly, shaking his

head. "You haven't called me that since . . . well, I don't think you ever called me that."

"I thought perhaps since you had inherited the title . . ." she began.

He released her to wave a hand. "Please, don't call me Hastings. That was my father. I will never fit in his shoes."

She frowned. "What do you mean? Did you not accede to the title?"

"Certainly. The good gentlemen of Parliament could hardly do less. But I will never be the man my father was."

"I think you are too hard on yourself," she informed him primly. "You and your father have much in common. He was such a nice man. Everyone liked him."

"I never realized how much until he died. Do you know there were over five hundred people at his funeral? And not one a paid mourner. Hard to believe he was the head of Britain's foremost espionage network."

Her eyes widened. "Lord Hastings was a spy?"

He chuckled, thinking how his father would have smiled at her incredulous tone. "No, only the spy master. He actively recruited, trained, and administered an elite troop of agents for His Majesty. He never volunteered the fact, but he never hid it either."

"I would never have suspected," she said in obvious awe. "He seemed so gentle, so dapper."

"That was my father," Leslie remembered. "Tie his cravat in a perfect Mathematical and send three men to the gates of hell, both without blinking. There wasn't a man under him who wouldn't have taken his place in that funeral casket. They told me so, every last one of them."

"You must have been proud," she ventured.

Pride did not begin to express the tumult of his emotions, but he hadn't been willing to name them all. He still wasn't. "Ah, well," he said, shrugging off the whole incident with far more composure than he felt. "That's all over now. Life is for the living."

"I imagine you're not even likely to see them again," she returned.

"Oh, I'll see them. My father's specialty was recruiting among the aristocracy. There are dozens of gentlemen in London who would be only too happy to do me a favor, for my father's sake, of course."

"Really?" She peered up at him, and he wondered what she was seeing. As usual, she did not hesitate in telling him. "I'm surprised, Leslie. I'd have thought your father would have recruited you to help him. With your love of adventure, you'd make a marvelous spy."

"Not according to my father," Leslie told her. She looked him askance, and he felt compelled to explain. "I assisted him any number of times, but he consistently refused to make me an agent."

She cocked her head. "Perhaps that was a compliment."

"What do you mean?" Leslie asked with a frown.

"Well, I don't know all that much about spying. But I would think spies generally have to be ready to fight at a moment's notice, kill anyone who gets in their way? Perhaps your father knew you were too kindhearted."

He started to laugh. She slapped his arm.

"Hush! You may pretend all you like, but you know you are. Who but a kindhearted fellow would allow a child to drag him all over the countryside?"

"A fellow who was bored out of his mind," Leslie

countered, refusing to see himself as the selfless martyr she painted him.

She shook her head. "You had chances for any number of other amusements. You were kind enough to stay with me. And you listened to me, for all like I was an equal, just like you're listening now. I vow I am rather good about droning on about my petty little problems."

He tapped her pert nose with one finger, a habit he had nearly forgotten he'd used when they were younger. "You aren't droning, Sprout. You are laying out your plan of attack, or at least trying to. And being very gracious about me interrupting you, I might add."

She smiled up at him. "You aren't interrupting. We are getting reacquainted."

They certainly were. He found himself far more fascinated with the woman Cleo than the girl. And in far more danger. Cleo Renfield had led him into forest hollows after game and river bottoms after fish. He might have ruined a few cravats, muddied his boots, threatened his favorite mount with a sprain. He'd even been chased by a maddened bull once while dashing after Cleo. Somehow, he had a feeling those escapades had been tame next to the adventures she could lead him through now.

He could hardly wait.

"So," he said, pulling her back against the wall so he could lean negligently, "you intend to prove to your sisters that you should be able to marry as you see fit by misbehaving. Explain this miracle to me."

She raised her chin. "It is simple, really. We will pretend we're courting."

"Unoriginal," he commented. "They already expect me to do so."

"Exactly," she replied. "But ours will not be the average, tame courtship."

"I should hope not," he quipped.

Her eyes flashed in warning. "You," she continued doggedly, "will pretend to lead me through any number of scrapes, thus proving you are not the man they thought."

"Ah," he said, with a sigh, putting a hand to his heart. "They shall see the cad that I am."

"In reality," she said, voice becoming even more stern, "we will carefully stage our misadventures so that no one is hurt."

"Thank God for that," he replied, thinking that the most likely thing to be hurt, besides Cleo's reputation, was his heart.

"When we have shocked them sufficiently," she concluded triumphantly, "I should be able to point out that you were their choice and that I was merely trying to please them and you. My own choice will thereby seem tame and acceptable in comparison."

"Your choice?" The pleasure he'd taken in teasing her the last few minutes evaporated as quickly as it had come. "I take it you have someone in mind?"

She started to shake her head, but his frown stopped her. He had to know the truth of it.

"Say a particular major?" he pressed.

Her face flamed. "How did you know?"

There was something lowering in that blush. "Lady Agnes mentioned him," he replied. "It's all right, Cleo. I like Tony Cutter. You could do far worse." Now that he'd seen the woman she'd become, a part of him agreed with Lady Agnes that she could do better, but he believed too strongly in her right to choose to say anything on the matter.

"I am not particularly attached to Major Cutter,"

she assured him, although Leslie found her protest hard to believe. "He has simply shown some interest. My goal is not so much about attaining his goodwill as my freedom. Will you help me?"

Her upturned face, still pink from her blush, was surprisingly appealing. He'd never noticed how long her lashes were, sweeping her fair cheeks with ginger fringe. Major Cutter was a lucky man. But he was not ready to give in just yet. He wouldn't like to find that his agreement to this plan landed him smack in parson's mousetrap.

"Tell me more," he prompted. "Do you have these misadventures planned?"

"Well, a few," she admitted, once more dropping her gaze. "I was hoping you'd come up with more. You do have a reputation for being a bit wild."

He shook his head. "Not me. That was Chas Prestwick. I generally made vague suggestions, or complained about being bored, and Chas filled in the delicious details of my salvation. More likely, he had something already planned and I simply went along for the fun."

"Really?" She looked so crestfallen that he could not help but be encouraged to try harder.

"Not to say that I never contributed," he said. "Give me tonight to think about it. If we are going to pretend to be courting, I imagine I'd better start by calling on you immediately. Will three in the afternoon do?"

"Three would be marvelous," she replied, offering him a bright smile. "And thank you, Leslie. This is very important to me. I know the plan is dicey, but I promise you, you won't regret helping."

Lady Agnes would scold him unmercifully, Cleo's sisters would see him hanged, and he would have to watch while she gave herself to another man. His heart quailed at the thought.

At least he wouldn't be bored.

He matched her smile. "I'll hold you to that promise, Cleo. I'll go along with your plan, on one condition: I expect you to give me the time of my life."

Four

"I think that went rather well," Electra offered, leaning back against the velvet upholstery of her closed carriage.

"He could not take his eyes off her," Andromeda agreed with a satisfied giggle, settling herself in beside her sister. "Absolutely besotted."

"Entirely too easy," Lady Agnes muttered, shifting in her seat next to Cleo, opposite them. "What are you up to, my girl?"

Cleo sat primly as the carriage set off for their town house. With the occasional light from outside coming through the shaded windows, she knew her sisters and godmother could not see her well and was glad for it. They might have recognized the danger in her smile. "I don't know what you mean, Godmother," she said, as if perplexed. "Was I not to attract Lord Hastings's attention?"

"Attract it, yes," Lady Agnes declared. "Monopolize it for half the evening, no. What exactly did you two talk about?"

Ellie and Annie leaned forward expectantly. Cleo stuffed her gloved hands deeper into the lap robe.

"The usual things, I suppose," she replied, not bothering to cover the yawn that followed. "You know, the weather, the cut of his coat, the quality of horses in his stable."

Her sisters sat back with a collective huff of disappointment. Lady Agnes snorted.

"That nonsense wouldn't have kept him interested for more than a quarter minute. I hope you plan to make better conversation when he calls."

"If he calls," Annie muttered.

"He will call," Ellie predicted. "I know that look when I see it in a man's eyes. He is too interested not to call."

"Actually," Cleo put in casually, "he did say he would call tomorrow, at three."

She saw her sisters' heads turn as they exchanged glances. Lady Agnes rapped her on the knee. "Good. And I shall have something to say in the matter when he appears. The two of you"—she pointed a finger at Cleo's sisters—"had better be absent."

Ellie drew herself up. "What do you mean?"

"We surely have every right to help chaperone our sister," Annie added. "Particularly now that a proper gentleman has shown interest."

"He doesn't like you above half," Lady Agnes told them. Cleo had to bite her lips not to laugh out loud. "You shall scare him off, mark my words. The best you could do for Cleo is to leave this whole affair to me."

Her sisters exchanged looks again. Cleo stiffened, ready to add her opinion to Lady Agnes's, but she felt her godmother's hand rest on her knee again. Glancing at her, Lady Agnes shook her head silently. Cleo said nothing.

"Very well," Ellie said at last. "I had an appointment tomorrow in any event."

"And I was due for a fitting," Annie put in hurriedly.

"Good," Lady Agnes said, removing her hand from Cleo's knee. "I will keep you informed of any progress."

Her sisters said little for the remainder of the drive home, and Cleo was just as glad to escape to the house with her godmother. Lady Agnes reached out to stop her, however, when she made for the stairs.

"A moment, young lady," she said, gray eyes narrowed. "I want you to know that while you may fool those doddering sisters of yours, you shall find me tougher material. Leslie Petersborough is a fine young man, much too fine to be played false."

Cleo raised her brows. "Played false? Lady Agnes, I assure you I would never do anything like that."

"Good," her godmother intoned, gripping the banister to haul herself up the stairs. "Then we have nothing more to say in the matter, at least for tonight. See you in the morning, Cleo."

Cleo followed her and pressed a kiss on her cheek before turning for her own room. "Until tomorrow, Lady Agnes."

She slipped into her bedroom to find Bess, the maid her godmother had hired for the Season, waiting. Cleo had entirely too much on her mind to spend another minute in company. Dismissing the girl, she sank before the dressing table and stared unseeing into the mirror.

The night had not gone as she had planned. For one thing, Lady Agnes was suspicious. That could prove dangerous to her plan. Of course, her godmother lived to argue, so perhaps her points this evening were not so much suspicion as a desire for debate. She would simply have to be more careful in her cunning.

The far more difficult matter was the case of

Leslie Petersborough. Who would have thought that the gangly young man from her summers would have turned out so magnificent? He exuded a certain attraction that left her rather breathless. There had been moments in their discussion when she had quite forgotten she was dealing with her old riding pal. Then she'd wanted nothing more than to cock her head and banter with him until she made that half smile turn for her alone. But of course, flirting with Leslie would never do if she was to reach her goal. He had been quite right to point out that she could not have it both ways. Leslie was a dear friend. Her goal was to have the right to make her own choices. Accepting Leslie as a candidate for her hand so quickly would be tantamount to giving Ellie and Annie control over the rest of her life.

The more pressing issue, however, was proceeding with her plan to shock her sisters. Perhaps the biggest disappointment of the evening had been to find that Leslie was singularly useless when it came to generating mischief. She had hoped he might be more help. At the very least, he could offer to race with her, as they had done so many times in the past. Perhaps she could suggest that tomorrow. She was probably being too hard on him, in any event. Now that she thought on it, she had been the one to plan their adventures in Castle Combe. But that had been in much more familiar territory. She needed guidance as to what was acceptable in London.

For all her learning the last five years at the Barnsley School, with all its rules and platitudes, she wasn't entirely sure what was appropriate. Some ladies seemed to be able to get away with a great deal more than what her sisters and godmother allowed. She wanted to be known as shocking, not scandalous.

She had told Leslie she wanted to walk the line between the two, but that line seemed rather fine at times.

Leslie might indeed come up with alternatives after a night's reflection, but she would need to lay out some plans herself. She wound one dark curl around her finger, frown deepening. There had to be something she could do before tomorrow that would set them firmly on the path she had chosen. Her eyes focused on the length of her hair glowing in the light of the candlesticks.

Cleo grinned and rose to get her sewing basket, and the sheers therein.

Leslie spent the evening at White's in an attempt to enjoy himself. He was surprised to find, however, that some part of his mind took his offer to Cleo all too seriously. He ruminated on the matter over a late supper in a quiet corner of the famous London gentlemen's club. He pondered on the plan over piquet in the card room. But everything that came to him seemed blasted improper for a young lady. His usual entertainments of racing, gambling, and sporting virtually excluded any woman of virtue. And the only other pastimes he seemed to be able to think about in connection with Cleo involved horizontal activities that no lady engaged in before marriage. Just the idea of those activities and Cleo cost him several guineas in lost hands. In the end, he had no choice but to give up and go home.

But even there he was not to have a moment's peace. As he undressed himself, having found the services of his father's aging valet entirely too depressing, he caught himself wondering just how shocking Cleo intended to be. Even one of her former activities would be enough to alienate her from the Ton. He had visions of her fishing knee-deep in the Serpentine, shinnying up a tree in Hyde Park, and hunting pigeons along St. James. In those visions, of course, she was the Cleo of old. He didn't want to think about what the new Cleo might do. Or rather, he knew if he thought too long about it, he wouldn't get any sleep that night.

By morning, he still had no answers. The fact made him not a little frustrated with himself. He had agreed to meet Cleo in the first place to show how much he had grown into his new role. It had been a noble sacrifice. Why was it he could think of nothing to help her now, when things might actually be considerably more fun?

He supposed the problem was him. He'd been a devoted follower for most of his life—first of his father, then friends, and finally of one particular friend, namely Chas Prestwick. There was a place for followers in the world, and he'd been a very good one. Why was it everyone, from Cleo to Parliament, suddenly insisted that he be the leader? It was discomposing, to say the least.

He very nearly called for the valet just to prove he needed help. But, in the end, he shaved and dressed himself as he had always done, choosing a bottle green coat, tan chamois trousers, and a very common fold in his cravat that would have made his dapper father shake his head in mortification. Then he breakfasted and read the morning paper before presenting himself at the door to the rented town house.

Only to find that Cleo had determined to be the leader after all.

"What the devil have you done to your hair!" he

yelped before she could even greet him in the drawing room.

Her hand flew to her head, eyes wide in her obvious dismay. "I cut it."

"Really?" he quipped, striding forward to poke at what was left of her silky tresses. "Have you gone maggoty in the brain, my girl? You look like a shorn sheep."

She grabbed his hand and pulled it down. "Shh, she'll hear you! I told Lady Agnes that short hair is your preference, so I cut it to please you." She lifted her head to allow her eyes to meet his gaze, which was surely as infuriated as he felt. "Does it really look so bad, Leslie? I tried to follow the picture in the ladies' magazine."

She looked so concerned that he felt his anger waning. And why was he angry anyway? He wasn't related to the chit; he wasn't even serious in his courting. If Cleo Renfield wanted to cut her hair or waltz at Almack's without permission, it was none of his business.

He angled his head and eyed the close-cropped curls. In truth, she didn't look all that bad. Without the weight of her long tresses, her hair twined in soft wisps around her head, framing her face and calling attention to her warm eyes. Indeed, the soft curls made her look taller somehow, more sophisticated, more womanly. The elegant look was entirely out of keeping with the simple pink muslin gown she had chosen to wear. He would have dressed her in something with more dash.

Or nothing at all.

He cleared his throat to clear his thoughts. "You'll do, Sprout," he told her. "The curls look a great deal better on you than they did on Caro Lamb, who started the whole dreadful trend. All right, I'll go along with it. Short hair is my undying passion."

She smiled. "Thank you, Les. Now, tell me quickly—what did you think of? We must hurry before Lady Agnes comes in. I'm sure she's only given us this time together so you can pursue your suit."

"My suit." He shook his head. "Sorry, Cleo, but my ideas are as nonexistent as my courting. Anything I'd do would be completely inappropriate for you."

"Such as?" she asked with a frown.

He had a sudden vision of Cleo riding naked through Hyde Park without her hair to cover her. "Oh, no," he declared. "I saw what you did on little provocation. I refuse to encourage you."

She opened her mouth for what he was sure would be a stinging rejoinder, but luckily Lady Agnes entered the room. Cleo snapped her mouth shut and resorted to a quick glare at him. As Mr. Cowls wheeled the parrot's cage into the room with a decided squeak that could have been the gilt wheels or the butler's joints, Leslie went to kiss his godmother's hand.

"Lady Agnes," he declared, "you grow more lovely each day."

Accepting his kiss, she waved off his praise with a rustle of her navy silk gown. "And you grow more bold. What were you thinking to ask Cleo to cut her hair?"

"What are you thinking to cart that parrot everywhere you go?" he countered. Purposely setting his back to her sharp gaze, he strode to the gilded cage and eyed the bird inside it. The parrot was as stiff as ever, hunching over its perch as if in some inner pain. He could almost hear the fellow's unhappy sigh.

Of course, it could have been Mr. Cowls.

"Pretty boy," Leslie said to the bird. "Do you know your name?"

A yellow-ringed, beady black eye regarded him steadily.

"You needn't cozen him," Lady Agnes barked. "He will not answer you. My nephew Thomas tried, his wife Margaret tried, my niece Catherine and her husband tried. Even Cleo tried. He simply refused to comment to any of them."

"He rarely even squawks," Cleo agreed. "I thought all parrots at least did that."

"He squawks well enough at dawn and dusk," Lady Agnes complained. "Ask my neighbors in Bath. He simply doesn't like London. A parrot generally needs the run of the house, but Electra did not stipulate that in her agreement with the owner of this wretched establishment. I am forced to keep him caged. Now he does nothing but brood."

"Perhaps he just hasn't heard a word that pleases him," Leslie mused, an idea forming. "Perhaps I should give teaching him a go." He turned to wink at his godmother. "What say you, Lady Agnes? Shall we have a daily tutoring session for your bird?"

Lady Agnes cocked her head, looking a bit like a bird herself. "Daily? You would come to see me every day?"

He could hear the longing in the old girl's voice, for all she tried to hide it. Even with Cleo for company, she was lonely. But he couldn't promise more than he knew he could give. "I will come to see your parrot as often as possible," he replied. "Though it goes without saying that I will pay my respects to you as well, if you are home when I call."

Lady Agnes sat taller, glaring at him. "You would come see the bird without seeing me?"

"I think it best if I work alone," Leslie explained. "That way, you won't have to be disappointed if we make no progress, and it will be a delightful surprise if we do. Cleo can assist me, if you like."

He caught a quick grin from Cleo before she masked it behind an indifferent look. His godmother must have seen the look as well.

"Impertinence," she scolded. "I see through you, young man. You think to win a few more minutes alone with Cleo every day. I would be a poor chaperone if I had the wool pulled over my eyes so easily."

"I assure you, I thought only of dear Hector here," Leslie returned with his most contrite smile. "But now that you mention it, I suppose my plan would give me an unfair advantage over Cleo's other admirers. I will have to be content to catch her only occasionally at home and let all the other smart young bucks and dandies have a chance at her. It is only sporting that she have her pick, after all."

Cleo was watching him from the corner of her eye, although anyone else looking would have thought she was studying her hands folded in her lap. Lady Agnes pursed her lips, as if considering his carefully laid bait.

"I suppose it might not hurt for her to help you," she mused, for all the world like a street vendor haggling over a piece of pastry. "You are an old friend of the family, after all. My own godson. And it would be very interesting if Hector would speak to everyone."

"Then we are agreed?" Leslie pressed.

She nodded. "Yes. You may start tomorrow."

"Lovely," Cleo agreed, and he would have sworn she let out her breath in relief. "We can start before our ride in Hyde Park."

Leslie felt a premonition of dread crawl up his back. He stared at Cleo, but her bright smile told him nothing. The determined set of her chin only served to scare him all the more. Somewhere in the space of time it had taken him to convince Lady Agnes to let him tutor the bird, Cleo had come up with a plan. If she had thought all night and decided to cut her hair, he hated to think what she'd come up with on a moment's notice.

"Did we agree to ride tomorrow, my dear?" he asked.

Her smile was tight. "Certainly, *my lord*. I'm sure that was what we were discussing before Lady Agnes joined us. You wanted to show off a particularly fine piece of horseflesh you bought recently, if I recall? The one you wanted to show Lady Agnes and me?"

Leslie nearly sighed aloud. Now he'd have to spend the afternoon at Tattersall's buying a horse. He hadn't been able to take much joy in his stables since his father's death. Certainly he had nothing new to show off, nothing his sharp-eyed godmother wouldn't have seen a dozen times. To put truth to Cleo's lie, he'd have to buy a new mount. He supposed there were worse things that she could have come up with.

"Yes, of course," he replied. "Your radiant beauty must have driven everything else from my mind."

"Then you also probably forgot that you agreed to accompany us to the Baminger ball this Saturday," Cleo continued doggedly.

Leslie's smile froze. That was decidedly worse. She had no idea what she asked. Lady Baminger couldn't stand the sight of him, ever since he and Chas Prestwick had made a scene at her annual ball last Season. Actually, Chas had made the scene by waltzing with Anne Fairchild and then backing the two of them into an unused room. Leslie, unfortunately, had been the one to whisk Chas out of the house before Lady Baminger's wrath could fall. Chas's parting shot, to call Lady Baminger's ball dull beyond words, had been repeated by many, to the lady's continuing embarrassment. She would be out for blood.

"I think you must be mistaken, my heart," he told Cleo, setting his face in stern lines in hopes she would have the good sense to desist. "I am certain I will be otherwise engaged on Saturday."

Cleo's dark eyes flashed. "It bodes ill for our courtship, sir, that you would so easily break a promise to me."

"A decided character flaw," Lady Agnes agreed, obviously unable to pass up an opportunity to needle him. "He has a problem in that area, make no mistake."

Leslie attempted to ignore her. "Perhaps we can discuss this tomorrow, sweetling," he said to Cleo. "In the meantime, I'll see if I can clear my calendar."

"That's all I ask, my friend," she returned with equal determination.

He bowed. "On that happy note, I shall take my leave of you. I have monopolized your time long enough." Knowing he was escaping, and rather glad of the fact, he moved to Lady Agnes and bent to kiss her soft cheek. "Good day, Godmother. Try to keep your charge in line, will you? The girl is impossibly strong-willed."

Cleo sputtered, but Lady Agnes's eyes twinkled.

"I will keep her on a tight rein," she promised. "Just see that you behave yourself."

"With your goddaughter as my inspiration, I could do no less," he replied, reflecting as he exited that it looked very likely that he would be doing far more.

Five

Five

Cleo would have let the day pass well satisfied with her progress if it hadn't been for some late afternoon visitors. Her godmother was still muttering about Leslie's admiration of short hair, and she was sure her sisters, when next they deigned to call, would be even more apoplectic. If she succeeded in getting Leslie to race in Hyde Park tomorrow, and she had no doubt she could appeal to his sense of adventure, she would be well on her way to ridding herself of her sisters' meddling.

Of course, she still had to convince him to attend the Baminger ball. Her sisters would never be sufficiently motivated by her behavior if she did not display it in a public place. Lady Baminger prided herself on inviting every member of the Haut Ton to her annual event, or so Lady Agnes had complained.

"It will be a dreadful crush," she had predicted when they'd gotten the invitations a fortnight earlier. "You mark my words."

Surely she and Leslie could find something to do at the event that would encourage her sisters' change of heart. She simply had to determine why Leslie was so adamant about refusing to attend and find a way to change his mind.

She was quite prepared to spend the rest of the

afternoon reading one of the novels she had gotten from the local lending library. With her favorite pastimes of fishing and hunting forbidden her at the Barnsley School, and riding generally lowered to nothing more exciting than a group plod on a circular track unless she pretended the horse ran away with her, she had learned that the world of literature could be almost as exciting as catching a brook trout. She was therefore surprised to find that before she had gotten through even one chapter of her novel, Cowls was standing in the doorway of the library, raspily clearing his throat to announce that she had a visitor.

She hurried across the hall to the little wood-paneled sitting room at the front of the house to find Marlys Rutherford waiting for her in one of the leather-bound chairs the room boasted.

"I had to come as soon as I could," her friend confided after they had exchanged greetings and Cleo had sat near her. She positively wiggled in her sunny yellow muslin dress that was nearly as bright as the smile on her round face. "Your conquest of Lord Hastings is the talk of the Ton. But what happened to your hair?"

Cleo knew she would have to get used to the question. "Lord Hastings prefers it short," she replied.

Marlys's brown eyes widened. "You cut it to please him? That is beyond anything! And so daring. My mother would have locked me in my room until it grew out. She only let me visit you in private so she could have a word with Lady Agnes." She raised a hand to absently finger her light brown ringlets. "He intends to offer, then?"

"Well," Cleo hedged, unable to lie to one of her best friends, "I cannot presume to know his mind, but I am committed to doing all I can to attach his regard. We grew up together, you know, and we are already so much more than friends."

"I see," Marlys replied, her smile fading. She leaned back and regarded Cleo solemnly. Cleo frowned at the sudden coolness, though in truth she had only expected as much. Falling in love so quickly was not ladylike, and Marlys wouldn't be allowed to remain friends with anyone less than a lady.

"Forget about all this," Cleo coaxed. "I am the same girl you knew in Somerset. Remember how many times we shared confidences?"

That wrung a smile from her. "I remember. I also remember how many times we had to mount a search party for you. Mr. Canterbury never did realize that the horses were not riding off with you, you were riding off with them."

Cleo giggled. "It got me longer time in the saddle, didn't it?"

"Certainly. And an excuse to spend more time in the stables to get over your . . . what did Miss Martingale call it?"

"My 'abnormal sensibilities toward equines,' " Cleo supplied. "You were wonderful not to give me away, Marlys."

"Well, it was us against the teachers in those days," she replied with a sad sigh. "A shame that had to change when the Season started. Now we must compete against each other for the prize."

Cleo felt chilled and wrapped her arms about herself. "It doesn't have to be that way. I could never see you as a rival."

Marlys smiled, but the sunshine had gone. "That is because you already have your beau. Besides, you were always prettier and more popular, Cleo. All this is easy for you."

"Not as easy as you might think," Cleo confessed. Just then, Mr. Cowls appeared in the doorway again.

"Miss Eloise Watkin to see you, Miss Cleo," he said.

Cleo rose even as Marlys paled. Their former classmate paused in the doorway, as if giving them an opportunity to admire the elaborate embroidering at the neck and hem of her soft blue muslin gown, the silky drape of her cashmere shawl, the perfect silk roses adorning her fashionable bonnet.

"I was just leaving," Marlys mumbled, scurrying past her for the stairs. Eloise watched her go with a slight frown, then ventured into the sitting room. Wondering what Eloise could want with her, Cleo returned to her seat. Eloise took the chair Marlys had vacated.

"I did not intend to frighten her away," she told Cleo. "I simply wished to speak with you."

"Her mother is upstairs with Lady Agnes," Cleo explained. "How can I help you?"

Eloise licked her lips, glancing back over her shoulder as if to be certain Marlys had gone. Her gaze, when it returned to Cleo, was dark, her emerald eyes shuttered.

"You know, of course, that I had to refuse Lord Owens," she said.

Cleo hadn't even known the handsome Scottish lord had been seriously courting her. "No. How very troubling for you, I'm sure."

Eloise sighed. "Very troubling. I had thought him quite the gentleman, but he was not all he appeared. He seemed to have developed a poor impression of me, if you take my meaning."

Cleo stiffened, afraid she took her meaning entirely too well. But how could Lord Owens know about Eloise's past? Cleo had promised Miss Martingale, the Barnsley School headmistress, never to speak of what she'd seen. "I'm sure you must be mistaken," she said. "Some gentlemen are notoriously afraid of being married."

As soon as the words left her mouth, she wished she could call them back. Eloise paled. "So, you haven't forgotten. Just how long do you intend to hold it over me?"

Cleo sighed. "I am not holding anything over you, Eloise. I have discussed the matter with no one but you and Miss Martingale, as I promised. You are the one who persists in dredging up the memory every time we speak."

"Oh, certainly," she snapped. "Blame me. Everyone else has. You might consider your own behavior. If you hadn't been spying in the stables that day, everything might have turned out differently. He loved me. He might have offered for me."

"I wasn't spying in the stables," Cleo informed her, though the guilt she always felt when reliving the day tugged anew. "I was just currying my horse."

"A nice excuse, but you did not have a horse. That spiritless nag wasn't any more your horse than this is your house. I know you have been beholden to your sisters for most of your life. You were jealous of me, and you wanted to catch me out. Admit it."

"I will admit nothing of the kind," Cleo replied, lifting her chin. "If you will remember, I spent a great deal of time in the stables, working with the horses, before you found another use for the place."

Eloise stiffened. "You were always better with animals than people. I do not find that so very admirable."

"There is nothing more I can tell you, Eloise," Cleo replied. "Did you have some other purpose in visiting than to insult me?"

Eloise's jaw was tight. "Actually, I had. I heard a distressing rumor that you were growing attached to one Major Anthony Cutter."

Cleo stared at her. "I do not know who could have told you that."

"Do not bother to deny it," Eloise declared. "I have seen the desire in your eyes when you look at him. Be warned, Cleo. He has been courting me for some time. I will not let you spoil that."

Cleo laughed, and Eloise started.

"You may determine anything you like," Cleo told her. "Major Cutter is an intelligent, well-bred gentleman. He is fully capable of determining which lady he chooses to favor."

"You intend to tell him about me, then," Eloise accused.

"Do you never tire of that nonsense? I assure you, I will be silent. I know how to keep my promises."

"See that you do," Eloise warned. "If I hear that you have been spreading stories about me, Miss Cleopatra Renfield, I will see that your reputation is served likewise."

"My reputation," Cleo informed her, "is not in question. If yours is, I would look to your own behavior and stop worrying about mine."

"Very well," Eloise declared, rising to shake out her skirts. "You have been warned. And one other thing: That haircut is atrocious. You will be laughed out of Almack's."

"Then you won't have a thing to worry about, will you?" Cleo replied with a smile. "Good afternoon, Miss Watkin. Pray don't trouble yourself to call again."

"I won't," she snapped, flouncing out into the entry hall.

Cleo felt herself shaking and clasped her hands

tightly together. The nerve of the woman! Why did she persist in believing Cleo incapable of keeping a secret? Cleo had never been her enemy. There had been moments before that day when Cleo had sincerely admired her. Eloise had been beautiful, smart, and generous. Unfortunately, her gifts were wasted on her driving need to capture the attention to herself. Still, Cleo had tried to show her a friendly face. Lord knew she had debated for several days before going to Miss Martingale to explain what she had seen that afternoon nearly four years ago now. Even Marlys had known how upset she was, though Cleo had not told her why. Only a fear for Eloise's safety had driven her to give the girl away. But did Eloise thank her? No, she had promptly made her her sworn enemy.

She shook her head and tried to steady her emotions. She had never been able to understand how Eloise thought. She wasn't even sure what Eloise hoped to achieve with her attention-getting ways. The best she could do was focus on her own plans. She certainly hoped, however, that Major Cutter was as smart as she had named him. Otherwise, he would very likely have his hands full.

Cleo was in a much better frame of mind the next afternoon when Mr. Cowls made his way to tell her that Leslie was waiting for her in the drawing room. She slapped the black-tasseled riding hat over her short curls and picked up the train of her amethyst wool riding habit to hurry down the corridor. But as she entered the room, she found Leslie cursing at the parrot.

"Did he bite you?" she cried, rushing to his side.

"Good afternoon," he greeted her so cheerfully

that she stopped in surprise. "And no, Hector here is very well behaved. He's quite the fine gentleman. And, as such, I thought perhaps he needed a more gentlemanly vocabulary."

Cleo raised a brow. "You're teaching him to swear?"

He grinned. "Rather appropriate, don't you think? It seemed to me the fellow would be dashed good at foul language."

She cringed at the pun, and Leslie laughed. She found herself chuckling as well. It only took a moment of his humor to set her at ease, no matter how handsome he looked. Today, he wore an aubergine riding jacket with black velvet lapels, and his hair was combed back under a high-crowned beaver. If she hadn't seen the light in his eyes, she could easily have mistaken him for a top-of-the-trees Corinthian.

"So, what have you taught him?" she asked.

He shook his head. "I was trying for something simple, like *hell,* but the fellow doesn't seem interested even in that."

She eyed the bird, who cocked his head, showing off the black and rose banding at his neck, and returned her gaze. "Perhaps he's more the evangelical type. What are the Methodists so fond of threatening? Hell and damnation?"

Hector spread his wings and let out a piercing squawk. Cleo was so surprised, she stumbled back, tumbling against Leslie. He caught her easily enough, his hands strong around her waist. Cleo stiffened as heat spread from his splayed fingers. Leslie didn't seem to notice. He merely righted her, keeping his hands at her waist, and drew her back against him, peering over her head at the parrot.

"You seem to have the right of it, Cleo," he maintained, making no move to disengage from her body. "Try again."

Cleo swallowed. Indeed, she wasn't sure she could utter more than a squeak with his hands clasping her this way. She could feel the length of his body pressed against her back like a forbidden caress. "I . . . I'm not sure I can," she managed.

"This is no time to be modest, my girl," he scolded. "I'm sure you had singing lessons at that school of yours." His right hand strayed to her belly, moving slowly up her rib cage, trailing fire in its wake. "You project, from here." He pressed just under her breasts. She stood taller, willing herself away from his touch. That only brought her backside against his thighs. She was surely supposed to do better than this when a gentleman was taking liberties. Only this was Leslie, and he surely wasn't trying to seduce her.

Was he?

"I think that's enough lessons for today," she said primly, pushing forcefully away from him so that she bumped Hector's cage. The bird spread his wings again and hissed in warning. She slipped around to put the gilded bars between herself and Leslie's confusing presence.

"Perhaps you are right," Leslie replied, rubbing his chin as he peered at the bird. "We shall try again tomorrow. Let me go and pay my respects to Lady Agnes and we shall be off."

She nodded and he quit the room. Then she collapsed onto the nearby sofa.

What was wrong with her? She lifted a shaky hand to her forehead and pushed her hat away from her face. She'd never reacted that way to any other fellow's touch. Of course, she hadn't been touched all that often, and certainly not in the way Leslie had touched her. Robbie Curry had held her hand longer than necessary at the Badgerly ball, and Donald Pelton had put his arms around her when lifting her from her saddle the one time they had gone riding. Neither of those times had affected her as the brief contact with Leslie had done.

Of course, she reminded herself sternly, she had gone weak at the knees the first time she had been introduced to Major Cutter. There was no comparison between how she felt around the darling major and Leslie. Leslie was an old friend. He was simply teasing her. She'd have to take herself more firmly in hand. She'd been in London for three months now; she certainly wasn't a schoolroom miss any longer. She could handle Leslie's attentions, if they became onerous.

Having convinced herself, she waited patiently until he returned from greeting Lady Agnes. Then they all had to troop down to the street to admire the rose gray gelding he had purchased. Cleo had to admit it was a fine animal, although something in the way his hand stroked the horse's shoulder made her riding habit feel unaccountably tight and itchy.

"So," Leslie said as they set off for Hyde Park, "what shocking behavior do you have in mind for today? You seem to have all your fingers and toes, so I take it you did not decide to cut off anything else."

She grimaced. "Certainly not. And my proposal for today is not so very shocking, although Lady Agnes and my sisters will likely think it so. I suggest we race."

Leslie grinned. "Capital idea. I am itching to try this fellow." He patted the horse again, and the gray shook out his mane. Leslie chuckled.

Cleo smiled as well. "He is a beauty. It's rare to

see such dark points on a gray. The markings on his legs make it look as if he's wearing boots."

"Exactly what I thought," Leslie informed her, sharing her smile. "I've decided to name him Hessian. Almost makes me forgive you for requiring me to buy him."

"Requiring you to buy him?" Cleo looked at him, brows raised. "How did I do that?"

"By telling Lady Agnes I had a new horse," he explained. "She's seen all my cattle, so I had to make good your lie. In future, you might ask before putting words in my mouth, or horses in my stable."

Cleo shook her head. "I think you took that far too seriously. If Lady Agnes had caught you in the lie, I could simply have said I was mistaken, or that I had not seen the horse, therefore, it was new to me."

Leslie eyed her. "Dashed good at lies, aren't you?"

She almost took umbrage, but she could hear the reluctant admiration in his voice. "I suppose I am," she allowed. "It was something I learned at school. I never lied when Mother and Father were alive."

"Except about trying to get into fighting matches," Leslie teased.

She smiled. "Well, I never got into any matches, so I didn't need to lie about it. It was only when Ellie shipped me off to boarding school that I found that a story or two made life a great deal more bearable."

"Where on earth did they send you," Leslie demanded, "a penal colony?"

She felt a twinge of annoyance. "Not at all. The Barnsley School for Young Ladies is a very fine institution. But as in any social situation, honesty is a questionable commodity. I tried it in the beginning; I was not thanked for it." Eloise came to mind, and she forced the memory away. "I found that life is easier if one keeps those in power happy. Wasn't it like that when you were at Eton?"

He frowned. "I suppose, although in truth, I never gave it much thought. There were enough fellows to pal around with that if some didn't wish to associate with me, I wasn't particularly concerned."

"An excellent way to look at it," Cleo told him. "But as the only son of a marquis, and in line for the title, I doubt too many dared treat you badly."

"And as a cozening little sprout, I somehow doubt you were shunned by all good society either," he quipped.

She could not help but remember how many girls had found her country ways atrocious, at least at first. Their teasing as well as her discovery of Eloise had only fueled her determination to regain control over her own life.

"We're almost to Hyde Park," she said, hoping he would not notice the abrupt change in topic. "Where shall we race? I want people to notice, but I should not want anyone to be trampled."

"Rotten Row," he advised.

Cleo frowned. She had never ridden on the sandy track that stretched the southern end of Hyde Park. Ladies did not ride on Rotten Row. But was this one of those rules she could break with impunity? "Perhaps I should see it first," she suggested.

Leslie was amenable, so they rode down into the park, following a riding path leading to the south and west. Immediately, she began to question the advisability of her scheme. Although it was still over an hour before the truly fashionable made their appearance, the park was crowded. Carriages jostled alongside each other, and knots of riders made desultory progress through the pedestrians and equipages.

Nurses walked while their charges cavorted through the mayhem. She could not see how anyone could safely trot, much less race.

By the time they reached Rotten Row, Cleo had all but decided to forget racing. Leslie, however, reined in where the track neared the Serpentine. He stood up in the stirrups to eye the riding path as it stretched down toward Kensington Gardens. The sandy path was just as crowded as the rest of the park, and Cleo despaired. Leslie shook his head, re-seating himself. Before she could turn her mount, however, he pointed his riding crop at her.

"See here, Miss Renfield," he declared in a tone so ringing that the nearest riders reined in to see what was happening. "How dare you impugn my mount. I tell you, I paid fifty guineas for this marvelous animal."

Cleo knew it was her cue to play along, but her heart had quailed. "Indeed, sir," she tried, meeting Leslie's teasing gaze straight on with an imploring one of her own, "I do apologize. I would never have guessed a horse could cost so much."

Leslie was not to be stopped. "What," he cried, "do you impugn my trading skills as well? You leave me no choice, madam. I challenge you to a race."

There was a scattering of applause from the gentlemen around them. The ladies tittered or made clucking noises at his bad form. Ladies, as they obviously knew, did not race.

"But the other riders . . ." Cleo protested.

"You there!" Leslie gestured to a stout gentleman on a roan mare. "Be a good chap and clear the path, would you?" He preened. "I should not want to fell anyone with this beast."

The gentleman seemed amenable, setting his horse at an ambling trot down the track. His deep-throated cries of "Clear the way" echoed back to Cleo on the breeze. Leslie shifted restlessly on his horse, which shivered in anticipation. She patted the sweet little mare Lady Agnes had procured for her, feeling her own excitement rise.

Leslie snatched off his top hat and cantered over to the side of the path, where a group of pedestrians had gathered.

"Would you mind, fair lady?" he asked, with as deep a bow as he could make astride. "I shouldn't want to ruin a perfectly good hat with all this fuss."

Cleo shook her head at his flirting, but then he pulled the horse to one side and she saw who he had favored with his attentions. Eloise's eyes were as narrowed as her smile as she gazed up at Leslie, accepting his hat. But far worse than that was the stiff line of her companion's mouth.

Cleo had never thought Major Cutter could look unpleasant, but standing possessively beside Eloise, she thought his usual gentlemanly glory quite dimmed. His short-cropped golden hair was all but obscured by the top hat, and the ordinary brown coat and chamois trousers were not nearly as dashing as the dress uniform he often wore to balls. No sooner had the thought crossed her mind, however, but the gentleman looked her way, and his vibrant eyes widened in surprise, drawing her in. As her cheeks heated in a blush, he inclined his head in greeting, touching his finger to his forehead in salute. Cleo sat a little straighter.

"Will you put this off all day, my lord?" she called sweetly to Leslie. "Your mount will surely expire from old age before you allow him a hoof on the course."

"Slander, madam!" Leslie accused, turning his horse back to her side. "You should beg me for a

Regina Scott

head start, because that is the only way you will ever be ahead of this magnificent animal."

"Done!" Cleo cried. "I accept. First one to the Kensington Park curve wins." She touched heels to flank and set her horse off down the track.

Six

Leslie stared as Cleo shot past him. The lovely lady who held his hat waved it at him frantically, as if he needed any encouragement. He had only a moment to register Tony Cutter's amused face as he stood beside the lady. Leslie tightened the reins on the gelding and pressed it into a gallop.

Trees shot past on either side, and he was certain he heard more than one cry of alarm at his recklessness. He ignored everything to focus on Cleo's retreating figure. She bent forward over the horse's stretched-out neck, clamping her feet against the one side to encourage it forward. He did likewise, feeling the gray's strides lengthening. His heart was pounding as loudly as his horse's hooves. Now *this* was adventure. Racing in Hyde Park, with a beautiful woman, on an untried horse. His father would have had his head.

And won a tidy sum betting on his win.

But despite his best efforts to urge the horse on, Cleo's lead continued to widen. He was clearly going to lose. Yet, somehow, he couldn't seem to care. Watching Cleo crouched in the side saddle, her nicely rounded backside moving with the horse's gait, he found himself far more enjoying the view. And her glowing face when he pulled up a sorry second was worth every bit of humiliation the defeat was likely to cause him that night at White's

"I won!" she proclaimed giddily, dark eyes alight, face splitting in a grin.

"Cheat!" Leslie accused, but he grinned back. "You were magnificent."

She tossed her head, short curls bouncing in the breeze. "I rather thought so. Even Major Cutter seemed to think so." She giggled.

The sound grated on Leslie's nerves, surprising him. "Yes, well," he stammered. "Mission accomplished, I suppose. Shall I return you home, or do you wish to circle the park in triumph?"

His tone must have betrayed his feelings, for she frowned. "Is something wrong, Leslie? Are you truly angry that I won?"

"Certainly not," he declared. "Why should I be upset that you took unfair advantage of me with a head start, enticed me into a race on an unfamiliar nag, and in short thoroughly trampled my reputation in front of any number of fair ladies?"

Now it was her turn to look annoyed. "Some of them," she informed him, "are not the ladies they appear." She seemed to recall herself and straightened in the saddle. "I'm sorry if I made you look ridiculous. I thought we were having fun."

"We are, Sprout," he assured her, poking her in the shoulder with his riding crop. "Take no heed of my mutterings. I simply thought that as you had achieved your objective, you might wish to retire from the field and plan your next battle."

"Oh, yes," she assured him. "I did want to speak with you about the Baminger ball. Would it be too painfully embarrassing to speak with our well-wishers first?"

He glanced back over his shoulder at the riders

who were ambling their way. Strolling in their wake, he spotted Tony Cutter alongside the dark-haired beauty who twirled his hat between her hands. Eloise Watkin, Cleo had named her. He wouldn't have minded making her acquaintance. For some reason, however, he had no desire to greet the good major. Besides, if he let the lady keep his hat, it would give him an excuse to look her up later. He returned his gaze to Cleo and nodded.

"Yes, having to face my ignominious defeat would be simply more than I could bear. Allow me to escort you home."

She glanced back at the approaching group as well and sighed. But she did not argue as Leslie set off for the Park Lane entrance.

"Les," she said after they had cleared the park, "I need you to escort me to the Baminger ball."

Leslie cringed. "I should have taken my punishment in the park. I cannot attend the ball, Cleo. That's deep into enemy territory." When she frowned at him, he explained. "Lord Prestwick and I caused a scandal at Lady Baminger's ball last year. I doubt I'd be welcomed back."

She made a face. "You're afraid of a year-old scandal? No one will remember."

"Lady Baminger will remember," Leslie predicted. "And if she somehow doesn't, I'm sure there will be some old snitch who will only be too happy to remind her."

"Can you not ask her forgiveness?" she pressed.

Leslie didn't try to suppress the shudder that ran through him. Lady Baminger was a patron of the arts. She sponsored composers, musicians, and artists. It was said, however, that while she sponsored operas, her husband sponsored opera dancers. For propriety's sake, she might have to turn a blind eye to her husband's extramarital pursuits. Indeed, her annual ball went a long way toward keeping her family acceptable in the eyes of the Ton. He who had damaged that acceptance would receive little mercy.

"I have no interest in trying," he assured Cleo. "There must be other parties we can attend together."

He glanced at her to find a decided pout on her pretty face. "I am not invited to other events nearly so public for the next fortnight. Even Major Cutter will be in attendance. After today, surely I must consolidate my advantage."

So it was Cutter who drew her to that reprehensible ball. Leslie felt his annoyance rising again and fought it down. She had never made any pretense that she did not enjoy the major's company. Why should her interest annoy him? He was only along for the fun. Perhaps he should point that out.

"So, you get your desire while I lose mine," he challenged.

She frowned. "What do you mean?"

"You promised me sport, Cleo. Facing Lady Baminger's wrath is hardly my idea of fun."

She did not seem to appreciate the obvious. Cleo set her face in stony lines, and they rode in silence for a while. Leslie enjoyed the thought that he had made his point, but as Cleo continued to stare resolutely ahead, he felt his enjoyment waning. Cleo annoyed was a rather chilling sight. He much preferred her happy.

"Perhaps I could learn where Tony Cutter plans to be over the next few weeks and gain us invitations," he offered.

She did not deign to look at him. "Major Cutter's presence is immaterial. I told you—a fortnight or more is far too long."

He wasn't convinced. But if the major was so inconstant that he could not wait a fortnight, he hardly deserved her devotion. Besides, Leslie could hardly fault her when he'd felt the same way about Lolly Dupray. And his inattention had indeed cost him the lovely dancer's interest, with her having accepted the duke only the day before.

"Perhaps we can contrive to cause another scandal in the park again," Leslie suggested.

"Perhaps," she allowed, but she did not seem hopeful.

Leslie sighed. "Are you always this obstinate?"

She stiffened. "I do not see how being true to one's purpose is being obstinate. I am disappointed in you, Leslie. I cannot believe you would let a little thing like Lady Baminger's opinion keep you from going where you want to go."

Leslie's fist tightened on the reins, making the gelding prance. "I don't give a hang for Lady Baminger's opinion," he informed her testily. "Her opinion in no way influences my behavior. I simply have no desire to endure the ringing scold she would no doubt like to give me. I told you, Cleo, my purpose is to have fun. Lady Baminger and fun do not inhabit the same sphere."

She cocked her head. "Perhaps they do. If I can find a way to make the evening enjoyable, would you relent?"

He sensed a trap but was intrigued nonetheless. "It would have to be jolly good," he warned. "I won't play the martyr."

"You won't have to," she promised. "But you may have to play the courtier. Let me think on it. We can talk more during your lessons to Hector tomorrow."

Leslie was far from satisfied with the answer, but he had no choice but to acquiesce and take Cleo home. He only hoped that fertile brain of hers would for once not be able to come up with a plan.

Though he rather thought he'd have more luck hoping that pigs might fly.

Cleo thought about the matter the rest of the afternoon. The race in the park had succeeded beyond her dreams. She had hoped the tale of her riding would spark comment, but they had definitely drawn a crowd. There had been enough whispering before they set off to assure her that tongues would wag. But she had to follow through.

There was no question in her mind that her attendance at the Baminger ball was now imperative. She had to enact another display to press her plan forward. She had hoped to spend the evening in contemplation, but she had not counted on gossip traveling so quickly. She had just sat down to a companionable dinner with Lady Agnes when Ellie stormed into the room. Mr. Cowls's phlegmy cough of discretion did no more than earn him her glare. Her black velvet cloak and long gloves proclaimed her intent to go out for the evening. The white ostrich plume in her gold lamé turban quivered in outrage.

"You!" She pointed an accusing finger at Cleo. "You are a disgrace to this family!"

Lady Agnes set down her silver even as Cleo felt herself pale. She sat straighter and merely raised a brow, while her insides churned. The battle was engaged.

"What's happened?" her godmother demanded.

"Have you not heard?" Ellie shook her head. "I am amazed no one saw fit to tell you. No less than three august personages hurried to my door with the tale. Cleo was racing in Hyde Park this afternoon."

"Impossible," Lady Agnes declared. "She was out with my godson this afternoon."

The cannon had been fired. Ellie stiffened as if hit. Cleo wanted to crow with delight. Instead, she bowed her head to hide her smile.

But she should not have counted the enemy as lost. "She raced *with* your godson," Ellie informed Lady Agnes. "I can only hope she did not give him a complete disgust of her."

A direct hit—they blamed her! Cleo's hands clenched in her lap even as her eyes rose involuntarily to meet her sister's angry gaze. "I'll have you know," she declared, "that he wanted to race. I only acquiesced to his wishes. Isn't that what you wanted?"

The return fire missed. "Ridiculous," Ellie maintained. "He was no doubt joking, and you took him seriously. Then you compounded the error by beating him. The poor man will never live it down."

Lady Agnes quirked a grin. "Beat him, did you? I'd have liked to see that."

The enemy marched forward. "Do not encourage her," Ellie commanded. "This outrageous behavior stops now, Cleo. I rather thought we had succeeded in taming you by sending you to school, but I see that the apple never falls far from the tree."

If Cleo had had troops, they would have been milling in confusion. "Exactly what do you mean by that?"

The enemy pursued her. Ellie shook her head, a small smile tilting the corners of her wide mouth. "Is it not obvious? I have tried to protect you, Cleo, from the way your mother raised you, but it is quite clear to me that she was a sorry example."

Cleo surged to her feet. "You leave my mother out of this! At least she loved me!"

"Sit down, girl," Lady Agnes commanded. "Your sister loves you too, in her own way."

"I'd like to have evidence of that," Cleo muttered, but she retreated, sinking back onto her chair, for her godmother's sake.

The enemy did not retreat so easily. "I shall not deign to answer that," Ellie replied. "My actions on your behalf should speak for themselves."

"Nonsense," Lady Agnes declared as Cleo's temper neared the breaking point. "What exactly have you done that's so praiseworthy?"

Ellie raised an eyebrow. "I rather thought paying for a wardrobe and taking out this house a substantial gift," she replied coldly.

"You picked her clothes without asking her, or me for that matter," Lady Agnes pointed out. "You chose the smallest town house on a secluded street at the very edge of respectability and furnished it with your cast-offs. Mighty charitable of you. Remind me never to ask you for favors."

Another direct hit! Ellie's eyes flashed. "I have done more than anyone could expect for a girl who is only a half sister. And further, I cannot be expected to provide for her indefinitely. I certainly cannot be expected to maintain a ramshackle husband with nothing to recommend him. Mr. Carlisle has made an investment in Cleo's education and upbringing these last five years, and he deserves to see a return. She will marry to advantage. I am only here tonight because she insists on endangering her reputation. If she is to have any hope of catching a husband, she must curb this wildness."

Cleo bridled anew. Lady Agnes snorted. "I doubt Leslie was put off by the affair. If I know my godson, he was likely delighted to have a good race. Just see to it the next time is in private, Cleo. I agree with your sister—you do have a reputation to protect."

The enemy turned suddenly on the intermediary. Ellie drew herself up to her full height. "Lady Agnes, might I have a word with you, in private?"

"No," Lady Agnes replied, picking up her fork. "As you can see, Cleo and I are eating. And you look as if you were on your way somewhere important. Be off, Electra. If we must speak, choose a civilized time tomorrow."

She had an ally! Cleo gazed at her godmother in admiration. Ellie stared openmouthed. Then she raised her head, accepting the challenge.

"You may count on it, madam," she snapped. She turned on her heel and strode for the door.

"Electra," Lady Agnes called, forcing Cleo's sister to pause and look back. "Remember that though your father's will names Mr. Carlisle as guardian, it specifies that I am to have charge of Cleo's Season. The fact might help you formulate your discussion for our next meeting. Have a nice evening, dear."

The enemy retreated with an utter lack of graciousness. Ellie left as stormily as she had arrived.

Cleo leapt from her seat and threw her arms around her godmother. "Oh, Lady Agnes, that was famous!"

"Hush, now," Lady Agnes replied sternly. She waited for Cleo to resume her seat before continuing. "Do not make me your champion, girl. I am just as determined as your sisters that you marry well." She set down her fork again and gazed at Cleo. She had never seen her godmother look so stern. "Make no mistake, Cleo," she intoned. "Your sisters will cut you off without a penny the moment you marry."

Cleo shrugged, picking up her own fork as her appetite returned. "I never asked for their money. It will not hurt me to lose it."

Lady Agnes shook her head. "Not if you marry well. But there is danger there too, my girl. They will also expect to receive a portion of whatever benefits marriage provides you."

"You mean they expect some kind of settlement?" Cleo asked, trying to remember what little she knew about marriage arrangements. "I thought the husband simply settled something on the wife, or she got to keep what she brought with her."

Lady Agnes's mouth was tight. "Normally, either of those examples might be the case. In your situation, however, I have no doubt Mr. Carlisle has something else in mind entirely."

"What has my sister's husband to do with this?" Cleo demanded. "He rarely even talked to me the few times I visited. Why should he care who I marry or what my husband offers, as long as I am no longer his responsibility?"

To Cleo's surprise, her godmother sighed wearily. "I am certain Electra is under considerable pressure from her husband to marry you off. Mr. Carlisle is a very prudent banker. As your sister pointed out, he has made an investment in you and will no doubt want a return."

Cleo rubbed her sleeves as the room seemed to have chilled. "You make it sound as if he expects to sell me to the highest bidder."

Her godmother stabbed at her salmon. "Your imagination is entirely too lurid, my girl. Just be warned. Your safest choice is to marry a man of integrity and substance who can protect you."

Integrity and substance? The image those words brought to mind was that of an elderly country squire, like her father. They were the last words that came to mind when she thought of a certain man about town.

"And you think Leslie is that man?" Cleo couldn't help her incredulous tone.

Lady Agnes barked a laugh. Then she pointed her fork at Cleo. "With your help he could be. Do not let Major Cutter's dash blind you to Leslie's possibilities, my girl. Now, finish your dinner before it gets cold."

Cleo returned to her food, but her mind continued to digest all she had learned. In truth, she knew little about George Carlisle, having only met him a few times when she had been forced to stay with Ellie during school holidays. But then, she didn't know a great deal about her sisters either. Although she hated their meddling, she had thought deep down that they did it over concern for her. Could they be motivated by greed instead? If so, her plan to shock them might never succeed.

But Lady Agnes was right that she had a chance. For this Season at least, there was only so much Ellie and Annie could do. She had not been aware that her parents' will gave her godmother such power. She had been too young to attend the reading of the will, and in the five years since, she had resigned herself to Ellie and Annie bossing her around. It did indeed look as if she were safe for the moment, but only so long as she looked for a husband. Once she made her choice or quit the field, she would be back under her sisters' control, their victim. Her plan had become vital to her future happiness. She had to succeed. And she would need all the help she could get.

Yet even as she thought about it, Leslie's face appeared in her mind and she smiled. Good old Leslie. Even if Lady Agnes was sometimes a fickle ally, Cleo could count on Les for help. She had no doubt she could convince him to escort her to the Baminger ball. She simply had to find a way for him to have fun.

And if she got considerable enjoyment out of the event, neither her sisters nor Lady Agnes need be the wiser.

Seven

"You want me to do what?" Leslie all but yelped when she confronted him the next day with the plan she'd hatched that night. As if sensing his agitation, Hector squawked obligingly, spreading his emerald wings until they stuck out on either side of his gilded cage.

"Shh!" Cleo cautioned Leslie. "You needn't sound so concerned. It will make all the difference, I promise you."

Leslie watched as she pursed her lips and made soothing noises to the parrot. Her slender hands reached through the bars to gently stroke the raised feathers until Hector lowered his wings back to his sides. Leslie rather thought if she stroked him that way, he would hardly be relaxed. He shook his head, as much at her logic as to clear his wayward thoughts.

"I fail to see how—what did you call it?—'dressing in sartorial splendor' will win me a place in Lady Baminger's affections."

"So that she will not regret allowing you on the attendee list," Cleo countered. "Besides, you wanted to have fun, didn't you? What could be more fun that being the most presentable gentleman at the ball?"

"Spoken like a green debutante," Leslie replied,

watching as she stiffened to glare at him. "May I hope you will be dressed in similar fashion?"

She turned from the parrot to eye him. "I always wear my best to balls."

"And quite demure and sweet you look too," he assured her. "Might I suggest that if you want your sisters to believe I am leading you astray, you might be better served to wear something other than white to a ball?"

She tightened her jaw. "I'd be delighted to, except that is all I own. My sisters chose my wardrobe. Insipid colors appear to be their favorites."

"So, what's to keep you from shopping?" he challenged. "I had to buy a blasted horse. A dress would not appear to be out of the question."

"It is entirely out of the question," she informed him heatedly. "I have no money of my own, and I refuse to accept anything more from Lady Agnes. She is already paying for most of the servants, as well as our stables. I won't ask her to clothe me as well."

So, that was why they lived at the edge of society with the odd furnishings. He was relieved to hear his godmother wasn't strapped for cash, although he found himself annoyed with Cleo's nip-farthing sisters. The least they could do was deck her out properly. He pulled a couple of guineas out of his pocket and flipped them to her. She caught them easily, eyes widening.

"Go on," he told her. "Get yourself a dress and have it fitted. I'm sure it will cost more than that. Use those to show the shopkeeper you are serious and have the bill sent to my solicitor. He's the same gentleman Lady Agnes uses."

She made a face and held the coins back out to him. "I can't do that, Les. Ladies do not accept clothing as gifts."

"A young lady should certainly be allowed to accept a gift from an old friend of the family," he corrected her. "Besides, if you think it is improper, tell Lady Agnes and your sisters I insisted."

She grinned. "That's very good. Quite shocking, actually. I shall do it, if you are certain you will not miss the money."

"I have plenty," he assured her with a smile.

"Then you won't mind having to buy new clothes for yourself," she replied, glancing up at him through her lashes.

He should have known better than to think he could distract her from her purpose. He gave a martyred sigh that made Hector shuffle on his perch. "I will look through my closet, Sprout, that much I'll promise you. Dash it all, but I begin to think you have no idea what constitutes fun."

She scowled, cinnamon brows dark over her little nose. "Very well, then, explain to me your concept of fun and I shall endeavor to fulfill it."

Leslie felt a smile tugging. He reached out and ran a finger down her cheek, watching with fascination as a blush blossomed from his touch. "Sweetling, you have no idea what you just offered."

Her eyes widened and her lips parted, drawing his eyes to her mouth. He'd wager her kiss would be as fragrant as the rose her lips reminded him of. He bent his head to find out.

"Well," Lady Agnes demanded, striding into the room in a rustle of dark silk, "does he talk yet?"

Leslie jerked upright. Good God, had he been about to kiss Cleo? By her look of wide-eyed amazement and deep blush, she evidently thought so too. He sent her what he hoped was a regretful smile and turned to greet his godmother. The only problem was, he wasn't entirely sure what he regretted—trying to kiss her, or failing.

"Good afternoon, Lady Agnes," he said, bowing. "And no, I fear our good friend Hector has yet to say a word."

"He is saying something," Lady Agnes returned, closing the distance between them so she could affix her bird with a steady eye. "I heard him squawking yesterday and today when you were here. That at least is an accomplishment."

"I've made an accomplishment as well," Cleo announced, forcing Lady Agnes to glance at her. Leslie could not imagine what the girl intended, but her announcements had the tendency to pick his pocket or inconvenience him. He narrowed his eyes at her in warning, but, although he saw her swallow, she continued on doggedly. "Lord Hastings has agreed to escort us to the Baminger ball."

Leslie closed his eyes for a moment, then opened them to find Cleo regarding him as if afraid he would strike her, and Lady Agnes regarding him as if afraid he'd lost his mind.

"Yes, well, I would be hard-pressed not to agree with anything the delightful Miss Renfield suggests," he replied truthfully. "At what time shall I call for you, Lady Agnes?"

"Nine-thirty," she answered, still watching him warily. "And see that you bring a large enough carriage for the three of us. No tricks to get Cleo alone."

At the moment, his only desire was to get Cleo alone so that he could wring her lovely neck. "Certainly not, Godmother. And since you have given me a commission, perhaps I should leave for the day. I shall want to pick the appropriate equipage to do justice to your celebrated beauty."

Lady Agnes snorted. Cleo frowned. "You are leaving?"

"Sadly, yes," Leslie replied, though sadness did not begin to describe his emotions. "I shall see you the day after tomorrow at half past nine, ladies."

"Won't you come to teach Hector tomorrow afternoon?" Cleo asked, rather plaintively, he thought. He bowed.

"No, I think not," he said as he straightened. "I shall be much too busy learning to dress in sartorial splendor." With a nod to his grinning godmother, he quit the room before Cleo's look of surprise could force a laugh to spoil his performance.

Cleo wasn't sure how Leslie would end up dressing. He might well wear something awful just to spite her. She *had* manipulated him. It was rather obvious that he did not like to appear less than perfect in front of their godmother. The trait was all too easy to use. Yet she was certain that her plan would succeed. If Leslie could just look like he belonged at the affair, Lady Baminger would have no choice but to accept him. Once Cleo got him in, she'd make sure he enjoyed the event.

His enjoyment, however, would not extend to a kiss. She could not imagine what he'd been thinking to lean toward her that way, his eyelids drifting lower even as his chin angled to avoid hers. Certainly she hadn't expected her heart to speed, her lips to purse, her own body to lean forward as well, expectantly, hopefully. Their teasing camaraderie must have made them both light-headed.

Of course, it was possible that she had misinterpreted his intentions. He was quite right to call her green, at least in the area of the intimacies shown from a man to a woman. She had never been kissed. She could not remember seeing her mother and father kissing, although she did remember they were wont to hold hands while walking down the country lanes near their home. Certainly she had never seen Ellie or Annie show the least bit of affection for the gentlemen they'd married. Most of her experiences came secondhand, through whispered conversations among equally inexperienced schoolgirls, and the brief mentions of courtly love in the novels she borrowed from the lending library.

Of course, there was her experience with catching Eloise and Jareth Darby. But in truth, she was still not a little confused by what had happened that day. When she had first heard the thumps and mewling overhead, she had thought perhaps one of the stable cats had somehow gotten stuck. The grooms were out attending to a riding lesson for the lower-form students, so she could scarcely ask them to intercede. She had clambered up the ladder and poked her head through the hole to find a gentleman lying in the hay with Eloise. Both were oblivious to her presence, and she could only stare in astonishment. The fellow's touch to Eloise's body had been tender, but Cleo could see tears on the girl's face. She had rushed to rescue Eloise from her supposed attacker. Snatching up a fork used to pitch hay down to the horses, she'd jabbed the fellow in the posterior. Even now, she had to squeeze her eyes tight shut to block out the scene that had followed.

Neither of them had been pleased by her attempted rescue. Darby, even then tall, wiry, and incredibly handsome, had easily disarmed her and coldly set about fastening himself up. He had clambered down a rear chute she had not known the stable possessed without another word to Eloise or her. Eloise had sobbed for what seemed like hours, during which time Cleo could only sit with hands folded tightly in her lap. Any attempt at conversation was met with fresh sobs. At length, she had simply climbed down and returned to the school.

She certainly hadn't realized she was injuring the prestigious Jareth Darby. At thirteen, she hadn't understood the nature of coupling. She still didn't. Only the pain she'd seen in Eloise's eyes had made her decide to tell Miss Martingale about the matter.

The entire scene had given her an awed curiosity about relations between men and women. Eloise had sobbed at Darby's defection, but she certainly had not looked or sounded as if she were having any fun when he was there with her. Leslie, on the other hand, was determined to have fun. It seemed unlikely then that he would wish to seduce her. She must have mistaken him.

The matter was not entirely driven from her mind as she tried to procure a shocking gown for the ball. She had told Leslie the truth. Her sisters had chosen simpering colors like pink, sky blue, and pale yellow that Cleo felt did not do justice to her cinnamon coloring. The most she'd been able to do was suggest a few alterations when the seamstress came to tailor them for her. The few pence she had to spend, a quarterly allowance also granted her by George Carlisle, went for accessories like gloves and fans and bonnets. But with two guineas in her pocket, and the promise of more if she needed it, she should be able to pick any gown she wanted.

The problem, of course, was time. She had only two days before the ball. No seamstress could whip up a dress so quickly. She racked her brain for a way around the issue, finally resorting to asking Bess about the matter.

"A gown ready by Saturday evening, miss?" the little brown-haired maid had mused. "You want one that just needs the fittings. A lady I heard tell of— well, perhaps lady is too strong a word—but she got her gowns ready-made from a clever woman who takes in gowns from the folks in need of blunt and fixes them like new. Might be she could help you."

It turned out she could. When Cleo and Bess managed to slip away while Lady Agnes was visiting her niece, Cleo found any number of fashionable gowns at the establishment on a back street in the heart of the city. Most were nowhere near her size, but several were close enough that simple fittings would suffice. One was shockingly daring, with a neckline square cut across the top of her breasts, and sleeves that were mere nothings at her shoulders. The apricot silk clung to her curves and swept gracefully to the floor in narrow folds. A deeper apricot satin ribbon just under her breasts further tightened a tiny bodice and left two long trails of sash down her thighs.

"I don't know, miss," Bess murmured while the rail-thin seamstress pinned the hem to Cleo's shorter stature. "I don't think her ladyship would approve."

"Really?" Cleo mused, though she was certain the maid was right. For all the gown's daring, however, the shade suited her coloring and the price was low enough that she had money left over from Leslie's gold. She completed the fittings and made the woman promise to deliver the finished gown in time for Cleo to dress the next day.

When she donned the gown that Saturday, however, her misgivings grew. She'd never seen so much skin. Surely she'd passed beyond shocking to scandalous. Bess agreed, if the tight set of her mouth was any indication. In the end, Cleo had found a cream lace fichu and wrapped it around her shoulders, pinning it to either side of her decolletage and filling the gap above with her mother's pearls. She could see her attempts at modesty ruined the line of the dress, but at least she did not feel naked. With a bandeau around her curls, she hoped she looked passable. It remained to be seen whether Leslie would approve.

Unfortunately, her extra care in dressing made her late going downstairs. Mr. Cowls had to point her to the sitting room, where her godmother and Leslie were already waiting. Cleo only made it to the doorway before stopping in shock.

Leslie was splendid.

His black hair shone in the candlelight. His slender frame hung with an expertly cut double-breasted velvet coat of a deep blue with silver filigree buttons. A sapphire in a silver setting sparkled from the folds of his pristine cravat, which was tied in a complicated fold that somehow drew her eyes across the breadth of his shoulders. His waistcoat, peeking out above the coat, was a black satin embroidered with silver veining. His silver gray satin breeches and white stockings were taut over muscular legs. Seeing her staring, he quirked a smile.

"Well . . ." she started.

"Hell and damnation," Hector squawked.

Cleo jumped even as Leslie compressed his lips in an obvious attempt not to crow with laughter.

Lady Agnes blinked. "Did he just speak?"

"He certainly tried," Leslie proclaimed, striding to the cage. "Pity we couldn't tell exactly what was on his mind. Good lad, Hector. That's enough for tonight. Wouldn't want to overdo it your first time." He snatched the cover from the top of the cage and blanketed the bars.

"What are you up to?" Lady Agnes demanded. "I distinctly heard him speak."

Leslie whirled to offer her his arm. "Now, now, Godmother, we wouldn't want to be any later than we already are. You can scold me tomorrow."

Lady Agnes rose slowly, frowning. "Exactly why should I be scolding you?"

While he waited for his godmother to join him, he offered Cleo his other arm. "I'm certain we can think of something. Coming, my dear?"

Still somewhat dazed, Cleo accepted. He bent his head closer to hers. "Stop staring, Sprout," he hissed. "You asked for sartorial splendor, remember?"

Cleo had no time to respond, for Lady Agnes had stepped up to take his arm.

"Your sisters," she told Cleo, "have atrocious taste in clothing. I wish you'd let me buy something more fitting."

"I'd say this particular gown fits Cleo rather well," Leslie countered.

Their godmother snorted but said no more about it as Leslie led them to the entry. He did not offer additional comment either. Just as well, she thought as they proceeded to get their wraps and walk down to the waiting carriage. She wasn't certain what to say anyway. She could not seem to reconcile her prankish partner with the stylish gentleman beside her.

"This will do nicely," Lady Agnes proclaimed as he handed her into the closed carriage. "I never knew you owned such a fine carriage."

Cleo glanced at the brown-lacquered sides and gold trimmings. Everything gleamed in the light of the lanterns on either side of the driver's box.

"I didn't own it," Leslie said beside her. He put a hand on her waist, and she stiffened. But his touch was light and gentle as he helped her up the little stair to the seating compartment. "It was my father's."

She could hear the sadness in his voice and felt her heart clench. This was the kindhearted Leslie she knew. She watched as he climbed into the carriage, but nothing in his smooth movements betrayed any emotion.

"Not much of a debater, your father," Lady Agnes ventured as he seated himself opposite them and signaled his driver to move off. "Far too much a gentleman to ever disagree with me. I hope you do not intend to follow in his stead now that you are the marquis."

Cleo thought she saw him grimace, but in the uneven light from outside, she could not be sure.

"Certainly not, Lady Agnes," he assured her. "I shall be only too happy to disagree with you, on any number of topics."

Lady Agnes snorted. "Tease. You are up to something, I can tell. Might as well admit it, for I shall find you out, mark my words."

Cleo stiffened, wondering just how much her godmother saw, but Leslie merely chuckled. "Why, Lady Agnes, I am honored you would think me so intriguing. I assure you, any secrets I have would not be worth your time. By the by, have I told you how fine you look this evening?"

He was avoiding the topic, and rather charmingly, Cleo thought. Unfortunately, their godmother did not seem to agree.

"You have," Lady Agnes declared. "Twice. That evasion will not suffice. However, I will settle for hearing you compliment Cleo."

Cleo put on a bright smile, even though she wasn't certain he could see her clearly. "That is hardly necessary," she put in hurriedly. "I am certain Leslie has other matters of more interest to discuss."

"On the contrary," Leslie replied, leaning forward as if to convince her of his sincerity. "Let me be the first to compliment you, for I surely will not be the last. Your beauty outshines the stars."

Cleo felt herself blush at the warmth of his voice. Lady Agnes barked out a laugh.

"Is that what you young men call a compliment these days?" she demanded. "Unoriginal and uninspired, I call it."

"Lady Agnes!" Cleo scolded.

Leslie sat straighter. "You challenge me, madam. Very well." His voice deepened, mellowing as he continued.

> *"She walks in beauty like the night*
> *Of cloudless climes and starry skies*
> *And all that's best of dark and bright*
> *Meet in her aspects, and her eyes."*

Cleo swallowed, heart jumping in her chest even as a slow heat spread up her face.

"Ha!" Lady Agnes declared. "Byron. You will not get off that easily."

Cleo started to shake her head, afraid of her own reaction should he persist. But Leslie seemed to know he had gone as far as he dared.

"Nor will you," he told his godmother. "Anything more I have to say to Cleo will be said in private. And now, madam, unless I am very much mistaken, we have arrived."

The carriage bumped to a stop and then shook as Leslie's groom sprang to open the door and lower the step. Leslie alighted to hand them both down, Lady Agnes first and then Cleo. As Cleo took his hand, he leaned closer to whisper, "Don't let her tease you, Sprout. You look divine. And if you need to hear more love poems to prove it, let me know."

She smiled as she stepped away from him, feeling absurdly pleased. Her pleasure was short-lived, however, as they joined the crowds entering the stately town house. First one of the waiting footmen stripped off her cloak, leaving her suddenly chilled despite the summer night. Then Lady Agnes began her usual complaining.

"I do not know why Lady Baminger insists on having these balls," she said as they were jostled through the entryway and funneled toward the receiving line just beyond. "She only has the one small ballroom on the main floor, with that ridiculous music room of hers. She ought to have done with it and rent Almack's."

Cleo was more than a little afraid that her godmother would say the same as they moved up the line to be greeted by their host and hostess. Lord and Lady Baminger were far more impressive than their ballroom. The tall, thin, dark-eyed lord nodded down his long nose at Cleo but went so far as to begin an argument with Lady Agnes, which seemed to please them both no end. The equally tall but far more substantial Lady Baminger was more welcoming, until she laid eyes on Leslie.

"Good evening, Lord Hastings," she intoned, refusing to do so much as offer her pudgy, ring-encrusted hand for him to bow over. "I want you to know you are welcome here tonight only because of your connection with Lady Agnes DeGuis. I have not forgotten last year's debacle."

Cleo tensed as Leslie cast her a quick glance. "I was certain you would not, madam. I assure you, the memory is indelibly etched in my mind as one of the worst moments of my sorry existence. That you are willing to forgive for my godmother's sake is testimony to your high moral standards."

Lord Baminger coughed into his hand, shoulders shaking. His wife sent him a quelling look before returning her frown to Leslie, who stood waiting patiently like a martyr about to face the lions for his faith. Cleo held her breath.

"I trust, sir," she said, "that there will be no repeat of last year's behavior?"

"Upon my honor," Leslie swore, executing a deep bow. "I shall be the complete gentleman. And may I add, Lady Baminger, that your magnanimous reception only proves the tales told of your long-suffering patience."

Lord Baminger choked. Lady Agnes tapped Leslie on the wrist with her fan even as Lady Baminger showed signs of thawing and Cleo let out her breath with relief.

"She is hardly ready for sainthood," her godmother snapped. "Now, come along, Cleo, before Leslie drowns in the butter boat."

She hustled them away from the door before Cleo could see how their hostess would respond.

"The evening had better improve, Sprout," Leslie whispered in her ear as they made their way into the ballroom.

"What?" she whispered back. "Didn't you find flirting with a dowager amusing? You do it so well."

He only grunted. Cleo bit back a giggle. A moment later, her breath caught in her throat.

Major Cutter, in full regimentals, stood framed by the doors of the music room on one side of the dance floor. The gold braid on his deep blue jacket shone as brightly as his pomaded hair in the candlelight. As Leslie moved them in his direction, his face broke into a smile, for all the world as if he had been waiting for her. All thought that he had set his cap for Eloise Watkin vanished from her mind. Her heart hammered uncomfortably in her chest, making the high waist of the gown entirely too tight under her breasts. Leslie put a hand against the small of her back. The pressure was amazingly reassuring.

"Courage, Sprout," he murmured before removing his hand to thrust it at the major. "Evening, Cutter. I believe you know my lovely companions?"

Major Cutter bowed. "Lady Agnes, you look younger each time I see you."

Lady Agnes snorted but said nothing. Her look to Leslie said exactly what she thought of this chance meeting.

"And Miss Renfield," the major continued, allowing his eyes to roam over her and setting her heart to pounding even faster, "always a pleasure."

He took Cleo's hand and brought it to his lips, pressing a fervent kiss against her knuckles. She wondered whether her legs could possibly support her.

"And may I say you look especially lovely tonight," he murmured as Lady Agnes pointed Leslie toward the dowagers' circle across the room. "Surely Lord Byron had you in mind when he wrote his famous lines,

> "She walks in beauty like the night
> Of cloudless climes and starry skies
> And all that's best of dark and bright
> Meet in her aspects, and her eyes."

Cleo stared at him. Leslie took her hand out of the major's grasp and transferred it to his own.

"Amateur," he muttered under his breath.

"Save me a dance, Miss Renfield," the major called as Leslie led her to safety at Lady Agnes's side.

Eight

Blast Leslie!

Cleo stamped into her bedchamber and yanked off her long gloves, telling Bess rather loudly to take herself off. The maid scampered out wide-eyed, but Cleo hardly cared. She was entirely too furious to want anyone at her side.

How dare he spoil her evening! He was supposed to be her ally. Instead, he had embarrassed her with his ridiculously high-flung praise, and then he'd completely ruined Major Cutter's flirtation by the very fact that he'd said it first.

The rest of the evening had been no better. She could scarcely look for an opportunity to do something shocking when Leslie had kept her so busy. Every woman present seemed to have developed a shocking lack of propriety where he was concerned. They simpered and flirted and flaunted themselves before him so that she was forced to stay by his side for fear Lady Agnes would suspect their courtship was a charade. But even her cold glare and possessive grip on his arm had not deterred them. He was supposed to be courting her, and not a single woman in the room seemed capable of realizing it.

To make matters worse, Eloise Watkin had been in attendance, and in rare form. Cleo had been forced to watch while she had no less than two dances with Major Cutter, setting tongues to wagging. Eloise had gone so far as to commandeer Leslie for a waltz, of all things, as if she knew Cleo could not dance it. The smile on his face while whirling the beauty around the floor had been far too knowing, Eloise's far too smug.

"Are you enjoying yourself, my lord?" Cleo had asked when he'd returned to her side near where Lady Agnes sat in the dowagers' circle.

He'd quirked his smile. "Thoroughly. And you?"

Her only response had been to stalk past him and accost the nearest male she knew, the older brother of a classmate, insisting that he had promised her that dance.

Perhaps worst of all, her single country dance with Major Cutter had been quite spoiled. She'd had to watch while he danced with three of her classmates, including an adoring Marlys Rutherford. When the dashing fellow had finally strolled up to inquire as to which dance she had been so gracious as to bestow on him, she'd shyly suggested the next dance. But Leslie had refused to relinquish her hand when the major requested it, forcing her to enact a small scene of pique. She was certain her face hadn't stopped flaming even by the time the dance ended.

"I take it you and Lord Hastings have reached an understanding?" the major had asked when the pattern of the dance brought them close enough for conversation.

"By no means," Cleo assured him, the words coming through clenched teeth. She glanced to where Leslie was supposed to be conversing with her godmother, only to find that no less than four young ladies clustered around him, fans waving so rapidly in their excitement, she wondered he did not immediately catch the ague. He seemed to know she was watching, for he raised his head to wink at her. She'd very nearly missed a step, and Major Cutter had been forced to pause to allow her to catch up. How could Leslie be so maddening?

She threw herself down on the stool before her dressing table and dragged the bandeau savagely from her curls. Her hand reached up to serve the pearls likewise and froze. What was the matter with her? Those were her mother's pearls, one of the few things that had not been sold or given away when her parents had died. That she would even think of treating them savagely surely showed how agitated she was. And for what? Was her anger with Leslie worth damaging something so precious?

And why exactly was she angry with Leslie anyway? She'd been the one to insist he dress better than usual. Of course, she'd hardly suspected how very splendid he'd look. Neither had the other ladies, she thought, for Leslie had seemed rather surprised by his sudden notoriety. She couldn't even say she was angry that he'd flirted with her. Theirs had been a teasing relationship from the first. She had to be honest. She wasn't angry with Leslie for quoting Byron first; she felt cheated because he had quoted the poet-lord better. His voice had been more impassioned, his admiration more sincere. In an unexpected test of manly ardor, Major Cutter had come off a poor second. And nearly every other woman in the room had recognized it before she had.

She let her head fall into her hands. She could not remember ever feeling so confused. Had her sisters' machinations succeeded in turning her into a mindless drone that she suddenly found the dashing major considerably less dashing? No, she could not be swayed from her course so easily! She could not let them dictate to her.

Determined, she raised her head and regarded herself in the mirror. Now that the tempestuous emotions of the evening were passing, she must force herself to think clearly. She had set herself on this course of action for a reason. She needed to keep that reason in sight. Some pain might be expected in reaching any goal.

She rose to unbutton her gown, thinking hard. Tonight had been sufficiently confusing, of course, that she had momentarily questioned her goal. It was impossible to forget her sisters'. Whatever their reasons, they wanted her to marry well. What, after all, did Cleo want?

She slipped off her shoes and placed them neatly in the bottom of her wardrobe. The gown followed into the clothes press. The clothes Ellie had bought for her stared back at her accusingly. Ellie had sold herself for a mess of porridge. Very good porridge, it was true, but porridge nonetheless. Is that what she wanted? To have fine clothes to wear and a finer carriage to port her about? It somehow did not feel ethical to base one's decisions on creature comfort alone. She forcibly put material matters from her mind as she pulled off her stays and chemise and wandered to the bureau to retrieve her linen nightdress. Surely there was a better purpose for her life besides dressing in pretty gowns and turning gentlemen's heads.

So, what did Cleo want? She slid between the covers and lay looking up at the canopy of her bed. The rose and green tapestries that hung from the posters were singularly uninspiring. No lofty thoughts filled her mind. She had never aspired to being more than a wife and mother. Indeed, now that she thought on it carefully, she wasn't certain she wanted to be anything else.

Of course, some women did not marry. Those with independent living like Lady Agnes did what they liked. She had no such living. Others became companions or governesses. She somehow thought her temperament would make her a bad choice for either vocation, even if they had appealed to her. Still others were more visible in their contributions to society. Certainly Hannah Moore had made her mark in people's lives with her advice on Christian living. Lady Mary Shelley had cut a swath through the literary world with that horror novel she'd written (a smuggled copy of which Cleo had read at the Barnsley School).

Yet those things, while fascinating, held no appeal for her own life. She thought she would be more than content to help her husband by managing his house and rearing his children. She could not remember helping her mother around the house, but certainly just seeing the way Ellie had decorated and furnished the town house set her hands to itching to do a better job. She could imagine sewing curtains and embroidering chair cushions, polishing brass and shining silver. While wives married to rich peers simply oversaw those activities, at least they made sure their homes were graciously appointed and efficiently run. She rather thought that would be an interesting challenge.

More than that, she wanted to be the center of her family. She remembered growing up under her mother's loving care. She did not think she could entrust her children to the care of nurses or governesses, as so many people seemed to be doing. She certainly would never abandon them to boarding schools. They would have tutors and governesses instead. Moreover, her children would have no doubts they were loved. In fact, she would very likely spoil them with her attentions. She could imagine tea parties with her daughters and tin soldier battles with her sons, and teaching them all to ride and hunt and fish.

But as she envisioned her future, she found it difficult to picture the gentleman who would be the father of all these sons and daughters. She flirted with the idea of Major Cutter filling the role. Yet if he was the right choice, surely the ghostly figure in her dreams would be wearing a deep blue coat with gold braid at the shoulders. Instead, she could not help but notice as she drifted off to sleep, he seemed to be wearing a blue velvet coat and smiling an amused little half smile.

Leslie fell asleep with considerably more difficulty. It took two hours of lounging by the fire in his dressing gown with a bottle of brandy at his side before he was even able to convince himself to try the bed.

The evening had not gone as he had intended. He had waited for Cleo to make some move to distinguish herself and ruin him forever in Lady Baminger's eyes, but she had not moved away from his side for more than a country dance. She had glowered at every female who had promenaded past, and when the interesting Miss Watkin had come to claim him for a waltz, she had all but snapped at the poor girl.

"I fear you must find me impertinent for thrusting myself upon you, my lord," Miss Watkin had murmured as they moved out onto the dance floor. "But I was uncertain whether Miss Renfield would be willing to let you go."

Leslie smiled at her, enjoying the feel of her considerable curves next to his body. "No more so than I am certain Major Cutter was loathe to part with you," he replied.

She dimpled. "Ah, but Major Cutter and I do not have an understanding."

She was leaving it to him to deny he had such an understanding with Cleo. He was more interested in her relationship with the major. There had been moments, like when she gave an exaggerated swing to her hips while walking, that he was tempted to believe she was less than an innocent. The gold lamé dress was molded to her frame. He would also have wagered a guinea to a groat that the luster of her lashes had been helped along by blacking, the blossoms on her fair cheeks by a rouge pot. Her smile as she glanced up at him was knowing, the way her body kept brushing his suggestively.

Another time he would have been more than happy to pursue the acquaintance. Now he simply wanted to know what exactly Tony Cutter was up to. The major had to know, between his appearance with Miss Watkin in the park two days earlier and the two dances he had favored her with tonight, that he was making a statement. Yet the girl did not seem to think him attached.

"The more fool he," Leslie had replied to her. "If he cannot see your worth, he cannot complain when others snatch you up."

She laughed. "Major Cutter knows how much I value his company. He has no need for jealousy. Do you, my lord?"

"Certainly not," Leslie told her. "The lady I loved would have no doubt as to my devotion, nor would I need to doubt her."

She sighed. "Ah, Miss Renfield is a lucky girl. Should I be offering her my congratulations?"

The minx was insistent. "Congratulations may be premature," he advised. "I assure you, when the time comes, all London will know."

"In the meantime," she murmured, glancing up at him from the corner of her emerald green eyes, "perhaps you would like to retrieve your hat? I shall be at home the next few afternoons."

He promised to visit in the near future, but in truth he found the prospect far less intriguing than he had in the park. In a contest of womanly virtue, Miss Watkin came off a poor second to Cleo's honest worth.

Cleo, on the other hand, had looked anything but intrigued when he returned to her after the dance. She had been cool to him the rest of the evening. He was certain by the set of her proud little chin on the ride home that she was much miffed with him, and he wasn't entirely sure why. It wasn't as if she could be jealous.

As far as he was concerned, he was the one who should be miffed. He'd been cheated. He had agreed to this whole charade as a favor to her and in hopes of fending off his growing lethargy since his father's death. While he could not claim to be bored, neither could he claim to believe any longer that he was helping Cleo. If anything, her plan was hurting her. The more scandalous she appeared, the more Major Cutter seemed to be interested. And Tony Cutter simply wasn't good enough for her.

He shook his head from his seat before the fire in the guest bedchamber. He could no more force himself to imagine Cleo with the major than he could force himself to sleep in the master bedchamber—his father's bedchamber, he reminded himself. He'd thought Cutter a fine fellow. He had obviously been mistaken.

He'd known Cutter for several years, ever since the fellow's return from the Peninsula following the Battle of Waterloo. With both of them men about town, it was inevitable that they might be drawn together for a game of cards or two. The major had at first been careful. He suspected the man had an innate distrust of his father and the gentlemen he recruited, for the military had long been skeptical of the ethics behind espionage. But once Cutter had learned that Leslie had little part in his father's activities, he had always treated Leslie with a politeness approaching friendliness. Leslie had always considered him moderately intelligent and affable.

Tonight, however, he had suddenly been stricken with the unfriendly desire to plant his fist in the fellow's knowing smile. By what right did the miscreant think he was on familiar enough grounds with Cleo to quote her a love poem? Never mind that Leslie had already quoted the same poem to her (and done a considerably better job, he might add). Leslie was a friend of the family, after all, and he and Cleo were attempting to make her family believe he was smitten. Tony Cutter, on the other hand, clearly had other purposes in mind. Leslie had seen the way the major's gaze lingered over Cleo's décolletage. He did not think Lady Agnes was right about Cutter being after Cleo's money. After all, she had none. Still, the fellow was obviously less than honorable, and Leslie'd be hanged before he let the fellow get his hands on Cleo.

Of course, he had to admit with a sigh that required a sip from the brandy snifter between his fingers, that wasn't the problem. He could easily find ways to keep Cleo and Cutter apart. Her family had already taken the fellow's measure. The problem was something far more intractable. How was he to justify keeping Cutter's hands off Cleo when all Leslie could think about was putting his hands on her?

He groaned, pulling his legs back under him and sitting up straighter in the wing-backed chair. This was ridiculous! Cleo was like a little sister to him. How could he burn with lust for a sister? The very idea should make him feel ill. He'd always resisted the suggestion that his wild activities made him less than a gentleman. Perhaps all those harping biddies of the Ton were right. He was utterly depraved.

Yet a part of his mind rebelled at that notion. Cleo was not, after all, related to him by blood or marriage, for all they shared was the same godmother. No church or legal decree would prevent a liaison. But he still could not convince himself that he was ready to marry, and he could not have Cleo any other way.

The thought that she'd make a rousing mistress did not survive its moment of life. Cleo was a lady and a virgin. She deserved to go that way to the husband she chose. He truly would become the reprobate everyone suspected he was if he prevented that.

No, the only choice lay in continuing to play the fool for her. He'd keep her from ruining her reputation and ward off her sisters. He would enjoy his time in her company, until the right man came along.

But somehow he didn't think boredom would describe his feelings when she left his life.

Nine

A good night's sleep was all it took for Cleo to awake once more determined to go through with her plan. She had not made enough progress last night. Lady Agnes had done no more than raise a brow when Cleo had danced with Major Cutter. She had to find a way to discredit Leslie in their eyes.

Normally, she would have a hard time even getting her sisters to take notice. They seldom called unless it was to upbraid her for some infraction of their rules. Once in a while she saw them at parties or the opera, but generally they did not move in the same company. Lady Agnes had at first insisted that Cleo visit each of them every week, but after the first few visits had proved uncomfortable in the extreme, her godmother had stopped suggesting it.

Luckily, today was Sunday. Lady Agnes and Cleo always walked the short distance to church to join Ellie and Annie for services. If she could just think of a reason, she might entice them to visit afterward. She was so deep in thought that she barely listened to the sermon. Only the vicar's parting quotation caught her attention.

"And so, in summary, look to the advice of Proverbs Fifteen: Twenty-two, which says, 'Without counsel purposes are disappointed: but in the multitude of counselors they are established.' "

She shook her head. Normally she liked going to the Bible for advice, but this time she could not accept it. What she had in her life were entirely too many counselors.

By the time the service ended, she still hadn't come up with a convincing excuse to get her sisters to return to the house. To her delight, however, Ellie insisted on taking them home. Lady Agnes bristled but finally acquiesced. She sat in the carriage, looking down her nose at them as if the very sight of them offended her, although her sisters were for once in fine looks. Ellie's plum kerseymere gown was elegantly tailored to her broadening frame, and even Annie's navy-striped silk was pressed and neat. Cleo tried to think what she might have done to warrant them inviting themselves along but could think of nothing. Then she remembered Ellie's threat to return and discuss Cleo's future with Lady Agnes. Clearly her older sister had brought Annie along for support. If she was right, Cleo vowed not to leave her godmother's side.

"What do you want?" Lady Agnes demanded when Mr. Cowls had seen them seated in the drawing room and wisely exited, shutting the door behind him.

Ellie and Annie exchanged glances, and Cleo knew she had been right in her guess as to their purpose.

"We have come to discuss Cleo's future," Ellie answered.

"In private," Annie added.

"Haven't we done that to death?" Cleo put in, even as Lady Agnes sat straighter in her navy silk gown. "Unless you have now determined that Lord Hastings is no longer worth my time, I fail to see what else there is to say on the matter."

"Well spoken," her godmother complimented her. "And if you have decided my Leslie is lacking, we do indeed need to have a talk."

Ellie stuck out her chin. "Lord Hastings still has our support. We simply question the method of attaining him."

"We are concerned about your chaperonage, Cleo," Annie added. "We are not convinced poor Lady Agnes has the stamina to keep up with your mad starts."

Cleo surged to her feet only to find her godmother alongside her.

"Stamina!" Lady Agnes cried, waving a gnarled hand in the air. "How dare you question my stamina? Perhaps you'd like a pointed demonstration of just how much energy I have."

Annie recoiled slightly, but Cleo could not help but put in her own defense. "Shame on you!" she told her sisters. "Is it not enough that you bully me? Must you insult Lady Agnes as well?"

"Hell and damnation!" Hector shouted, spreading his wings.

Annie gasped. Cleo blinked. Ellie stared at him as if he'd grown horns.

"Did he just speak?" she demanded in the silence that followed.

"Yes, he did," Lady Agnes declared, hurrying to the cage. "Clever boy, Hector! Clever, clever boy!"

"He swore at us!" Annie protested. "I heard him. He distinctly said—"

"What he said," Ellie interrupted haughtily, "is immaterial. We did not come here to talk to a bird. We came to talk to Lady Agnes."

"Couldn't we all just talk to each other?" Cleo ventured, hoping to get them away from the subject of Lady Agnes's abilities and on to the subject of

Leslie's unsuitability. "I am told some families find it interesting."

"We," Electra intoned, "are not like other families."

"Certainly not," Annie agreed with a sniff.

Cleo frowned. "And why is that, do you think?"

"A very good question," Lady Agnes pronounced, obviously giving up on the bird, who had returned to his silent brooding. "What exactly has put a spoke in your wheel, Electra? Why do you insist on badgering the girl?"

"I do not badger," Ellie replied. Her stiff pose dared anyone to argue with her. "I merely do my duty, as I see it."

"We are her older sisters, after all," Annie put in. "Her only blood relatives, as you know full well."

"Hell and hell," Hector said obligingly.

Lady Agnes chortled with delight. Annie paled, waving her hand in front of her face as if she feared she'd faint. Ellie narrowed her eyes at the bird.

"Someone," she declared, "has taught this bird to speak."

"Yes," Cleo agreed merrily. "Lord Hastings. Hasn't he done a marvelous job of it?"

"Splendid," Lady Agnes proclaimed.

"Does he know anything other than obscenities?" Annie managed weakly.

"Not that I can tell," Cleo told her.

"Obscenities?" Lady Agnes frowned. "I heard nothing out of the ordinary. He very clearly said Helen Ell. I grant you it makes little sense, but it's a marvelous start."

Now Annie regarded the bird as well. "Helen Ell? Well, that is a relief. I rather thought he said—"

"Will you stop prattling on about that bird?" Ellie demanded, hands on her generous hips. "Mr. Carlisle is expecting me home by half past four. I do not have time to waste."

"Well, neither do I," Annie retorted with a toss of her head. "Lord Stephenson expects to go out tonight and I shall need sufficient time to dress."

"Then perhaps you both should leave," Lady Agnes remarked.

"Now, now," Cleo put in. She could not help but be pleased that at least Annie had noticed the bird's misbehavior, but she needed more time to sufficiently shock Ellie. Her mind cast around for anything she might use to her advantage. She had not gotten a reaction from her dress last night, but of course she had ruined its affect with the fichu. The whole idea had been a waste of Leslie's money. Then again, perhaps she might turn the leftover funds to good use.

"Can't we be civil?" she begged. "If you will not talk, perhaps a hand of cards?"

Ellie grew even stiffer, if that were possible. "Cards?" she all but sneered.

Annie wrinkled her nose. "I have little interest in whist, I assure you."

"Takes entirely too much intelligence," Lady Agnes agreed, earning her a scowl from Annie.

"I was thinking of something more daring," Cleo confided. "Leslie, er, Lord Hastings has been teaching me silverloo. I'm not terribly good yet, but I'd like to practice."

"Gambling, on the Lord's Day?" Ellie waved away her offer with a limp hand.

"Of no interest whatsoever without real money behind it," Annie agreed warily.

"Well," Cleo said casually, "I do have some money put aside."

Ellie looked thoughtful even as Annie narrowed her

eyes. "You have money?" Annie demanded. "Why didn't you tell us?"

"Lord Hastings gave it to me," Cleo said innocently. "He advised me to buy a dress with it, as he does not approve of your taste in clothing. I found the most interesting shop where the lady was only too happy to fit me. She is a very talented seamstress. I cannot imagine why she only seems to attract actresses and opera dancers."

Annie choked. Lady Agnes shook her head. Ellie glared at her.

"Were you seen going to this shop?" she demanded.

Cleo shrugged. "I don't know. I did not make any attempt to hide. It cannot be so very bad a place if Lord Hastings likes the dresses, can it?"

Ellie pursed her lips. "As Lord Hastings is an old friend of the family, I suppose it is permissible for him to suggest a change to your wardrobe."

"If you clothed her better," Lady Agnes put in, "he would not have to."

"Be that as it may," Ellie continued, eyes narrowing, "I hope that in the future, Cleo, you will consult Lady Agnes or one of us before making a purchase."

"Really, Cleo," Annie added with a sniff, "Lord Hastings must think you a complete muttonhead for accepting his money and then squandering it on some inappropriate mantua maker. I am amazed you haven't given him a complete disgust of you."

"Me!" Cleo could barely squeak the word, she was so incensed. "He showers me with gold and sends me to shop with harlots and you question *my* intelligence?"

"Showers you with gold, is it?" Annie challenged. "Do you not think he expected some kind of return on it?"

"I'll have you know," Cleo countered, "that I bought a perfectly delightful dress and had it fitted, with money to spare."

"That was not what she meant," Lady Agnes muttered, leaning forward so that Annie was forced to lean back in defense.

"Never mind that now," Ellie said with a sudden sweetness that sent chills up Cleo's spine. "Lady Stephenson, you are being obstinate. Our sister has graciously invited us to play a round of cards with her. Even if it is Sunday, I do not see how we can refuse and still claim ourselves to be civil. Silverloo, is it? I might be persuaded. If you would join us, Lady Agnes?"

Lady Agnes frowned at her. "Do you cheat?"

Annie gasped again even as Cleo bit her lips to keep from laughing. Ellie merely regarded the old woman as if she might be a new form of fungus. "I have no need to cheat," she replied. "For the simple reason that I always win."

Lady Agnes cackled, rubbing her hands together. "Now, there is a statement I cannot allow to stand. Ring for Mr. Cowls, Cleo. We shall have a game right here."

Cleo had to own that the afternoon had only been a partial success. Annie and Ellie had spent their bickering on the game, thus saving Lady Agnes from whatever scold they had been determined to provide. Unfortunately, even in gambling on the Lord's Day, and doing it rather badly, Cleo had failed to shock them in the slightest. She had come off the worse in her confession about the dress, and Hector refused to help things along by cursing, watching their play silently with his beady black eyes. Worse, Ellie's words had proven true. She won nearly every hand and was obviously only too happy to divest Cleo of the rest of Leslie's money and what was left of this quarter's allowance from Mr. Carlisle. She also managed to pocket a considerable portion of Lady Agnes's pin money, leaving Cleo's godmother to complain about having to make do with last Season's gloves for their next outing to Almack's.

Even so obviously pleased with her winnings, Ellie could not resist a parting shot at Cleo's expense.

"You appear to have captured Lord Hastings's eye," she said as she settled her bonnet on her tightly wound curls. "I expect an offer from him shortly, but see to it that he makes it a good one."

"I understand his father left him rather well off," Annie added as Cleo bristled. "He ought to be good for a tidy dower settlement. And a title to boot." She sucked her teeth as if she had just eaten a tasty caramel.

"Not a penny," Cleo started, but Lady Agnes put a hand on her arm in warning.

"What did you say?" Ellie demanded, pausing in the act of straightening her bonnet.

"She said you are not likely to see a penny," Lady Agnes replied, "if you do not let her get on with her courtship. Leave it to me. The boy will be brought up to snuff."

"I certainly hope so," Ellie replied, turning for the door. She paused again and looked back over her shoulder at Lady Agnes. "I know you have your own inheritance, Lady Agnes, and you certainly have been more than generous to Cleo. I am sure Mr. Carlisle can make it worth your while to see Cleo well settled."

She was offering a bribe! Cleo wanted to scream at her. Lady Agnes merely shook her head.

"Tell Mr. Carlisle to keep his blood money," she told Ellie. "I understand what he expects. I will see Cleo well settled. Good afternoon, girls."

She waved as Mr. Cowls hobbled forward to open the door for them. As he closed the door, he peered back at Lady Agnes.

"Steps need sweeping, mum," he murmured.

Lady Agnes cackled. "Right you are, Mr. Cowls. That's what happens when I let trash accumulate."

Mr. Cowls let out a chuckle before lowering his gaze and shuffling back toward the kitchen. Cleo shook her head.

"I'm sorry, Lady Agnes," she said, following her godmother back to the drawing room. "I seem to come with some rather shocking baggage for sisters."

"Everyone has a flaw," Lady Agnes replied, moving around the card table. "Your sisters are yours. Insufferable, pompous popinjays. I cannot wait for the day when you can spit in their faces."

"Lady Agnes!" Cleo scolded, but she could not help but spoil it with a giggle. "I would settle right now for picking their pockets."

"You will have to do better than you did today," Lady Agnes predicted. "Whatever was Leslie thinking to teach you to play so badly?" She ambled up to Hector's cage and poked her finger at him. "But at least he taught my baby to talk when in company. Say something, clever boy!"

Hector cocked his head and eyed her.

"About his language . . ." Cleo started, but Lady Agnes waved her off.

"I am certain his diction will improve," she said. "The more he speaks, the better we will be able to understand him." She turned back to Cleo. "Leslie will visit tomorrow to continue the lessons, will he not?"

Cleo shrugged. "I suppose so."

Lady Agnes peered at her, looking suspiciously like Hector. "You do not sound enthusiastic. Did you and Leslie have a falling out?"

"No," Cleo replied, trying to brighten. "You must have seen how devoted we were to each other last night."

Lady Agnes snorted. "What I saw were two people who were too busy preening to talk to each other. You will be married a long time, girl. You should be making sure you are getting a good bargain."

"I thought you *wanted* me to marry Leslie," Cleo accused.

"I do," Lady Agnes retorted. "Make no mistake about it. But I am not an ogre like your sisters. If I thought you truly hated the boy, I would call it off."

Cleo smiled. "Really?"

Lady Agnes scowled. "Don't you get ideas, young lady. I can spot insincerity a mile away. You have known Leslie far too long to take him in sudden dislike. Much as I hate to say it, Cleo, I agree with Electra. The sooner you marry Leslie, the better. He will suit you well."

"Hell and damnation," Hector squawked.

"I couldn't agree more," Cleo muttered under her breath.

Ten

Leslie arrived for Hector's swearing lessons the next afternoon full of righteous determination. Playing the martyr was at least a new experience for him, and he was surprised to find how easily his spirits conformed to the role. He had fully convinced himself that Cleo was an impressionable young lady, whom he bore some responsibility to serve and protect. Such was the proper role of a gentleman. He intended to start by convincing her to safeguard her reputation. He did not expect to find her in a towering rage.

"What's happened?" he demanded as soon as Mr. Cowls had shown him into the drawing room.

Cleo was pacing and muttering, the skirts of her pink muslin gown hissing about her legs. Her agitation was such that even Hector was affected. He shuffled back and forth on his perch and clicked his beak against either side of the cage.

"They are determined that I marry you," Cleo said by way of explanation. "I will not be forced, Les. They cannot run my life."

"Certainly not," he agreed in his new role of protector of the innocent. "Don't concern yourself, Cleo. I refuse to offer, so you cannot be forced into marrying me."

"Do you think it will be that easy?" she challenged, pausing to glare at him. "They shall find some way to have you, they are that determined. I have tried everything I can think of to sway their opinions, and all they can see is the size of your estate and the height of your position."

He shook his head. "They have a rather dismal opinion of you if I'm the best they can hope for."

That drew her up short. "Nonsense, Leslie. You're a prime candidate, make no mistake."

He felt absurdly pleased, but she continued on as if she hadn't noticed. "I completely understand why they are so determined to settle me on you," she told him. "You are well liked and well heeled. You have a very nice title and are favorable on the eyes, when you take the trouble to dress properly."

"Thank you," he managed, even as he couldn't help glancing down at his brown cutaway coat and tan trousers, wondering whether she found them acceptable. Shaking his head at his own vanity, he refocused on her harangue.

"As persnickety as they are about propriety," she was saying, "I had thought a few misadventures would be enough to get them off your scent. I obviously underestimated their potential for greed."

"So," he mused, leaning one hip against the writing table near the door, "what do you suggest we do now?"

She frowned, and suddenly her shoulders slumped. "I don't know. I'm completely out of ideas."

His first instinct was to cross to her and take her in his arms to comfort her. It was the action of a lover, but certainly a protector might do the same. Yet he hesitated, unsure of his motives.

"Come now," he tried joking. "You've outlined schemes all your life. Surely this is no different."

She shook her head, setting her curls to bouncing. Even her delightfully short hair looked dejected. "I've tried and tried, Leslie. I explained you told me to cut off my hair and they only scolded me for it. I told them you instigated the race, and had to endure another ringing scold. I detailed how you gave me money for a dress and they advised me how to spend the money wisely! To top it all off, Hector nearly cursed Ellie and Annie out of the house yesterday and Lady Agnes refused to believe he'd said anything the least offensive."

Leslie eyed the parrot, who rocked back and forth on his perch before turning away from him. "Hector cursed?"

"Beautifully. At least, it was clear to me. Annie thought so too by the way she went on. Lady Agnes scolded her for thinking her precious Hector would be less than a gentleman."

Leslie grinned. "Perhaps I should try some words with greater impact."

"It wouldn't matter," Cleo said with a sigh. "You could teach him to curse in seven languages and my sisters would only tell me I don't deserve to marry such a clever fellow. Nothing seems to make them take you in dislike."

"They should have dinner with me," Leslie joked. "I assure you, I am quite capable of forgetting my manners. I might even be able to develop a disgustingly deep belch if called upon."

She made a face. "That wouldn't bother Annie. I've heard Lord Stephenson do the same the few times I've visited. I tell you, Leslie, I am sunk. I even tried to cheat at silverloo yesterday, thinking to blame you for teaching me, but I only succeeded in losing all my money, and a considerable portion of Lady Agnes's. I am hopeless!"

She sounded so forlorn that his good intentions flew out the window. He crossed to her side and drew her into his arms. Her dark cinnamon curls rested against his chest. If he had bent his head, he could have pressed a kiss against her crown.

"Buck up, Sprout," he murmured. His hands itched to stroke her slender back, his fingers to tease the curls in her hair. Instead, he held himself straight and proper and tried to ignore her scent of jasmine and fresh soap that tickled his nose. "We'll think of something. You know I fully support your right to control your own destiny."

"I know," she murmured against his vest. "You have no idea how much comfort I take from your support." One hand came up to toy with the velvet collar of his coat, her fingers stroking the material. He was certain she made the gesture without thinking, but his mind easily tumbled to visions of her hands stroking his bare skin in a far less innocent manner. He set her away from him, swallowing his rising desire.

"I'm always glad to be of service," he assured her. His voice cracked on the sentiment. He cleared his throat and continued more firmly. "What we need now is a strategy. What has Lady Agnes planned for you in the next few days?"

"We have tickets for Almack's," she replied, head cocked in thought. "Between now and then I believe we have been invited to a garden party at Mrs. Enwright's and a musicale at Lady Monke's. Do you see any opportunities there?"

"Doubtful," he told her. Mrs. Enwright was a frail old lady whose conversation was as wispy as her hair. It would take little to shock her, but he'd have to risk giving the poor dear heart failure. Lady Monke, on the other hand, was of a sturdier physique, and an earthier mind. She was on her third lover this Season. Somehow he doubted anything he and Cleo could do would shock her.

Cleo sighed. "What must I do to sway these people? Walk naked in Hyde Park while you play on the flute like some Indian snake charmer?"

Where did she get these images? Was she out to torture him, or was God trying to test his resolve? He straightened, determined to stay in his role of protector.

"Perhaps we should try something else," he suggested. "Perhaps we need only look for a gentleman who pleases you as much as he pleases your family."

She put her hands on her hips. "I thought you were on my side! You promised to help me, Leslie Petersborough. Don't you dare try to back out now."

Leslie sighed. So much for logic. Perhaps he could scare her. He placed his hands on her shoulders, forcing himself to ignore the feel of her beneath his fingers. "I'm not backing out, Sprout. I am becoming concerned for you. I want you to be fully frank with me. You said at the beginning of this that our misadventures would cause no one harm. If you truly intend to go through with this plan of yours to shock your sisters, it looks as if we may have to cause a little harm."

"I would not harm innocents," she said with a frown.

"I would not advise harming anyone," he replied. "But if you want to succeed, I'm afraid that's exactly what we'll have to do."

"Do you mean my sisters?" she probed. "Much as I despise their methods, I would not want anything bad to happen to them. And I know you cannot mean hurting Lady Agnes."

"Never," he promised. He gazed at her until her

eyes met his. How easy it would be to lose himself in those depths! He focused on his task. "I'm not talking about other people, Cleo. I'm talking about the two of us. If we go forward to meet the goal of your original plan, there is every chance that my reputation or yours will be damaged. I daresay mine will survive. I'm not sure yours will."

She bit her lip before responding, and he hoped he had gotten through. "It makes little sense to damage the only thing I have been told will gain me a husband," she said.

"I agree," Leslie replied. "But you must understand how narrow is the path upon which we walk. There is a very fine line between shocking your sisters and shocking the Ton."

She shrugged out of his grip to resume her pacing. "What do you ask of me? On the one hand, I will be entrapped in a loveless marriage. On the other, I am forced to live my life by their odious, ridiculous rules. I will likely die an old maid."

"Worse," he intoned, intent that she understand the gravity of the situation. "Before you die you will have to live with being a shamed woman, ostracized by society. No one will visit you. No one will be willing to employ you. You will have to rely on the dubious charity of your sisters."

She shuddered. "You paint a bleak future. But I still say better a life as a charity case than a life of empty longing. Besides, no matter what happens, my true friends will not desert me."

She was indeed innocent. He had no doubt they would not be able to wipe the sand from their feet fast enough. "At the very least," he joked, "you will discover who your true friends are."

She turned to move, stalking back to his side. Her nearness threatened to overpower his resolve, and he scuttled away until he fetched up sharply against Hector's cage. The parrot spread his wings and squawked, but Cleo, as if sensing nothing wrong, pursued Leslie, turning her face up to his.

"You would not desert me, would you, Les?" she asked, lips parted.

"Never," he swore, wanting only to cover those upturned lips with kisses. "Whatever happens, Cleo, you can count on me."

To his combined relief and regret, she stepped back, spreading her hands with a smile. "Then I have nothing to fear. I am clay in your capable hands. Mold me, shape me, do with me what you will."

There she went again. His imagination seized on the analogy, and he was forced to face Hector instead of her so that she could not see the desire on his face. "You are determined to go through with your plan, then? Even if it shocks Major Cutter?"

He did not have to see her to know her smile had faded. "What do you mean?"

"I am not convinced he is a gentleman," Leslie replied, feeling like a craven child for tattling.

"Why?" Her tone had become chilly.

How could he explain? What woman would want to hear that a man she admired saw only her bosom? But this wasn't any woman, this was Cleo. "Didn't you think he was a bit familiar the other night?" he asked.

"At the Baminger ball?" She moved around the cage so that she could peer at him around Hector's watchful form. "I barely spoke above three words to him all night. How is that familiar?"

"Did he ever look you in the eye?" Leslie demanded.

She frowned. "Certainly, a few times. Is it not customary for a gentleman to refrain from staring into a woman's eyes?"

"Certainly," he agreed. "But it is no less polite to remain staring at her chest."

Color flared to her cheek and she stalked around the cage to confront him. "Leslie Petersborough, that is disgusting! How dare you malign Major Cutter in that way! I assure you, he never, he wouldn't . . ." She stopped, breathing hard, staring up at him. "Did he really stare at my chest?"

My God, she was flattered! If that was all it took to cozen her, he'd cheerfully keep his eyes at mid-level for the rest of his life. Of course, the knight-protector protested such an ungentlemanly thought.

"I've said quite enough on the matter," he told her. "Suffice it to say, I need you to tell me you want to go through with this plan of yours."

She tossed her head. "Nothing you have said has deterred me."

"Very well," he replied, sealing her fate, and his. "We'll do something reprehensible at Almack's, then. Be ready on Wednesday."

"Clever boy," Hector squawked.

By Wednesday, Cleo had steeled herself for the worst. The last two days had passed pleasantly enough. Her sisters had not called, but several of her friends had. Marlys Rutherford was conspicuously missing. No doubt her mother prevented her from calling. Cleo's infamy was obviously spreading, even if it did not serve to upset her sisters. However, none of the girls who called was the least offended about her racing, although they all teased her unmercifully for her short hair. She rather hoped they would be similarly friendly after she finished with her crusade.

In addition, she'd spent part of every afternoon alone with Leslie and Hector. Lady Agnes was in transports over the new words Hector had managed to produce (most of them proper, for all of Leslie's threats), and Leslie had been cheerful, even if he refused to tell her his plans. Best of all, Major Cutter had singled her out at Lady Monke's musicale. His manner at intermission had been polite but warm, and she had felt his eyes on her for the rest of the performance (and considerably higher than her chest).

Several other gentlemen sought to further their acquaintance, including Mr. Mortimer Dent, a saffron-haired fellow who was causing quite a stir with his drawings. While Cleo had found his impassioned discussion of the importance of light in composing art interesting, Lady Agnes had rejected him out of hand.

"He wasn't good enough for Lady Agatha Crawford's niece," she told Cleo after the gentleman had been shown out. "He followed her about all last Season like a lost puppy. Fancied himself a poet then— wrote awful stuff like odes to hunting dogs. Do not encourage that connection. Electra would eat him for supper."

She decided not to argue. Time enough to assert herself once her sisters were cowed. And that all depended on Leslie and their scandal at Almack's.

She was already on the floor in a staid country dance with Robbie Newcomer, the older brother of Mary Newcomer in her class, when she spotted Leslie entering the famed assembly rooms. He had returned to his conservative evening wear, dressing himself in a somber black coat and breeches that were at odds with the misadventure he had proposed having. No sooner had she seen him, however, than the dance demanded her attention, and she lost track of him among the crowd. Robbie had not apparently noticed her lack of concentration, for the tall blond-haired fellow kept up an easy stream of conversation whenever the dance brought them close enough to speak. But as he bowed to her at the end of the set, Leslie stepped to her side.

"Good evening, Newcomer," he drawled, threading Cleo's arm possessively through his. "Good of you to keep Miss Renfield company in my absence."

Cleo raised a brow at his high-handed tone, but Robbie bowed. "Your servant, Lord Hastings. But perhaps you should be warned about leaving a lovely woman like Miss Renfield alone. Too many gentlemen would be sorely tempted to take your place in her affections."

"Do you malign my constancy, sir?" Cleo teased, rapping him lightly on the arm with her fan.

"Have a care, Newcomer," Leslie growled with sincerity that made Cleo stare at him in surprise. "I should hate to have to call you out for insulting the lady."

Robbie's blue eyes twinkled as he laid a hand on the chest of his green velvet coat. "You wound me, sir. I sought only to compliment the fair lady, I assure you." He bowed again to Cleo. "Your servant, Miss Renfield. Might I hope to call on you later in the week?"

Cleo smiled, offering him her hand. "I look forward to it, sir."

He did not kiss her fingers, merely giving them a squeeze, before nodding to Leslie and moving off to find his next partner. Leslie pulled on her arm, leading her toward the nearest wall.

"So," he snapped as soon as they were out of hearing of the dancers and those promenading by, "you've decided that Newcomer would make a better candidate than Cutter."

Cleo blinked. "Not at all. Mr. Newcomer is the brother of a school friend. Of course I'll receive him when he calls."

He stared across the room to where Robbie was leading a simpering young miss onto the floor. "I suppose he's a congenial fellow," he allowed. "Old family, solid fortune I hear, reasonably handsome."

She couldn't help but chuckle. "Good teeth too, solid legs. Ought to run the quarter mile in under a minute. Think what I could get for him at Tatt's."

Leslie shook his head. "Your point. I was merely trying to list his many qualities. You could do worse in a husband."

Cleo frowned. "I'm getting very tired of hearing how much worse I could do. I want to do better, sir. And I want the opportunity to choose for myself."

He nodded just as the musicians began the unmistakable strains of a waltz. Leslie took her hand. "Shall we?"

Cleo stared at him. "But Leslie, I haven't been given permission."

"I took the liberty of asking for you," he assured her. "You do know how to dance the waltz, don't you, Sprout? I should not like to embarrass myself."

"I practiced any number of times," Cleo assured him tartly. "So, yes, you makebait, by all means, let us waltz."

She waited for his grin to appear, but his bow to her was courtly, his expression serious. He led her onto the floor as if to present her at court.

It was one of the more complicated of waltzes, but

Cleo was undaunted. Indeed, she felt her stomach flutter with excitement as Leslie linked hands with her. He held her lightly, moving effortlessly with her around the floor. If it hadn't been for his serious expression, she would have thoroughly enjoyed the first few moments.

But as the dance progressed, from closed to open waltzing and back again, Leslie's expression softened. Was it her imagination or did he hold her just the slightest bit closer so that their bodies brushed? Certainly she was aware how the white silk of her skirt slid past his thighs. Her heartbeat quickened. As they reached the interlude where they clasped hands over her head, her gaze met his and she nearly gasped at the warmth in those dark eyes. The image of hot chocolate was forever replaced by smoldering coals. She wondered that her curls were not singed.

What was even more alarming was the response of her own body. She seemed drawn yet closer to him, aware of the touch of his hand at her waist as they resumed the closed waltz. She noticed the size and strength of his fingers engulfing her own, the width of his shoulders, the flare of his hips. She inhaled the smell of him—warm leather and crisp mint. Indeed, Leslie seemed to fill her senses until even the music was a dull hum in the background. She was lost and she didn't much care whether she was ever found.

He drew her to a stop and bowed. She could not think why, then realized the dance had ended. She struggled to slow her breath and her racing pulse. Indeed, she was surprised to find she felt not a little faint. She had never noticed how warm Almack's could be.

"You are magnificent," Leslie declared, straightening from his bow, his eyes assuring her of his sincerity. "Now, be strong and follow my lead. We are about to cause a scandal."

Eleven

Cleo blinked, then turned to follow his gaze to where Lady Agnes was bearing down upon them with no less than the undisputed queen of London society, Lady Jersey, beside her. Lady Jersey's finely molded head was up, like a horse ready to gallop, and her elegant pistachio-green silk gown swirled around her long legs. Cleo gulped in a gasp, pasting what she was sure was a sickly smile on her face. Leslie surreptitiously squeezed her elbow in encouragement.

Lady Agnes had fire in her gray eyes, but it was the redoubtable Lady Jersey who spoke first. "Miss Renfield," she intoned, bearing dignified while all the while managing to impart her displeasure. "Your godmother assures me there has been some mistake. Did one of my sister patronesses give you permission to waltz, for I am certain I did not."

Cleo felt as if the air had suddenly chilled. Around them, gentlemen were staring and women whispered behind their fans. What had she done? Could she have mistaken Leslie? She glanced quickly at him, but for once his usually open face was hooded. Loyalty insisted that she refuse to make him the villain.

"I understood I had permission, Lady Jersey," she replied humbly. "I assure you, I am as shocked as you are to find I was mistaken. I am terribly sorry. Can you ever forgive me?"

The utterly spineless grovel would have been enough to assuage Ellie or Annie, but Lady Jersey was obviously made of stronger stuff. Cleo had heard that all the patronesses took their roles as social arbiters quite seriously. Indeed, Lady Jersey herself had once refused admittance to the hero of Waterloo, Lord Wellington, when he arrived seven minutes late and wearing trousers rather than the knee breeches the ladies had dictated as proper attire in their hallowed hall. Now Lady Jersey merely narrowed her eyes.

"I do not condone lying, Miss Renfield, any more than I condone impertinence," she said in tones that only served to chill Cleo further. "Surely you are aware that you must personally request permission. Lady Agnes cannot intercede for you."

"Nor did I," Lady Agnes put in even as Cleo felt herself blanching. "But you are far off the mark if you think my Cleo a liar, Sally. Someone is clearly trying to make trouble for her."

"Perhaps," Lady Jersey intoned. "And perhaps you are misled by your devotion to the girl. Haven't I heard any number of exploits recently? Racing in Hyde Park? Stealing other young ladies' beaus? You have only to look at her hair to know she has wild tendencies."

Cleo's hand rose involuntarily to her curls. More people were gathering. Indeed, she'd never felt so many eyes upon her. Some people smirked, exchanging knowing looks, as Ellie and Annie were wont to do. Others shook their heads in dismay at her obvious downfall. She had never felt so humiliated in her life.

"The wild tendencies," Leslie said, loud enough to carry to all those listening, "are mine. I wished to waltz with Miss Renfield. When she very rightly refused me, I told her I had your permission."

Cleo stared at him as there were hushed gasps on either side. Lady Agnes rolled her eyes. The lady patroness raised a gold-rimmed quizzing glass off her elegant chest and raked him from top to bottom through it. Leslie stood with a negligent grace and a cold expression, as if their petty concerns bored him. Cleo, knowing this must be his plan and that he was doing it for her, felt as if her heart would burst with pride at his performance.

"I am severely disappointed in you, Lord Hastings," Lady Jersey said, allowing her quizzing glass to drop back in place. "But then, you have consistently been a disappointment, haven't you? First to society and then to your dear father. Small wonder your one-time friend Lord Prestwick has chosen not to associate with you."

Cleo thought she saw Leslie grimace, but the moment passed so quickly, she could not be sure.

Lady Jersey continued as if she had seen nothing. "You are banished from Almack's, sir, for the rest of the Season. Do not dare approach any of us or we will give you the cut direct. Come along, Miss Renfield."

Lady Agnes shook her head at him, but turned her back even as Lady Jersey did. All around them, people did the same, contemptuously, coldly, the only sound the soft rustle of the women's dresses as they moved away. Leslie stood isolated, back straight, head high.

Cleo hesitated. Surely she'd seen a flicker of pain from behind those dark eyes. She couldn't simply leave him like this. She caught his gaze.

"This is what you wanted," he hissed. "Your family won't stand for our marriage now—society means too much to them. Go on."

People were beginning to whisper again. Lady Jersey did not turn back, but Lady Agnes turned long enough to order Cleo to her side with one imperious wave of her hand. Another moment, and she'd undo everything he was trying to achieve.

"Meet me at the house," she murmured. "And thank you."

Although her heart protested, she hurried after her godmother, leaving Leslie to make his way to the door.

Utterly alone.

The rest of the evening was mostly a blur to Cleo. After an initial time of awkwardness, in which everyone made sure that Lady Jersey was not in fact wroth with her, she was again claimed by her various partners to dance. Most of the gentlemen were unrelentingly proper, unendingly kind, and utterly unremarkable. Which was just as well, for she found it difficult to give them her complete attention. Her mind kept reviewing the scene of Leslie's humiliation.

He had been hurt by Lady Jersey's censure, for all he had brought it on himself. She could not have mistaken what she had seen. He had removed himself from good society for her sake. After warning her what might happen if they succeeded in shocking her sisters, he had taken all the burden on himself. She had to find a way to make it up to him.

The one bright spot in the night was the appearance of Major Cutter. He appeared at her side late in the evening, very politely requested her hand for a line dance, and complimented her on her looks.

She could not deny that he was in rather good looks himself, with his uniform nearly as crisp as the medals hung upon his broad chest. He made the usual conversation as the dance allowed, asking after her sisters, commenting on the weather. When they stood out for a round at the end of the line, however, his conversation grew more familiar.

"I had no idea you were such an accomplished dancer, Miss Renfield," he began, bringing a blush of pleasure to her cheeks. "That waltz with Lord Hastings was remarkable. But did I understand correctly that Lady Jersey found fault with it?"

She knew her blush had deepened. She had no idea he had been in the room to see the fated dance, nor that anyone would not know the story Lady Jersey was telling by now. Indeed, the fans had not stopped moving for a full hour as the gossip spread from one group of women to another. "Lady Jersey found fault with Lord Hastings," she explained. "I'm sure it was a dreadful misunderstanding. Lord Hastings is a gentleman."

"Oh, quite," the major replied with a nod. She watched in fascination as the candlelight glinted off his golden hair and turned his blue eyes to azure. "A more rousing comrade one could not find. I am pleased to hear you support him, Miss Renfield. It tells me you are a particular friend of his."

She wanted to be warmed by his praise, but something about the way he said the phrase made her uneasy. It was as if he'd deliberately hit the wrong key in the middle of a moving sonata. Still, his smile was for her alone, and she found it hard not to be in charity with him. "I have known Lord Hastings since I was a child," she told him. "Some of my warmest memories are of times we spent together."

His smile deepened as he took her hand to lead

her back into the dance. "May I hope," he murmured, pressing her fingers, "that I might have the opportunity to give you warm memories of me as well?"

Cleo's heart turned over. "Certainly, sir," she all but stammered. "I would be more than delighted to further our acquaintance. Please feel free to call any time."

His smile had been triumphant as they went through the motions of the dance, and he returned her to Lady Agnes with a sweeping bow and the promise to see her soon. She was afraid to hope he might keep that promise.

On the other hand, she did not have to guess about her godmother's feelings. Lady Agnes only waited until they were safely ensconced in her small carriage before letting Cleo know of her disappointment.

"What were you thinking?" she demanded. "And do not repeat that Banbury tale of Leslie lying to you."

"I thought you believed me!" Cleo protested, humiliation rising anew.

"I believe someone lied to you," Lady Agnes informed her. "But I will not believe my Leslie would do so. What I believe right now is that the two of you are cooking up mischief. I demand to know what."

"It no longer matters," Cleo replied, steadfastly turning her face to the window. "Any mischief we might have made is at an end with Leslie banished from all good society for the Season."

"A harsh punishment," Lady Agnes predicted. "The boy is a social animal. He cannot think for himself."

"That's not true," Cleo protested, resolutely refusing to meet her godmother's gaze, which was no doubt as militant as her own.

"Give me one good example of anything he ever thought of on his own," Lady Agnes challenged.

Cleo would have been delighted to tell her about Leslie's brilliant plan tonight, but of course she couldn't. She thought hard. Truthfully, she had led him into most of their escapades. But surely he had done something noteworthy before now. "He thought of teaching Hector to speak," she tried.

Lady Agnes snorted. "Only after I brought up the idea. The boy is a follower. Nothing shameful in that, unless one happens to follow the wrong people. That's why this banishment is bound to be bad for him. I have never liked his tendency to run with the wrong crowd."

"What are you talking about? Leslie seems quite presentable to me."

"He would," Lady Agnes grumbled. "He seems to take great pains to show his better side to you. I doubt whether he has mentioned his more deplorable habits."

"Perhaps he hasn't mentioned them because they are a figment of a gossip's imagination," Cleo replied tartly.

Lady Agnes barked a laugh. "Loyal, aren't you, girl? I appreciate that. But Leslie is not ready for sainthood yet. He gambles too heavily, even if he has yet to put a dent in his fortune. He drinks too much, even though he never has a headache in the morning. He races horses and carriages far too recklessly. I thought his father's death might cure him of that. Does he want the title to go into abeyance? But no, Leslie is only interested in one thing—having fun. If he cannot have it with the Haut Ton, he will find it elsewhere. Mark my words, his censure by Sally Jersey will only drive him deeper into the arms of depravity."

Cleo whirled to face her. "Well, I like that. First Leslie is the most saintly gentleman in London and I should swoon to have my name coupled with his, and now he consorts with the hounds of hell. You, madam, cannot have it both ways."

"Neither can you," Lady Agnes replied. "You take great pains to show your sisters how wicked he is. Now will you balk if I do the same?"

Had she given her plan away? Cleo felt herself paling and was again thankful for the uneven light. "I cannot think what you mean. You know I consider Leslie a friend."

"Such a friend that he nearly ruined your Season," her godmother pointed out. "And all for his own gain, or so he claims."

Again Cleo was sorely tempted to tell Lady Agnes exactly how selfless Leslie had been, but she could not do so without making his sacrifice worthless. She snapped her mouth shut and returned her gaze to the window.

"And do not think you shall be the only one to hear my scold," Lady Agnes warned her. "I plan to scald Leslie's ears off the next time I see him. I only hope he dares to come calling tomorrow, so I have tonight to think of an appropriate barrage."

Cleo cringed. She rather hoped Leslie had ignored her whispered plea to meet her at the house. He hardly needed more verbal abuse tonight, particularly from their godmother. Luckily, no crested coach awaited them at the door of their town house. She could only pray that Lady Agnes was wrong about his wicked tendencies and that Leslie was somewhere safe for the night.

Twelve

If Cleo had seen him that night, she could not have thought him safe. Nor would she have thought he had left his predilection to mischief behind. He had marched into his town house, demanded a bottle of port, and sequestered himself in the library. And none of his servants had seen him until morning.

Leslie woke with a groan. It wasn't that he was hung over. Far from it. Chas Prestwick had always complained that while Leslie was the first to feel his liquor, he was also the first to recover. He seldom felt the least effect of the alcohol the next day, no matter how many drinks he'd managed to put away the night before. So today there was no pounding headache or wretched stomach to remind him of his folly. There was simply the unalterable fact that he had ostracized himself from Society. Some marquis he'd turned out to be.

He should never have started on that bottle of port. But in truth he hadn't expected the pain that had accompanied Lady Jersey's words. He should not have dwelled on them; they were, after all, only the prideful ravings of a woman who took her power in Society too seriously. But having started on the bottle, he couldn't seem to stop. It was as if she had found the one hole in his armor and neatly slipped the dirk into his heart.

And twisted it.

In truth, he hadn't been certain how she'd react to his willful disobedience to one of Almack's most sacred rules. He'd rather hoped she'd give him a playful slap on the wrist and tell him how naughty he was. He'd wanted to shock Cleo's sisters, not the world. No such luck. He was in exile, banished from good Society until the harvest.

But perhaps he deserved his banishment. He groaned again, throwing an arm up over his unshaven face. He was failing dismally at keeping his gentlemanly protector role with Cleo. Each time he saw her he wanted to take her in his arms. Dancing with her last night had made his body sing. He'd tried to be the good friend, but instead had succumbed to his desires, pulling her closer to him, wanting only to feel their bodies touching.

Well, that was done now. He was not likely to be given the chance to dance with her again. Surely her sisters would send him packing. He had only to make his obligatory appearance to his godmother today to receive his notice. Cleo would be allowed to make her own decisions. He only hoped one of those decisions might involve remaining friends with him.

He did not reckon on company that morning, particularly female company. He had gone upstairs to bathe, change, and shave himself, then arrived in the breakfast room ready for a hearty meal. Bertram, his father's stiff-necked butler, who seemed to be no more easy than Leslie about the new lord of the manor, stood even straighter than usual when he came to the breakfast room. Leslie paused in wolfing down his breakfast of steak and eggs to wait curiously to learn the reason for the interruption.

"My lord," Bertram intoned. "There is a woman here to see you."

Cleo. Leslie bolted out of his chair. "You didn't let her in, did you? Damnation, Bertram, she could be ruined coming to see a gentleman like this."

Bertram raised his long nose and audibly sniffed. "I tried to dissuade the person, my lord, I assure you. She is adamant. I deposited her in the sitting room."

How like Cleo, Leslie thought, throwing down his napkin and striding for the door. In fact, he was rather surprised she hadn't brazened it out completely and bearded him at breakfast. Bertram did not bother to point out that he was still in his shirtsleeves. The fellow looked more than happy to step out of his way and absent himself in the nether parts of the house. Leslie was sure he would soon be regaling the rest of the staff of this new indication of their young master's depravity.

"What do you think you're doing?" he demanded, striding into the sitting room.

Eloise Watkin, resplendent in a silk walking dress of a bright saffron hue, turned from her perusal of his father's gilded world globe. "I apologize, my lord. Is this a special memento for you?"

Leslie skidded to a stop, his Hessians making a decided dent in the Oriental carpet. "Miss Watkin. I didn't expect, that is, I thought . . ." He sounded like the veriest schoolboy! Raking a hand quickly through his hair, he collected himself and bowed. "Your servant, Miss Watkin. How may I assist you?"

She crossed to the settee, where his top hat reposed on a cushion. "You did not come for your hat, my lord. I thought perhaps I should bring it to you."

Leslie smiled stiffly, moving forward to accept it from her. "Very thoughtful of you, I'm sure. But you must have a care for your reputation, my dear. Do you not know that ladies are not supposed to visit gentlemen?"

"I know the dictates of Society," she replied with a pretty blush. "I took precautions. My maid is waiting at the front door. It is early, before most of the Ton will even be awake. Indeed, I left my chaperone at home asleep."

"Very wise of you," Leslie returned, wondering whether she made a habit of these early morning visits. Still, he could not fault the view. Unlike their previous meetings, she did not appear to be overly primped. Her dark lashes swept pale cheeks and her lips were moist, as if with dew. His smile deepened in appreciation.

"I want you to understand how seriously I take matters," she said, keeping her gaze on the tips of the half boots that peeped out from under her full skirt. "I assure you, I would not have come at all except that I feared I would never see you again otherwise."

He had been remiss in not furthering the acquaintance, as he had implied he would do. "My apologies for taking you out of your way," he told her. "I should have called."

"I understand how busy you must be," she said humbly. "You have been much sought after. However, after last night, I was afraid you could not call. You see, I heard about the contretemps at Almack's."

How many people had heard of the contretemps at Almack's? he wondered. Probably a better question was how many people *hadn't* heard, given Sally Jersey's predilection to gossip. "I'm even more amazed you would deign to visit me, madam," he replied.

She sighed, laying a hand on his arm and giving it a squeeze before quickly withdrawing. "My lord, that is the very reason I knew I had to call. This accusation against you is most unfair. I simply wanted you to know that your true friends will not abandon you."

He could not help but be touched by her devotion. Only a few days ago he had wanted to be touched, by more than her devotion. Now, however, he found himself merely content with her friendship. "You are too kind, madam," he said. "Unfortunately, I must insist that this visit will only bring you harm. I would not see a true friend censured because of me."

She gazed up at him, head cocked. "You are sending me away?"

"I am returning your friendship by ensuring your good reputation," he returned. "Thank you for coming, but I must insist that you leave before any harm comes to you."

"I do not believe any harm could come to me when I am with you," she said, gazing up at him. Face upturned, eyes half closed, lips dewy, she begged for a kiss. Leslie swallowed.

"You honor me, madam," he said, stepping away. "I am certain my man will be ready to see you to the door."

He could only hope Bertram would have had the sense to station the footman somewhere handy. He thought perhaps she might persist, but she merely smiled.

"Very well," she murmured. She wandered to the door, only to pause to look regretfully back at him over her shoulder. "Good day, Lord Hastings. I do hope I shall see you again soon."

Leslie bowed, keeping his eyes on her and straightening slowly in a sign of devotion. She seemed content with that, moving out into the corridor. He heard the sound of her heels on the polished stair. Only then did he allow himself a wry smile.

"Perhaps this banishment won't be so bad after all, Leslie old boy," he murmured aloud.

Indeed, that proved shortly to be the case. Before he could even think of making his way to Cleo's for his lecture from Lady Agnes, he received no less than a dozen notes of support. Several were from gentlemen, like Lord Trevithan, who had been agents for his father. Others were from fellows like Mortimer Dent whom he had known at Oxford. The one that touched his heart most was from Chas Prestwick, assuring him that he and Anne would admire him even when "he chose to make an ass of himself." Enclosed in the note were directions to the boxing match that afternoon between the Mighty Bull of Lancaster and the Giant of Seven Dials. At least some of the finer things in life were not barred to him.

Cleo, of course, had no way of knowing this. She could not erase the memory of his sorrowful retreat the previous night. She fully expected him to be just as miserable that morning when he called. She was therefore surprised when Leslie was shown into the drawing room before noon, as Lady Agnes had commanded, his cravat unspoiled and his smile chipper.

"How are you?" she asked solicitously as Mr. Cowls hobbled off to fetch their godmother.

"Hale and hearty," he declared, strolling over to poke a finger at Hector. "Why do you ask?"

Cleo raised a brow. "You looked rather pained last night."

He shrugged, but something in the stiffness of the gesture told her that he was not as cavalier about the matter as he pretended. "You mustn't dwell on that, Cleo," he said. "I knew the risks before I acted. I had hoped for a better outcome, but such was not the case."

"But you sacrificed yourself for me," Cleo protested.

"Not at all," he insisted. "I'm the one determined to have fun, remember?"

"And being banished from Society is your idea of fun?"

He turned from the parrot to grin at her. "As you predicted, my true friends have stood by me. They have gone out of their way to give me their support. Chas, Lord Prestwick, has even invited me to a boxing match this very day."

Cleo grinned back, relieved that Lady Agnes's dire predictions had not come true. "Oh, Les, how marvelous! May I come too? You know how much I've wanted to see one."

His smile faded. "This would not be a good time."

"Why?" she asked, feeling her own smile fade.

Leslie ran a hand back through his hair, a sure sign he did not want to deal with the subject. "Ladies," he tried, "do not attend boxing matches."

"Ladies also refuse to be seen with fellows who have been blackballed by the patronesses of Almack's," she informed him. "Do you want me to stand by *that* rule?"

"I would rather you did not."

Cleo stepped forward and looked up at him in entreaty. "Then take me with you. Please, Les? You are the only one I can ask."

He returned her gaze, face stiff, and she wondered whether she'd finally pressed him too far. Perhaps this was one area she shouldn't encroach upon. But then his look softened and he touched her cheek with the back of his hand. "Why do I have such a hard time refusing you?"

Cleo felt her grin returning. "Because I'm a cozening little sprout. Is that a yes?"

"Yes. But Lady Agnes won't approve, so mum's the word, my girl. I'll think of some way to get you out of the house."

She nodded, then clamped her mouth shut as their godmother moved into the room.

"And there you are, thick as thieves," she declared. "Come and sit down, Leslie. We must talk. Cleo, I want you to stay and listen as well."

Cleo didn't mind the excuse to stay. She wanted to hear the resolution of their plan. She only hoped Lady Agnes wouldn't roast Leslie over the coals. Despite his protests, she still felt he had done all this for her sake. "Certainly, Lady Agnes," she said as Leslie moved to comply. "My sisters did say I should do everything to please Leslie. Perhaps I should share his blame."

"Loyal, ain't she," Leslie quipped, settling into one of the wing-backed chairs and stretching out his long legs before him. "Puts me in mind of a Spaniel I had once."

Cleo stuck out her tongue at him. Leslie barked a laugh.

Lady Agnes shook her head. "Merry as griggs, the two of you, and I'd like to know why. Do you like being a disgrace?"

"There is nothing disgraceful about Cleo," Leslie said, demeanor suddenly serious. "As was proven last night, the blame for this misadventure falls squarely on me."

Cleo waited for her godmother to agree, but as usual, Lady Agnes had her own opinion.

"Not entirely," she informed him. "I have already had three notes this morning canceling engagements with Cleo. I suspect more will follow. And heaven help us when Electra and Andromeda find out."

Leslie's frown matched the one Cleo could feel on her own face. She had not realized she might still be in trouble.

"But I thought it was understood that I acted alone," Leslie protested, leaning forward.

"You may have concocted that lie alone," Lady Agnes replied, "but you acted with Cleo. Coupled with her curls and that race, you must admit the evidence is damning."

"Hell and damnation," Hector squawked.

"My thoughts precisely, old boy," Leslie said, even as Lady Agnes frowned at the bird.

Cleo ignored them both. "Lady Jersey also accused me of beau snatching, and we all know that is a humbug. Surely this storm will blow over."

"I would not count on it," Lady Agnes said.

Cleo shook her head. "But I have been the proper debutante up until now, done everything anyone asked of me. I cannot believe I am so lightly esteemed that I will be cut from Society."

"Leslie's foolishness has entertained them for years," their godmother replied with a sniff. "Yet you see how easily they throw him over. There are rules, Cleo."

Cleo rolled her eyes. "I am so tired of hearing about rules. Who made up these ridiculous rules? Why does everyone blindly follow them?"

"That doesn't matter," Lady Agnes maintained. "The fact is, there are rules, and woe betide the young lady who flaunts them."

Cleo snapped her fingers. "That for their silly rules. I haven't done anything that some other young lady hasn't tried. Look at Lady Lamb!"

Leslie shuddered. Lady Agnes shook her head.

"Caro Lamb," she pronounced, "is an unhappy widgeon who will likely die of the French pox for all her licentious behavior. Pray pick a better example."

"Your daughter-in-law, Lady Thomas DeGuis, then," Cleo supplied readily. "She works with fallen women and supposedly did so before she was married."

"Danced the waltz before it was popular too," Leslie commented with a fond smile.

"Margaret is an Original," Lady Agnes informed them sternly. "Cleo hasn't the panache to pull that off."

Cleo drew herself up. "That, madam, is your opinion."

"Now, now, Sprout," Leslie put in as her godmother bristled. "The lady has a point. There isn't anyone quite like Margaret. I'm not certain the Ton could stand more than one of her."

"Precisely," Lady Agnes declared. "You may posture all you like, Cleo, but the facts are before you. You are facing ruin."

Cleo shook her head, fully ready to keep fighting. Leslie cleared his throat.

"Not to be disrespectful, Godmother," he said, "but didn't you intend to ring a peal over *my* head? I'd rather you left Cleo alone and got on with it. I have other engagements this afternoon."

Cleo bit back a laugh as Lady Agnes glared at him.

"Insufferable puppy," she scolded. "Very well, if you want it baldly. Your behavior is the outside of enough."

"Ah," Leslie replied, leaning back once more. "Now, that is more like it."

"Oh, you may well laugh," Lady Agnes told him,

scowling. "You have gotten yourself banned from Society and are threatening to take Cleo with you. There is only one solution to this mess."

"Shall I drink hemlock or fall on my sword?" Leslie quipped.

"Neither," Lady Agnes snapped. "The only gentlemanly thing to do is offer for Cleo. This minute."

Thirteen

Cleo surged to her feet. "No!" she cried even as Leslie barked a laugh.

"If Cleo is drowning," he told Lady Agnes over Hector's agitated squawk, "the last thing she needs is to be tied to a millstone. If you will remember, I was the one banned from Society last night. I fail to see how marriage to me avails Cleo."

"Exactly," Cleo agreed, forcing herself to sit back down as Lady Agnes shook her head.

"You might think what it avails you," she scolded Leslie. "Do you understand the magnitude of being banished from Almack's?"

Cleo was beginning to get an inkling of how drastically he might have been served. He didn't seem worried, but if she, who had been given Lady Jersey's reluctant forgiveness, was still being cut, Leslie would be ostracized. If such thoughts were going through his head, he did not show it. Leslie merely frowned, studying the toes of his boots as if lost in contemplation. Then he jerked upright and struck his palm against his forehead, making her jump.

"My God!" he cried, face screwed up in obvious shock. "What have I done? I shall no longer be forced to don knee breeches. I shall have to forego the pleasure of stale cakes and weak lemonade. Oh, the horror of it; I shall have to find some other amusement for Wednesday night. However shall I survive?"

Cleo could not help but laugh. Lady Agnes reached out and rapped his kneecap with her bony knuckles. Leslie yelped theatrically.

"Stop that, you jackanapes," she demanded. "This is far more serious than a loss of momentary amusement. You have been pointed out as beyond the pale. Your friends will shun you."

"My friends have already told me that my mistakes are forgiven," he informed her, grin still merry. Cleo smiled in relief. His next words, however, only made her hackles rise. "A very lovely young lady made so free as to appear at my door this morning in support, and Chas Prestwick has let me know that nothing I can do would earn his wrath."

Who would be so bold as to visit him at home? She did not dare repeat aloud the name that sprang to mind. Surely Eloise Watkin would not be so brazen. Had she learned nothing from her encounter with Jareth Darby? A lady should never put herself in a position where she might be tempted to give her favors away before marriage. Even Cleo would not be so foolish as to break that rule. She fought to focus on the debate.

"Chas Prestwick has never been a leader in Society," Lady Agnes was saying. "And any young lady who comes to a gentleman's door can by definition not be a member of good society. Face it, my boy, you are lost. Do you wish to have no one but scoundrels and miscreants to associate with?"

He shrugged, half smile evident. "Those are my associates, according to you."

"And do you prefer those to be Cleo's associates?" she countered.

"Godmother, really," Cleo began, but Leslie cast her a sharp, appraising glance.

"Certainly not," he said, smile fading at last. "Which is why I do not intend to marry her."

"That is hardly the reason," Cleo scolded him. "I don't believe any of this rubbish about you anyway. Scoundrels and miscreants indeed." She turned to her godmother, who was regarding her with narrowed eyes. "Leslie doesn't love me, Lady Agnes. Nor I him. I am sorry we had to deceive you. We felt it necessary at the time. We are the dearest of friends, but nothing more."

She expected her godmother to scold her unmercifully, but she merely threw up her hands as if in praise. "Thank goodness for that," she declared. "You will be nothing more than friends with a gentleman until the day you wed, if I have anything to say in the matter."

Cleo felt herself blushing. "I still will not marry Leslie."

Lady Agnes let out a huff. "Fine. Have it your way. But if you refuse Leslie, what do you propose? Your sisters will not sit idly by, Cleo. Indeed, I am shocked they have not pounced upon us already. Make no mistake; if the gossips were happy to tattle about your horse race, they are even now filling your sisters' ears with this latest debacle."

"We can always flee for the Continent," Leslie offered.

Cleo smiled at him. "I don't think that will be necessary."

"Very likely," Lady Agnes maintained. "Once they determine your chances with Leslie are lost, or decide Leslie is not worth the trouble, they will choose another candidate. I shudder to think how inappropriate this one will be."

"I am hoping for another result," Cleo told her godmother. "Might it not be that my sisters will finally realize their inadequacy at making my choices for me?"

Lady Agnes blinked. "Why would they do that? Do you expect them to suddenly acquire sense or the ability to see logic? Might as well wish for the moon, my girl."

Cleo frowned, but Leslie leaned forward. "Are you saying her sisters will insist on marrying her off against her wishes?"

"I will not let them," Cleo blustered.

"You do not have a choice," Lady Agnes replied. "George Carlisle is your guardian. He can marry you off to whom he chooses. We should be thankful he hasn't settled on someone like that reprehensible Major Cutter."

Before Cleo could protest that Major Cutter seemed quite all right to her, Leslie stepped in. "I agree. Tony Cutter is not the gentleman I thought him. I will not countenance him for Cleo's hand."

"You won't countenance him?" Cleo stared at him, feeling her temper rising. "Will you order me about as well? When did you have anything to say in the matter?"

He uncoiled so rapidly to thrust his face toward hers that she flinched back. "When I became your *dearest friend,* remember?" he snarled.

Cleo refused to be cowed. She could not imagine what had gotten into him, but she could not allow him to join the ranks of those who dictated to her. "That doesn't give you the right to tell me who to marry," she retorted.

"I think I've jolly well earned that right," he challenged. "I've played the courtier and the martyr for you, Cleo. I won't play the fool any longer. If you know what's good for you, you'll stay away from Tony Cutter."

"You're jealous," she accused, unable to think of any other reason for his actions.

"Ha!" he cried. "How can a *dear friend* be jealous?"

"That is quite enough," Lady Agnes commanded. In the silence that followed, Cleo took a deep breath. She had never seen Leslie so angry. Indeed, she wasn't sure she'd ever seen Leslie angry at all. A muscle worked in his cheek, his dark eyes blazed, and his face was nearly as red as the carpet at her feet. She noticed her own hands were balled at her sides and carefully opened them.

"You are both making fools of yourselves," Lady Agnes continued when neither of them spoke. "Let us come to a truce, and I will propose the terms."

Cleo took another deep breath. "You may propose," she said as civilly as she could. "I do not promise to obey."

Lady Agnes glared at her. "Don't be impertinent with me, miss. Do you think I agreed to be your chaperone for the fun of it?"

Cleo blinked. Indeed, she had rather thought that was why her godmother had sought her out as school was ending. Then she remembered the conversation between Lady Agnes and Ellie. It was an obligation for Lady Agnes to shepherd Cleo through the Season. Though she knew Lady Agnes loved her, this hectic Season could not have been her first wish. Looking at her godmother now, she suddenly noted how thin she was, how translucent her skin, how filmy her gray eyes. For all her fuss and furor, she was aging. Lady Agnes caught her look and grimaced.

"I am not dead yet, girl," she said, as if reading Cleo's mind. "With any luck, I have a few years yet to go. But I've been around long enough to have learned some things. Now, you listen to me."

Cleo nodded, sitting back in her chair. Leslie had leaned back as well, but she could not help but notice that his stance was far from relaxed. He looked more like a lion ready to pounce.

"First," Lady Agnes said, "Leslie will propose."

Leslie scowled. Cleo grit her teeth.

"You will accept," Lady Agnes continued, forestalling her intentions to refuse immediately. "You will have six weeks while the banns are read to find another candidate for your hand. If you find one, you will cry off, and the Ton will give Leslie their pity. That way he just might make it through the Season without offending someone again."

"Your faith in me is inspiring," Leslie drawled.

Lady Agnes ignored him. "If you cannot find another gentleman to your liking, however, and bring him up to scratch within six weeks' time, you will marry Leslie."

Cleo opened her mouth to protest.

"Done," Leslie proclaimed, rising. "Excellent strategy, Godmother. That concluded, I think Cleo needs some air. I'll take her for a drive. Don't expect us back before dinner."

Cleo stared at him. So did Lady Agnes.

He smiled charmingly. "Don't stand there gaping, Sprout. Fetch your spencer and bonnet and let's be off."

"Have you gone mad?" she managed. "You agree to that preposterous plan?"

He was already moving toward the door. "Certainly. I was sure I said as much. Good day, Lady Agnes. Come along, Cleo."

Cleo continued to stare at his retreating back. How could he have simply given in? She was certain he'd support her, even if he had taken a strange dislike to Major Cutter. Looking at her chest, indeed. He hadn't so much as lowered his gaze past her lips last night. She cast a glance at her godmother, who was shaking her head.

"You'd better go after him," she told Cleo. "I'm not entirely certain he's safe."

Cleo nodded. "I quite agree. I'll try to bring him back in time for dinner."

Lady Agnes nodded as well, rising. "Good. And may I say, Cleo, that I am most pleased by your calm reaction to my proposal. It bodes well for us being able to rescue your reputation."

"I'm glad you're pleased," Cleo replied, heading for the entry hall, where she could hear Leslie bellowing for Mr. Cowls to fetch her things. "But as for my reputation, we will have to wait and see."

Lady Agnes frowned, but Cleo knew she spoke the truth. She wasn't sure how the Ton would react when word of her engagement leaked out. She wasn't certain she could find her own true love and bring him up to snuff in a mere six weeks.

But she was entirely sure of the satisfaction she would feel when she strangled Leslie with the carefully tied folds of his pristine cravat.

Leslie settled back against the squabs of his father's coach, meeting Cleo's militant eye. He was rather surprised she hadn't strangled him by now. Even the reminder that he had gotten her safely out of the house, with no questions asked, to see the illicit boxing match had failed to remove the righteous anger from her gaze.

"You admitted defeat without even asking me," she accused him.

"Not at all," he replied as the coach set off. "We lost the battle, dear Cleo. I refuse to believe we lost the war."

That at least seemed to mollify her. The grim lines around her sweet mouth relaxed. He smiled.

"Don't give up on me yet, Sprout. I still have a few cards to play. I never let you down before, did I?"

Her arms fell to her sides, and she returned his smile sheepishly. "Never. I'm sorry, Leslie. I just never thought it would come to this. Do you realize what we agreed to? I have six weeks to find a husband."

"Easy as that." Leslie snapped his fingers.

She raised a brow. "Oh, really? I have been on the town for months and have yet to find the perfect fellow. Unless you count Major Cutter."

Just the name set his hackles rising, but he promised himself to behave like a gentleman. "Yes, I understand you favor him. Is he a viable candidate?"

He steeled himself to hear a glorified account of the fellow's dubious merits, but to his surprise, her gaze wavered, then turned away from him entirely.

"Truth be told, Les, I'm not entirely sure. He is thoughtful and handsome, and my heart beats faster whenever I'm near him, but . . ." She trailed off.

"But?" Leslie encouraged, feeling craven for hoping she might have discovered the fellow's flaws.

She shook her head. "But that seems woefully little on which to base one's hope for the future. These wretched rules keep us from having more than a five-minute conversation when we meet. It would be nice to have an opportunity to get to know him better."

Although he knew it was the logical next step, part of him quailed. "Could it be that he is only interested in a flirtation?"

"Perhaps," she acknowledged as she stared out the window. "Oh, I don't know, Les! I wish Mother was alive. I know she'd be able to advise me."

Leslie might not have been able to remember a great deal about Mrs. Renfield, but he somehow thought she'd been a canny soul. Certainly she'd see more to this major than Cleo did. Mothers, in his experience, knew all about cads like the major. However, he knew how Cleo felt. Over the last year he had wished for his father's wisdom any number of times. He could almost hear the old fellow now.

"Well, this is an interesting scrape you've gotten yourself into, my boy," he'd say with that grave voice, the twinkle in his eyes the only sign that he was more amused than incensed. "What do you propose to do about it?"

Leslie, of course, would propose something entirely outrageous, but his father would never feign shock or offer censure. He'd merely stroke his curling mustache and say, "Indeed. An interesting approach. Have you considered this?" And then he'd proceed to question and probe until Leslie was painfully aware of the many flaws in his plan and his father had given him the seeds of a far more useful way to solve the matter. It would certainly be interesting to see what he would do with this coil. How exactly would he deal with Cleo's interest in the odious major?

"I don't suppose Miss Renfield is likely to come to the same conclusion herself?" he'd have asked. "Being the smart little chit you claim she is and all."

Which would have set Leslie on a quarter-hour rant about Cleo's cleverness, citing any number of examples from her childhood on. What a pity his father wasn't here. But that was part of the problem.

He sighed. "Well, I suspect there comes a time

when we all have to move forward on our own," he told Cleo.

She turned from the window to eye him. "You miss your father, don't you?"

Leslie blinked. "Am I that obvious?"

"To a mere acquaintance, no. But I think I know you better than that." She cocked her head. "Lady Jersey was wrong, you know. I will not believe you disappointed your father."

"Perhaps not," Leslie replied. "But the fact of the matter remains: I will never be the marquis he was. How can I be expected to take his place?"

"You can't," she agreed. "For the simple reason that you are not your father."

"No," Leslie said. "I'm Les."

She cringed at the pun. "That is not what I meant. I meant that you are yourself—kind, gentle, sweet, funny. You are not less than your father; you could be far more."

Gazing into her warm brown eyes, he could almost believe her. When he was around her, there were moments he felt like the mighty Marquis of Hastings. Of course, there were also moments he felt like a green schoolboy fresh from the country. "We are a pair, Cleo. Neither of us is making any progress in getting what we want."

She smiled. "We are rather dismal. And I don't think we're asking for so very much either."

"Just the right to control your life," he reminded her.

"And the right to have fun," she countered. "In truth, however, I suspect we both want someone who will care for us no matter what scrapes we get into."

"I already have someone like that," he said, watching her. "You."

She blushed, but the light in her eyes told him she

was pleased. "And I have you. Thank you for sticking with me through all this, Les. I wish I could say it will be more fun from here out, but I simply do not know."

"It's all right, Cleo," he replied, letting his heart bask in the glow of her approval. "I'm not sure what happens next either, but at least we can face it together."

The next two days would prove just how wrong he could be.

Fourteen

Cleo had to admit that the boxing match was as exciting as she'd hoped, if for slightly different reasons. She really had no experience with how such things were run, but she had imagined she'd be sitting close to the front of the event and watching two gentlemen jabbing civilly at each other in a show of manly strength and agility. As it turned out, nothing could have been further from the truth.

In the first place, she wasn't even allowed near the ring. As the carriage drew close to the site for the match, Leslie's coachman opened the panel that separated him from the interior of the coach.

"Nearly there, m' lord," he called down, round face red from the wind. "Do you want to go afoot or shall I try for yer father's old spot?"

Leslie hesitated, casting her a quick glance. "The edge of the field will be fine," he replied to his man.

Cleo eyed him. "Can we see anything from the edge?"

Her voice must have betrayed her suspicion, for he chuckled. "Enough," he promised. "My father used to take in the fights from his carriage, and he could see enough to trounce me in the betting books. Besides, we really should try to minimize the damage to your reputation."

She wrinkled her nose. "If you only know that one note, pray stop harping. Am I not allowed any time to enjoy myself?"

He reached across and tapped her nose. "Impertinent miss," he snapped in a high falsetto that was a near perfect imitation of Lady Agnes. Cleo laughed.

"If I didn't agree with you," he said in his normal voice, "I wouldn't have brought you."

Cleo turned to watch as Leslie's coachman brought the carriage to a stop on the edge of a wide field already teeming with people. Dandies jostled costermongers for places around a circle cleared in the flattened grass where the fighters would take their stances. At least a dozen other carriages ringed the area. Unfortunately, even with the height of Leslie's carriage, Cleo could catch only glimpses beyond the heads and shoulders of the people in front of her. Frustrated, she clambered up onto her knees on the seat.

A quickly drawn breath made her glance at Leslie, but he merely offered her a strained smile.

"Comfortable?" he quipped.

She followed his gaze to where her dress had ridden up to reveal her stocking-clad ankles and calves. Even though they were only displayed for Leslie, she felt herself blushing and hastily tugged down her skirts. "Yes," she lied, returning her embarrassed gaze to the window. "How soon will they start?"

He must have pulled his watch from the pocket of his vest for she heard the click of the cover opening. "A few more minutes yet. Listen, you can still hear the bookmakers calling for wagers."

Outside the noise was indeed mounting. Friends called encouragement to each other, bookmakers shouted odds given, and vendors hawked their wares.

A dirty-faced lad ran by with a fist full of almonds, and some industrious soul had brought a keg of ale on a wagon and was selling drafts for a penny a pint.

"Sounds as if the Giant is the favorite," Leslie commented. "Pity. I put my money on the fellow from Seven Dials, Jabberton."

She smiled at him. "Do you always favor the odd man out?"

He returned her smile with a good-natured shrug. "Seems to be my lot in life. Would you like to make a wager?"

"Oh, Leslie, that would be famous!" No sooner had she said the words than she realized she could do no such thing. "Or perhaps not. I lost all my money playing silverloo, and I won't see any allowance from Mr. Carlisle until next month."

Leslie spread his hands. "I would be happy to advance you the blunt, Sprout."

"Done!" she declared. "A quid on the fellow from Seven Dials. Industrious gentlemen should be encouraged."

Leslie grinned, reaching up to tap on the panel above his head. When the face of his coachman appeared, he tossed up a coin. "A quid for Jabberton, Jack. From the lady."

"Right-to, m' lord," he barked with a grin. "And if I may be so bold, tell the lady I'm only too happy to take her money, for mine's on the Bull."

Cleo laughed as the panel snapped shut.

Her amusement, however, quickly evaporated as the fighters failed to appear. By the lengthy conversation going on between several gentlemen near the center of the circle, she could only conclude that something had gone wrong. The crowd shouted the louder for the match to begin.

"What happened?" she asked Leslie.

He shook his head. "I cannot tell. There may have been a change in plan. The magistrates frown on these matches, at least in public. Perhaps there's been a change in venue to keep all parties happy. Those gentlemen"—he pointed to the ones arguing in the center of the ring—"are the seconds for the fighters. I have yet to see either the Bull or the Giant in the throng. Neither do I see Prestwick. We may have come for no purpose, Sprout."

She frowned. "I shall be highly disappointed, if that is the case. It isn't likely I shall get a chance to see a fight again soon."

"One never knows," Leslie replied mysteriously. Before she could question him, however, he continued. "The most interesting thing about any London social event, even boxing, is the people who turn out for it. For example, look at that beefy fellow on the right of the circle."

Although any number of the people outside the coach could have been labeled beefy, Cleo immediately saw who he meant. A very large gentleman stood with a tankard in one hand and a sausage in the other, alternatively swigging from either. All the while his face grew redder and redder until Cleo thought he must explode.

"He likely has a wager on and isn't pleased it's about to be declared void," Leslie commented. "And what about that young fellow there, with the yellow feather in his cap?"

Cleo spotted the young man easily enough. His confident swagger and cries to customers were spoiled by an occasional hiccough that shook his slender frame. "The one selling the brandy balls?"

"Looks as if he's been sampling his wares," Leslie replied. "And I see we aren't the only members of the Ton present. See that toffee-colored coach? That's Lord Darton's equipage."

"Will Lady DeGuis be here?" Cleo asked, glancing about.

Leslie shook his head. "Not likely. Margaret has little interest in fighting of this sort."

His tone rang with admiration. Cleo eyed him. "And you applaud her for that, don't you?"

"Certainly," he agreed readily. "I admire many things about Margaret. She's honest, caring, intelligent, and rousing good fun."

Cleo caught herself wondering whether he'd describe her with such passion. She wasn't entirely sure she'd behaved honestly or with a great deal of care or intelligence lately. Well, at least she had provided him with some fun. She turned back to the window in time to see a familiar face in the crowd. She stiffened, heart jumping to her throat.

"Oh, look, Leslie! It's Major Cutter."

Leslie peered out his own window. As Cleo watched, the major made his way through the throng. He was dressed in civilian clothes today, a bottle green coat and chamois trousers tucked into gleaming Hessians. To her surprise, he seemed to be heading for Leslie's carriage.

"He's coming this way," she gasped, hands fluttering to tug down her spencer and smooth down her skirt. "Oh, Leslie, this could be my chance. Will you invite him to join us?"

Leslie hesitated as she turned an entreating face to him. "You will not mind him seeing you in a questionable situation?" he asked.

Cleo shook her head. Then, remembering her ankles, she scrambled back into a proper sitting position. "Please, Leslie?" she begged.

Still Leslie hesitated, regarding her steadily. She

felt her blush growing. "What? Is something the matter with me?"

He sighed. "No, Sprout, you are utterly adorable, as always. Allow me to fetch your hero for you. But somehow I doubt I will be thanked for it, by either of you."

She frowned, but he had already lowered the window on his side of the coach, calling the major by name. Cleo swallowed, hardly daring to peer out the window to see whether the man would respond. But a moment more and the door handle was turning. She felt herself trembling as violently as the coach as Major Cutter climbed in to join them.

She wasn't sure how he would react when he saw her, but to her delight, his questioning smile grew to one of obvious pleasure, and he seated himself beside her rather than joining Leslie on the other side of the carriage.

"Miss Renfield, how nice to see you," he said, taking her hand and bringing it to his lips. His mouth pressed fervently against the back of her hand, sending her heart to her throat. No doubt that was why she was only able to stammer out a greeting.

"Good of you to join us, Cutter," Leslie snapped out, in an obvious attempt to break the spell.

Major Cutter's gaze held Cleo's even as his hand refused to release hers. "The invitation could not have been more welcome," he answered.

Cleo swallowed, willing her boneless fingers to pull away from him.

"Who do you favor?" Leslie persisted.

Major Cutter's mouth lifted in a smile that sent heat to the center of her stomach before he turned to Leslie at last. "The Bull, naturally. He has the longer reach, the greater height, and the better reputation."

"He also has the least motivation," Leslie argued. "Miss Renfield and I favor Jabberton. He still has passion for the sport."

"Ah, yes, passion," Major Cutter replied knowingly. "An important quality in any number of situations, as I believe you both know."

Cleo frowned. She quite agreed with the basic sentiment, but something in the way Leslie's dark eyes flashed and Major Cutter smiled told her that something else was being said. She wasn't entirely sure what, but she could not help but feel that it had something to do with her.

"Ah, look," he continued smoothly, as if unaware of the tension in the coach. "The Bull has arrived at last."

Cleo turned eagerly to the window, but sitting in the ladylike position afforded her a view no better than the backs of those nearest her. Climbing on her knees with Major Cutter present was unthinkable. She allowed herself a small sigh.

"You'll appreciate his stance, Miss Renfield." Major Cutter's voice, so near her ear, startled her, and she realized he had slid up close behind her. Her heart started pounding so hard and fast that she could barely hear his next murmured words.

"You can see how he holds his hands loosely, as if he's ready for anything." She tensed as his hand grazed her shoulder, his fingers brushing the curls at the nap of her neck. "His body is confident in his power. At any moment, he might lunge at his opponent, conquering him."

The coach was surely heating in the afternoon sun. She could not imagine why Lord Hastings had painted it in so dark a color. She slid away from Major Cutter, pinioning herself up against the cool of the window, and tugged at the collar of her spencer. Outside a cheer went up, and she wished she could see what had caused it. Anything to take her mind off the major's closeness.

"Ah, Jabberton is down already," Major Cutter supplied with a shake of his head that somehow allowed him to close the distance between them. "I knew the Bull would prove the dominant fighter. He takes what he wants."

Cleo's head spun. She couldn't seem to catch a breath. *Oh, Lord, please don't let me faint,* she prayed. *I refuse to be one of those milk-and-water misses.*

"Here, Cleo." Leslie's voice came gently through her fog. "I think you'll find the view better from my window."

She blinked and focused with difficulty on Leslie's smile. Her legs trembled under her as she rose, but she managed to cross the small distance without mishap.

Leslie had piled up the bolsters so that she could still sit like a lady and see out. With a smile of gratitude, she perched on her new throne and peered out at the ring.

She was hoping the fight might distract her from the heated thoughts Major Cutter had engendered. But there was no help outside for her flushed constitution. She was quite shocked to find that both the gentlemen were naked from the waist up. Already sweat poured down the rippling muscles of the Mighty Bull of Lancaster, making his tanned skin glisten in the sunlight like polished mahogany. Jabberton, scrambling up from the ground, was peppered with dirt, but that only emphasized his chiseled frame. She tried to focus on the action rather than on either of them. Unfortunately, they continued to swing at each other until the Bull managed to close with the smaller Jabberton. Their grunting reached her ears even over the roar of the crowd. It only served to remind her of Eloise in the hayloft. Face flaming, she dropped her gaze to her clenched hands.

It wasn't until Jabberton had managed to trip the Bull and slam his head into the ground (as Leslie described to her later), thus ending the fight, that she was able to raise her gaze. Then it was to find Major Cutter regarding her with narrowed eyes. When he saw her staring, he smiled, but this time the gesture did not delight her. She felt as if someone had doused her in cold water.

"So, you've won your wager, Miss Renfield," he said as Leslie rapped on the roof to signal to his coachman to go fetch their winnings. "It would appear passion won after all."

"Luck," Leslie proclaimed before Cleo could respond. "Miss Renfield is a good-luck charm. I never fear when she is at my side."

His sunny smile smacked of ownership. Cleo bristled.

"Nonsense, Lord Hastings," she declared, using the hated title deliberately, "you do very well without me, if the tales I hear are true."

"He plays the game well," the major agreed graciously. "He's quite lucky, at cards. Speaking of which, I've discovered a delightful new gaming establishment. Select clientele, tasteful atmosphere, well-moderated play. Perhaps you'd care to join me?"

The question had been framed to Leslie, but Cleo saw no reason not to include herself. She turned an eager face to Leslie. "Oh, could we, Les? I've always wanted to see a gaming hell."

"This isn't a hell, infant," he informed her with a scowl. "And you have no business out in public at a place like that."

"I quite agree with Lord Hastings," Cutter put in even as Cleo took umbrage at Leslie's high-handed tone. "Although I suppose it would be all right if we were both there to protect her."

"She shouldn't be someplace she needs two grown men to protect her," Leslie told him heatedly.

Cleo returned his scowl. "It hardly sounds that dangerous."

"It isn't," Major Cutter insisted. "However, I would not want to advise you against the wishes of your protector, Miss Renfield."

Leslie's body went stiff, and Cleo glanced at him in surprise. The muscle was working in his cheek again, as if he'd clenched his teeth, and his eyes burned into the major. "I am not Miss Renfield's protector, Cutter," he said with an edge of steel in his voice. "We are old friends, nothing more."

Cleo glanced at the major, who had raised his chin and was regarding Leslie with equal heat. "Then you will not mind if another gentleman shows interest."

"I don't understand," she said, cutting through their locked gazes. "Why are you two being so hostile to each other?"

It was probably not the ladylike thing to say. Undoubtedly she was breaking some rule that said she was to sit politely like a bone between two dogs and wait until they were through tearing each other apart. Certainly Leslie looked at her as if she'd grown a second nose. Major Cutter merely inclined his head in her direction.

"I shall allow Lord Hastings to explain, my dear," he replied. "Perhaps I should leave him to it. Thank you for allowing me to view the fight with you. If you change your mind, Hastings, about any of the topics we've discussed, please feel free to contact me at White's this evening. Miss Renfield, your servant."

Cleo watched as he moved to open the coach door. She glanced at Leslie, but his face was shuttered. Despite the uncertain undercurrents, she could not let the major leave like this. She reached out and put a hand on his arm.

"Thank you for the invitation, Major," she said. "And may I return the compliment by inviting you to call on me at home?"

She was being forward and he obviously realized it. His face was suddenly as shuttered as Leslie's. "Always happy to oblige a lady, Miss Renfield," he returned. "Enjoy your winnings."

She let him go and watched as he shut the coach door behind him with a snap.

Fifteen

As soon as Cutter took his miserable, womanizing hide out the door, Cleo rounded on Leslie, as he knew she would.

"Explain yourself immediately," she demanded. "You were unconscionably rude to Major Cutter. I want to know why."

He couldn't answer her. No matter what he tried, he was continually put in a position where he had to shatter her innocence. Perhaps he should simply tell her of his suspicions and have done with it.

"He called me your protector," he said. "Do you have any idea what that means?"

She frowned. "I assumed it was something of a guardian, like Mr. Carlisle is to me."

He snorted. "Oh, it's nothing like that, I assure you." She gazed at him quizzically, and he raked a hand back through his hair. How could he explain this to her? "Damnation, Cleo, you're putting me in an impossible position."

"Why?" she asked; then, as he groaned, she laid a hand on his arm. "Leslie, what is it? I felt the tension between the two of you, so I know something of import transpired. Shouldn't I know what?"

She had a right to know, but he still couldn't find

the words to tell her. He sighed. "Do you know anything about your sisters' marriages?"

She cocked her head. "A little, I suppose. Why do you ask?"

Why did he ask? Why couldn't he simply say it? "Do you know why your sister's husband, Lord Stephenson, is rarely received?"

"He gambles," she answered readily enough. "And he flirts with other men's wives."

Leslie took a deep breath. "Everyone gambles. And it isn't the flirting that bothers them, Sprout."

Her face flamed. "You're talking about taking a mistress."

"Do you understand what that means?" he asked, watching her.

She hung her head. "Very little."

God, how he hated this. "How little?"

She squirmed. "Must we have this discussion?"

"Not in the slightest," he replied. "As long as you don't ask me why I nearly called Tony Cutter out just now."

She let out her breath in a sigh of exasperation. "But I must know, Leslie." When he said nothing, she shrugged. "Very well. A mistress is someone a gentlemen kisses who is not his wife."

"Close enough," Leslie declared, offering a prayer of gratitude that he did not have to elaborate. "When a woman agrees to be a mistress, she goes under a man's protection. He generally pays for her upkeep the way a man might keep his wife. The man who keeps her is therefore known as her protector."

She stared at him, and he could see the comprehension dawning behind her eyes. "You must be mistaken."

He barked out a laugh. "Oh, no, Sprout, I assure you, I am not mistaken."

"But Major Cutter would not use the term that way," she protested, nearly making him gag with her misplaced loyalty. "He could not believe that we . . . that I . . ."

"Anyone with a grain of sense would know you cannot be my mistress," Leslie assured her. "You are a lady, and my tastes tend to run in other directions."

That brought the color flooding back into her cheeks, and he cursed himself. "You have a mistress?" she demanded to know.

"No," he snapped. That was only the truth, for at the moment, Lolly Dupray had gone over to the duke and he had been far too busy with Cleo to find himself another likely candidate.

She took a deep breath. "Well, I'm glad to hear that. It doesn't strike me as a very gentlemanly thing to do."

Most of the gentlemen of his acquaintance would have disagreed, but he did not want to encourage her thoughts along those lines. "Now do you see why I disfavor Cutter?"

She scowled. "No, for I cannot believe he would do such a thing either. Nor do I believe he finds me a woman of easy virtue."

He threw up his hands. "Then I can't help you, Cleo. For I believe he would and he does."

She gazed at him a moment before shaking her head. "Then we are at an impasse."

"We seem to be," he agreed. "And in that case, I think we should decide upon our next course of action, which should be to find you a husband."

She shook her head again, but this time more vehemently. "I don't understand you, Leslie. I thought we agreed that my best course was to spend additional time getting to know Major Cutter. Surely that is the only way to tell whether he has my best interests at heart. Why not accept his offer to attend the gaming hell?"

Why not indeed? The idea had merit. Give the girl some proximity to the infamous Major Cutter and she'd soon see through him. But Leslie wasn't sure he could stand to watch the process. He had nearly exploded watching Cutter's practiced seduction in the carriage this afternoon. The fellow had all but put his hands on her! Each comment had been murmured with the heated purr of a lover, each phrase calculatingly couched in innuendo. Leslie had had to ball his hands into fists to keep from grabbing the villain by the too-perfect folds of his cravat and tossing him out of the coach.

And Cleo! She had only made matters worse. He knew she had no idea what the miscreant was trying to do. But even minutes after the major had made his escape, Leslie's blood was still boiling in his veins. Small wonder he'd refused an invitation for an encore performance. Small wonder he hadn't shot the fellow where he sat!

"Nothing Major Cutter did or said this afternoon concerned you?" he challenged.

She blinked. "Concern me? I . . . I'm not sure what you mean."

Her eyes were wide, but they did not quite meet his gaze. Had she, in fact, been discomposed by the major's none-too-subtle flirting? He pressed his advantage. "Did you like how he talked to you? Did his choice of topics amuse you?"

He had obviously been mistaken in her concern, for she relaxed, shrugging. "He talked about the fight. As did you, as did I. I will grant you, he isn't the most original conversationalist, if that's what you mean."

"Indeed," Leslie quipped. "I have seen it done far better to far more experienced ladies than you."

"What are you talking about?" Cleo demanded. "Do not start with this odious accusation of Major Cutter's opinion of me again. I will grant you, there were moments when I thought him the least bit familiar, but that is not the same as taking me for your mistress."

"Familiar, is it?" Leslie replied, determined that she understand. "Very well, Miss Innocent, you leave me no choice but to demonstrate what you must learn for your own safety. If you would kindly gaze out the window at the rapidly disbanding crowd."

Her frown remained, but she did as he bid. Leslie sat for a moment, steeling himself, watching as his driver returned with their winnings and resumed his seat on the box. Under cover of the swaying of the coach, he slid closer to Cleo.

"See the people moving about, Miss Renfield," he murmured near her ear. He was so close, a dark curl teased his cheek like a silken finger. "There is such grace in moving limbs, swaying, joining."

"Leslie," she growled in warning.

"Watch the crowd, if you please," he instructed. Then he gave into temptation and let his gloved fingers brush her hair as he inched closer.

"Fighting is such an exertion," he murmured, inhaling her smell of jasmine. "I much prefer other forms of exercise, something more entertaining for both partners, something more intimate."

She stiffened, but he could not stop himself, didn't want to stop himself. He bent and brushed his lips against the nape of her neck, sighing against the sweetness of her skin. He could have sworn she tasted every bit as warm and honeyed as she looked.

His heart pounding, he straightened and waited for her to slap his face.

She did not disappoint him. She whirled from the window, face blazing, hand up. But the blow never came. She merely glared at him. "Point taken," she snapped. "It was annoying and flustering when he did it. When you do it, it feels like . . ."

"Betrayal?"

She nodded, swallowing, and the anger went out of her. "So, you are asking me to believe that Major Cutter is a miscreant who would also betray me. But I have never heard anyone say anything bad about him, never smelled the least whiff of scandal. If he is so awful, why hasn't he shown it by now?"

She had him there. Until Cleo had taken an interest in the major, Leslie had always considered him the best of good fellows. Was he wrong in what he saw? He remembered the cunning words, the clever hands that had nearly driven him mad. No, Tony Cutter had definitely been set on seduction. But were his actions any worse than that of any other buck of the Ton? Did his insinuations imply anything more devious than the urgent desire to make the lady his? Was Leslie simply a jealous fool?

"I have only my own experiences and intuition to guide me," he admitted. "Both tell me Tony Cutter is looking for a mistress, not a wife. Lady Agnes thinks he is after money."

Cleo barked a laugh. "I have no money. You know that." She paused with a frown. "Still, it would explain his interest in Eloise Watkin. Now *she* has money."

"Either way, I would not see you harmed, Cleo."

"I assure you, neither would I," she replied fervently. "But you know our agreement with Lady Agnes, Leslie. I must find a husband in six weeks' time.

I refuse to compromise you on the altar of matrimony."

He wanted to groan aloud at her choice of analogies. His brain continued to seize on them all too easily. He would have been only too delighted to have her compromise him anywhere she pleased. "We will find someone else, Sprout," he maintained, reaching up to tap the panel and signal his driver to start for home.

"I am not ready to give up on Major Cutter yet," she said, raising his bile once again. "There must be a way to prove his true colors."

"I suppose," he allowed as the coach set off. "If our good friend Major Cutter sees fit to call on you in all propriety, I will rethink his intentions. But until he does, I want you to promise me never to be alone with him."

Her eyes widened. "You don't think he would accost me?"

Leslie shook his head, trying to hide the fact that his blood turned cold just considering the possibility. "I have no idea. I simply think it wise to take precautions." He reached out and touched her cheek, wishing he could be so bold as to remove his glove and stroke the softness. "Don't be afraid, Sprout. I don't intend to let you out of my sight until the day you are safely wed."

She sighed, rising to move to the opposite seat as if dismissing him. "I'm very much afraid, Leslie," she said. "For if Major Cutter is not the man I think him, that day may never arrive."

If Cleo thought her afternoon was surprising, her evening faired no better. Leslie drove her home and stayed for an early dinner. After he left, Ellie arrived, and Cleo had to endure a ringing scold over the Almack's contretemps before her sister quieted down enough to let Lady Agnes announce the fact that Leslie had proposed. Then Ellie was all knowing smiles. Indeed, she insisted that Lady Agnes leave them alone to explain the changes that would soon occur in Cleo's maidenly status. Luckily, Lady Agnes protested.

"I'm her chaperone," her godmother declared, shaking out the skirts of her black silk gown. "It's therefore my responsibility to prepare her for her marriage bed."

"You?" Ellie thrust out the chest of her amethyst satin gown. "Need I remind you, madam, that you are a spinster?"

"What has that to say about anything?" Lady Agnes challenged. "I know how horses mate, and I'm certainly no mare."

Cleo felt her cheeks heat in a blush, but in truth she was too curious about what her sister wanted to impart to stop the conversation.

"So you say," Ellie replied to Lady Agnes. "But as Cleo's oldest sister, I feel it my duty to pass along my experience, just in case."

Lady Agnes leaned back in her chair. "If you have so much experience in the area, I'd like to hear it. Maybe I'll learn something as well."

Ellie glared at her for a moment before turning her gaze on Cleo. "Once a gentleman has committed himself to a lady," she began, "he feels he has the right to touch her wherever he sees fit. It will be up to you to depress such notions."

Cleo frowned. "I'm not quite sure what you mean," she said, although the memory of Eloise in the hayloft intruded. "Why would a gentleman want to touch me?"

Ellie compressed her lips even as Lady Agnes leaned forward for an answer.

"Gentlemen are by nature more prone to giving in to their base natures," Ellie said with arch superiority. "They are only satisfied if they can indulge their senses. I am certain Lord Hastings will be no exception. You must remember that a short embrace, a discreet touch on the shoulder, or perhaps a kindly kiss on the cheek is acceptable. Anything else should be discouraged."

So, neither Major Cutter's touch on her neck nor Leslie's kiss had been acceptable, even if they had been engaged to her. Of course, Leslie's had only been done in demonstration, even if the very thorough demonstration had served to send heat to the center of her being. Major Cutter's had obviously been motivated by something else. The question remained as to what.

"I daresay," Lady Agnes interrupted far more gently than was her wont, "that all that changes with marriage. When there is love and respect between husband and wife the, er, touching is more likely to be pleasurable to them both."

Cleo smiled, even as Ellie rolled her eyes. Now, that answer made sense. It fit with the warm, comfortable feeling she had sensed between her mother and father. It fit with the tension she'd felt between Jareth Darby and Eloise Watkin. Perhaps Eloise was right that some sort of love had been present, but respect seemed to have been missing. The answer even explained her response to Major Cutter, who she had respected but not loved. Small wonder his touches had made her feel faint.

Ellie had some other pointed advice about keeping her eyes shut and watching for her time of the month, but Cleo didn't pay much attention. The events of the day seemed to crowd in on her, and she was glad when her sister dismissed her at last.

As she climbed into bed, however, Lady Agnes walked in. She leaned over the bed and pulled the coverlet up under Cleo's chin.

"No one's done that since my mother died," Cleo told her with a fond smile.

Lady Agnes shook her head. "Your sisters never did know how to handle you. Did Electra's disgustingly inadequate description tonight trouble you?"

"No," Cleo replied. "Your clarification made a great deal of sense."

Lady Agnes snorted. "Of course I make sense. Thank goodness you did not put much stock in your sister's wisdom. I may never have had a lover, but I've seen how happy my friends and family are in their marriages. I find it hard to believe every one of them simply shuts their eyes and makes the best of things when the lamp is blown out. Look at Margaret and Thomas, for goodness sake—happy as griggs, the pair of them, and she's even been known to kiss him in public."

On that cheery note, Cleo kissed her godmother good night.

Sixteen

Leslie's evening fared far worse. He had escorted Cleo home and ate dinner with her and Lady Agnes, escaping the house as early as he could for the quiet of his club. White's was hardly silent, if one counted the thrum of civilized conversation, the chime of fine crystal, or the shuffle of cards against green baize. But Leslie was long used to those noises. He was far less used to the sound of his own brain, furiously working. He could not seem to get Cleo's problem off his mind.

Normally, he would have found little time to contemplate the issue. He was a well-known figure at the club and generally did not lack for invitations to dine, to play cards, to converse. Tonight, however, it was obvious that his presence was awkward. Gentlemen who could be counted on to stop and chat now barely nodded in passing. Fellows he had considered more than acquaintances suddenly found it expedient to be elsewhere. One set of lords actually stopped playing when he expressed interest in their game, and Robbie Newcomer, the lad who had stood up with Cleo before their now infamous waltz, went so far as to give him the cut direct. Sally Jersey's edict was being enforced far beyond the bounds of Almack's.

The censure was extreme, but he could not say it

troubled him as much as he had expected. Cleo knew his motives had been pure. He resigned himself to a quiet night and retreated to an armchair near one of the fireplaces to ponder. He was therefore surprised when someone deigned to join him. And even more surprised when that someone proved to be Cutter.

"Lord Hastings," he greeted. "Might I have a word with you?"

Leslie raised a brow. Cutter merely regarded him with a slight frown. Snapping a nod, Leslie motioned him to the opposite chair. Once safely ensconced, the major lost no time in explaining himself.

"I had no idea you had offered for Miss Renfield," he said, hands braced on the thighs of his white breeches.

Leslie frowned. "Who told you that?"

"The betting books closed today when it became known that Lady Agnes DeGuis had sent the notice to *The Times* of your engagement. You must have been ready to call me out for my behavior this afternoon."

Leslie clenched his teeth. He had not counted on his godmother to move so quickly. "I was," he admitted. "I don't mind telling you, Cutter, that your methods are a dash familiar."

"My apologies," Cutter replied humbly. "I promise you, I'm not the type to poach on another man's territory."

Drat his godmother! How was Cleo to get another man to show interest without making the engagement a lie and Lady Agnes a liar? A neater trap he had never seen. Cleo would simply have to come up with a logical explanation as to why the banns were being read even as she sought a husband. Perhaps he and Cleo should come up with something together, so their stories matched. In the meantime, he supposed he should discourage the notion that the lady was taken.

"I'm not impressed by your actions," Leslie told Cutter. "However, I think Miss Renfield highly regards you. I would be a fool to stand in the way of that regard."

Cutter leaned forward. "Do I understand you correctly? Are you encouraging me to pursue Miss Renfield, even though you are now engaged to her?"

Leslie met his gaze. "I am encouraging you to be honest in your dealings with her. If you are interested, do not let my supposed engagement to the lady stand in your way."

"I appreciate your candor, Hastings," he said. "And I cannot help noticing that you are a bit friendless at the moment. Let me return your kindness. I would be happy to have you join me at Madame Zala's gaming establishment. A gentleman with deep pockets is always welcome there. Say tomorrow evening?"

Leslie couldn't see that kindness had anything to do with it. If Major Cutter wanted to pick his pockets at the gaming table, a private establishment looked to be the only way he could do it, as he was clearly unwelcome at White's. Still, there was something wrong about the whole affair. He simply couldn't put his finger on it. "I shall consider it," he replied.

Cutter stood and snapped a bow, and Leslie nodded in farewell. As soon as the major strolled away, he frowned. It seemed the best thing he could do was figure out what Cutter was up to. For that, he needed decidedly more information.

Perhaps the best ear man in twelve counties could help.

* * *

Morning was always good for brightening Cleo's outlook. She awoke determined to find a way out of her predicament. The logical first step was to determine whether or not Major Cutter was the blackguard Leslie thought him. To do this, she clearly needed to spend time in the gentleman's company. She could not sit around waiting for him to call. Yet, she certainly could not call on him. She hadn't the foggiest notion where he lived, and ladies did not call on gentlemen, regardless. She could scarcely haunt the front steps of White's, and she could not rely purely on the chance that he attend one of the balls she was to attend over the next week. She had to think of something else.

The answer was dropped in her lap by the unlikely person of Eloise Watkin. Surprise could not describe Cleo's emotions when Mr. Cowls announced the visitor and ushered the girl into the drawing room, where Cleo had been thinking. Eloise looked as lovely as ever in a green-sprigged muslin gown, but as Cleo motioned her to a chair, she could not help noticing that the girl's green eyes were rimmed by red.

"I know you told me not to call again," Eloise said as soon as they were alone, "but I had nowhere else to turn."

"I apologize for speaking so harshly to you the last time you were here," Cleo replied sincerely. "I wish you would believe me that the memory of that day is as unpleasant for me as it is for you."

"It cannot be." Eloise rose and wandered about the room, hands clenched before her. "I thought I loved him and he loved me. I would have given him anything and very nearly did. You would think I would have learned." She stopped and regarded Cleo steadily, head high. "No, I *have* learned. I know you must think me a horrid flirt, Cleo, that I am forever bringing myself to a gentleman's notice. It is my way of testing them. I will not let a gentleman close unless he has proven himself worthy."

Cleo nodded in understanding. "I am not certain I would do the same, but I can see how you might have come to that. But why do you tell me this?"

Eloise returned to her seat. "Because I need your help. You are the only one who will understand how important this is to me." She paused, swallowing, as if unsure of her reception. "I am interested in Major Cutter, and I need to know whether his intentions toward me are honorable."

Cleo wanted to laugh at the irony, but she was afraid of hurting Eloise's feelings. "I'm afraid I cannot help you, Eloise. I am also interested in the major and having no better luck determining his motives."

Eloise stared at her, and Cleo thought she might spring up and depart that minute. Instead, her lips compressed in a determined line. "I am sorry we are rivals. If you remember, I did try to stop that in the beginning."

"You tried to warn me away from him," Cleo corrected her. "You should know better. I am far too stubborn for that tactic to work."

Eloise shook her head with a wry smile. "Yes, I should have known better. But our problem remains. You must have seen how slippery he is about making commitments. I have hinted and postured as much as I can. He will say nothing that one can pin one's hopes upon, yet he seems to expect complete devotion from the lady. How can either of us know his intentions?"

Cleo could not answer the question, but Eloise did not appear to expect an answer. "I tell you, Cleo, I

will not be betrayed again. After seeing my fall, I
would think you would feel the same."

Indeed, Cleo found she did feel the same way. She
remembered her reaction all too clearly the day before, when Leslie had demonstrated seduction. Betrayal by someone you loved had to be the worst hurt
of all. She had been witness to Eloise's betrayal the
first time. Perhaps this time she could prevent it.

"I understand," Cleo told her. "And I am certain
it will surprise you to learn that I agree with you.
We must know Major Cutter's true colors."

Eloise cocked her head. "Then you have a plan?"

Cleo nodded. "The beginnings of one. But before
I can start it, I must know. If Major Cutter proves
himself a gentleman, are you willing to let him
choose which lady he would like to pursue?"

"Certainly." Eloise's charming smile told Cleo that
she had no doubt who that would be. Cleo wasn't so
sure, but she found it did not matter. She smiled as
well.

"Very well, then. We are agreed to work together
to determine Major Cutter's motives."

"And woe betide him," Eloise added, "if he should
prove to be a villain."

Agreeing with Eloise was always a rare occur-
rence, Cleo knew, but she somehow thought getting
Leslie to agree would prove far more difficult. Still,
she resolved to try that very afternoon when he came
to teach Hector. Although the lessons were no longer
necessary for either her plan or Hector, the ruse
proved a good excuse to spend time together. She
was certain Leslie would appear at three. Neither did
he disappoint her. It was only his insistence that Mr.
Cowls stay and chat that surprised her.

It surprised the butler as well. He raised a thin white brow and leaned toward Leslie as if he could not have heard properly. "A conversation, Lord Petersborough?"

"Yes, Mr. Cowls, if you would be so kind." Leslie turned eagerly to Cleo. "I thought of this last night. Mr. Cowls is an expert at reconnaissance, according to Lady Agnes. I thought he might shed some light on our friend Major Cutter."

Cleo brightened and turned to the elderly retainer. "Oh, yes, please, Mr. Cowls. Tell us anything you know."

Cowls glanced back and forth between the two of them, then slowly straightened and closed his eyes. Cleo glanced at Leslie with a frown, but he looked just as perplexed. They both jumped as Cowls began to recite rapidly, as if reading off the insides of his eyelids.

"Anthony Gervais Cutter, born fifth February, seventeen-eighty-eight, to Mrs. Marva Cutter of Sussex, husband deceased. No marriage lines available. Schooled by the local rector. Entered His Majesty's forces at fifteen. One of the few to be promoted to an officer on recommendation rather than purchasing his commission. Colonel who recommended his appointment to major died shortly afterward in battle. Passed most of his career in London but served at Waterloo. Currently serving at half pay at his request. Owns two horses, rents a small flat outside Mayfair. Gambles, badly. Currently owes debts of over six thousand pounds to people of rather unsavory reputations. Favorite club appears to be Madame Zala's, where one should never drink the wine. Applied for a loan to remove his debt and was summarily dismissed."

Leslie whistled, and Cleo shook her head, as much

in astonishment at the amount Cutter owed as admiration of Mr. Cowls's skills. The butler slowly opened his eyes and blinked twice. "Will that be all, my lord?"

"How do you know all that?" Cleo couldn't help asking.

"I regret, Miss Cleo, that I am not at liberty to say. Might I be excused?"

Leslie nodded, and he bowed himself out. Cleo took a seat on the sofa, still shaking her head.

"How does he do that?" she asked as Leslie sat beside her.

"Apparently by listening to conversations," he replied. "I can see why Lady Agnes treasures him. So, Sprout, did that answer your questions about Cutter?"

"No. He is in debt for a great deal, Les, with no apparent means of repaying it. Yet if he was a fortune hunter, why pursue me?"

Leslie tapped his finger against the knee of his chamois trousers. "You received no inheritance from your father or mother?"

"None. We were never rich. Mr. Carlisle may provide me with a small marriage dower, but not nearly enough to pay a debt of that size."

"No rich great-uncle waiting to pop off and endow you with all his worldly goods?"

Cleo giggled. "Not a one. Only a dear godmother with her own inheritance. And Lady Agnes would never pay my husband's debts."

"I grant you it is unlikely. So, where does that leave us?"

"With having to determine Major Cutter's worth," Cleo replied firmly. "I must do it, Les."

"He means so much to you?"

She thought she heard more than curiosity behind the comment, but Leslie's face was composed. "Yes.

Leslie, I have made up my mind. I want you to take me to this gaming hell he spoke of, but only if we can be certain he will be in attendance."

She expected to have to fight him over the request and readied her arsenal of reasons.

"We can be certain he'll be there," Leslie said grimly. "We shall go tonight."

Cleo stared at him. "You agree?"

Leslie rose. "You overwhelm me with your gratitude," he quipped, going to face the parrot. Hector shrugged and turned his back. "As do you, old boy. Don't you have a squawk for the fellow who taught you to say 'Hell and damnation'?"

"Hell and damnation," Hector grumbled.

Cleo rose to join him. "Leave him be for a moment. I know I should simply thank you, Leslie, but your turnabout confuses me. You do not trust Major Cutter. Why agree to meet him?"

Leslie hunched a shrug, reminding her for all the world of the parrot at his most recalcitrant. "I decided you have the right of it. The only chance you have to see him for himself is to spend some time with him. I shall send a note round to tell him we'll join him tonight at eight. It's early enough in the evening that the heavy players will not yet be out. That should keep the company moderately respectable."

"That also puts us in conflict with Mrs. Winston's ball," Cleo informed him. "I believe it starts at nine. Lady Agnes has already written to have you included in the invitation."

Leslie frowned. "Mrs. Winston? Another high stickler. I can imagine her frustration when she receives Lady Agnes's note. She'd have been only too happy to cut me, I'm sure, but she will not like to offend the DeGuises." His frown deepened. "Still, she's not likely to get through the receiving line before ten. That should allow us an hour or so at the gaming establishment."

Cleo grinned, giving his arm a squeeze. "That would be perfect. Now we just have to get Lady Agnes to agree to let us go to the ball without her."

That proved all too easy. Her godmother started in her usual argumentative state of mind, but by the time Leslie was through, she was demanding that he swallow his pride and take Cleo to the ball without her. All that remained was to dress for the fateful event and wait for Leslie to return for her.

Dressing did not prove difficult. She dismissed Bess and did the task herself. Having decided to put Major Cutter to the test, Cleo donned her scandalous gown, tucking the lace fichu she had used earlier into her reticule, along with some pins. She certainly didn't want to look seductive at Mrs. Winston's ball, not with everyone already gossiping about Leslie. She regarded herself in the mirror, noting the height of her color and the depth of her décolletage. She could not bring herself to dampen her petticoats, but surely the clinging silk and the vast amount of her neck and shoulders that were in evidence would be enough. She cinched tight the apricot satin ribbon under her bosom and let the ends hang tantalizingly down each thigh. With her long gloves and pearls, she fancied she looked ready for intrigue.

The hardest part of all was waiting. She finished her toilette early and paced her room for a quarter hour before going down the stairs and repeating the performance in the entry hall. Mr. Cowls ambled past twice, once with her brown velvet evening cloak and another with a glass of sherry. When she accepted the glass with a questioning frown, he shrugged.

"You seem a bit nervous, miss," he ventured with

his usual wheeze. "Would you like me to fetch your godmother instead?"

"You needn't fetch anyone," Lady Agnes informed him, coming down the hall. "And remove that alcohol from my goddaughter's hand immediately. Do you want Major Cutter to think her a drunkard?"

Cleo gasped, fingers suddenly as numb as the rest of her as she handed Mr. Cowls the glass. "Godmother, I . . ." she started.

Lady Agnes waved a hand. "Don't bother to lie. You do it rather badly."

She reached the entryway and raised a quizzing glass to look Cleo up and down, reaching out to pluck open her cloak with her free hand. Not sure what to think, Cleo spread her skirts and did a pirouette.

"An all-out assault, I see," her godmother quipped, dropping the glass to her chest. "You stay close to Leslie tonight, my girl. I quite understand wanting the gentleman to appreciate your assets, but make sure you save something for marriage."

Cleo felt herself flaming. "You don't mind, then?"

"Of course I mind," Lady Agnes replied, moving toward the sitting room. "You know I don't like the fellow above half. But you're obviously not willing to accept my word that he's a miscreant, and I'm not sure I'd want you to. So, go. Prove to yourself he's not the fellow for you. Just don't be too late to Mrs. Winston's. The old termagant will never let me live it down if you and Leslie cause a problem at her event."

Cleo rushed forward and plastered a kiss on her godmother's cheek. "Oh, thank you, Lady Agnes! I promise we will be good."

Lady Agnes snorted, but she patted Cleo's hand

where it rested on her shoulder. Then the knocker sounded, and the adventure began.

"Did Lady Agnes give you any trouble?" Leslie asked as he saw her seated in the carriage.

Cleo shook her head. "No, but she gave me a fright. She knows, Les. Don't ask me how, but she knows."

"If she and Mr. Cowls weren't as old as Methuselah, I'd think they knelt at keyholes," Leslie replied with a chuckle of reluctant admiration. "She must have some other source, though I don't know who could have heard us."

Cleo stared at him. "Hector!"

"Hector? Of course!" Leslie chuckled. "No wonder the old bird picked up swearing so easily. I'd wager he's talked to Lady Agnes for years and she's never let on. Of course, she appears to have other sources, for some of her information could not come from the bird." He shook his head. "You have to credit our godmother for being resourceful."

It was a short distance to the establishment, which sat back from the street in a turreted town house. The elegantly dressed couple entering just as they arrived went a long way toward reassuring Cleo as to the propriety of the place. But Leslie did not appear appeased. Indeed, his face darkened and he muttered under his breath as they climbed the stairs and rapped at the red lacquered door. She could not ask him what troubled him, however, for the door opened immediately to reveal a fellow nearly as large as the Mighty Bull of Lancaster, and twice as battered.

"We're friends of Major Cutter," Leslie told him when he growled an explanation for their presence. "I believe we were expected this evening."

"Mayhap ye were," the giant grumbled. "Yer names would be?"

"The lady's name is not important," Leslie replied with a coolness to match the man's heat. "I am the Marquis of Hastings."

The giant swept the door wide. "Yer very welcome, yer lordship. Enjoy yer evening."

Cleo clung to Leslie's arm as they walked into the cavernous entry. The door swung silently shut behind them. A liveried footman stepped forward to take their cloaks, and she tried not to shiver as the air hit her bare skin. Leslie paled when he caught sight of her gown, but he only rolled his eyes as he straightened the white silk of his cravat, in sharp contrast to his otherwise black evening wear.

Trying to ignore her growing unease, Cleo glanced surreptitiously about, not sure what she expected, but the entry looked little different from those of the other town houses she'd visited. Landscapes graced the satin-draped walls, which were painted a soft green. A marble-tiled floor, with small green blocks alternating with larger white ones, spread down a short corridor to what was likely the dining room. A white stair with a black iron banister curved to the upper floors. The crystal chandelier over her head and the sconces set high along the stair led her eye up, to where a woman waited on the landing.

Cleo swallowed. She had done her best to attempt what she thought would be a seductive style, but this woman had obviously mastered it. Her dress—what there was of it—was black and dripped with jet beads that reflected the light. It was impossible not to notice her creamy skin, for so much of it was displayed—her shoulders, her arms to her hands, which were encased in black lace gloves, and most of her chest. In fact, as she leaned on the balustrade to regard Leslie, both bare arms were propped so that it was possible to gaze straight down her impressive cleavage. Cleo's eyes widened.

"We won't stay above a half hour," Leslie whispered near her ear. "Let's find Cutter and get on with it."

He started for the stairs and as his hand was on her elbow, she could do nothing but do likewise. The woman straightened slowly as they climbed, so that by the time they reached her, she was fully upright and smiling in welcome.

"Lord Hastings," she greeted, extending her hand palm down. The movement was languid, yet Leslie stiffened, as if she had suddenly drawn a knife. "A pleasure to have you join us. And this must be Miss Renfield."

Cleo nodded and started to drop a curtsy, but Leslie's grip tightened, forcing her to remain upright.

"I trust," he growled, "that that is the last time I will hear the lady's name in this house."

The woman raised a finely etched brow. While it was a black as deep as her dress, her hair, Cleo couldn't help noticing, was a soft gold piled high on her head. Jet drops fell from tiny ears. She was beautiful, and Cleo could only stare in fascination as her reddened lips raised at one corner and she withdrew her hand. "As you wish, of course, my lord," she murmured. "We specialize in discretion. Allow me to show you around."

Leslie eyed her a moment more before inclining his head in acceptance. She moved ahead of them into the room that opened off the top of the stairs. Cleo wanted to gaze all about her, but she only got a glimpse of gold and scarlet and green before her eyes were drawn to the woman again. Her hips had looked no different than Cleo's, but they certainly moved in a way Cleo had never experienced. Her whole being swayed most poetically as she glided into the card room. Cleo suspected a gentleman would find the movement even more compelling. She glanced at Leslie, but his mouth was set in a grim line. If the woman's grace was intriguing to him, he didn't show it.

Their hostess paused partway into the room. "This is our main salon," she said, voice low and husky. "To your right are the tables for hazard and vingt-un. To your left are the tables for silverloo and faro. The more interesting play is generally at the tables toward the back of the room, where there is more privacy. Should you prefer even more adventurous play, I'd be happy to escort you to one of our private rooms."

"That won't be necessary," Leslie assured her, his grip on Cleo's elbow once more tightening, as if he expected her to be torn from him.

"Good evening, Madame Zala," came a familiar voice, and Cleo straightened as Major Cutter in evening wear as black as Leslie's stepped up to the woman. He raised her hand and brought it to his lips in salute. Cleo tried not to stare. Their hostess merely smiled.

"My dear Major, how lovely to see you again. And how thoughtful of you to recommend us to your friends. I'll have a bottle of champagne sent round to your usual table."

Major Cutter inclined his head in thanks, and she glided off. Cleo pulled her eyes away from the woman's walk as Major Cutter stepped closer to her.

"Miss Renfield," he intoned, "a pleasure as always." He raised her hand, turning her fingers at the last moment to press his kiss deeply into her palm.

Cleo tried not to shiver as the touch made her stomach roll over.

The game had begun. It remained to be seen who would be the winner.

Seventeen

Leslie watched as the delicate skin of Cleo's shoulders turned pink with her blush. He wanted to rip the cloth off the nearby table and swathe her in it from head to toe. What had he been thinking to insist that she buy a scandalous gown? It left nothing to the imagination. Or rather, it inflamed his. He could picture just how easily it would slide to the floor if he could put his hands on those blasted ribbons.

By the appreciative gleam in Cutter's eye, he could imagine the same thing. Leslie tightened his grip on Cleo's arm and felt her wince. Realizing he was hurting her, he hastily let go. She stepped away from him, rubbing her elbow, and he felt suddenly chilled by the loss of her body next to his.

"I've never played faro before," she was saying in an utterly insipid fashion that set Leslie's teeth on edge. "Perhaps you could teach me, Major."

The good major was only too happy to agree, and she accepted his arm. But as they moved toward the table, Leslie found himself frozen in place. Cleo's hips swayed rhythmically side to side, taunting him. Him? They taunted every man in the room. She had obviously been observing the fair Madame Zala, but the movement on Cleo's curves was, in Leslie's opinion, far more potent. Swallowing, he hurried after her.

He had thought playing faro might take his mind off Cleo's unfolding seduction, but there was no escape at the table. After explaining the situation to the gentlemen present, and using Cleo's name in the process, Leslie heard with chagrin, Cutter requested their permission for her to share his hand. The knowing smiles of agreement only set Leslie's hackles higher. To make matters worse, the Duke of Reddington joined the set. Leslie had seen him enter as they had arrived, with none other than Lolly Dupray at his side. Now the perfidious Miss Dupray draped herself on his shoulder as tightly as her spring green gown draped her curves. She leaned over to run her hands along the cards in a proprietary fashion. Glancing up, she surreptitiously winked at Leslie. Leslie cringed inwardly.

The night got no better. Cutter let Cleo hold the cards, but one of his hands cradled hers. The other lolled along the back of her chair, grazing her bare shoulders. Cutter's head bent to her ear as he whispered suggestions for play, and Cleo dimpled at his words. Leslie grabbed the champagne flute offered him by a passing waiter and guzzled the contents.

Cleo won, of course. That made her throw back her head and laugh with delight, her curls dancing, the slender length of her throat exposed. Several of the gentlemen playing grinned. Reddington went so far as to raise a quizzing glass to stare at her in obvious appreciation. Lolly had to nip his ear with her teeth to get his attention back to her. Cutter's hand slid with proprietary confidence from Cleo's shoulders to her waist. Leslie refused another glass.

Cutter led her next to the vingt-un table and played a round with her at his side. She seemed delighted to watch him play, leaning over to murmur questions.

Her movement was entirely too much like Lolly's. Their continued closeness made the alcohol burn in Leslie's stomach even though he continued to refuse the wine offered him.

He lost track of time. He lost track of the games they played. The only game he cared about was the one Cutter was playing with Cleo. When the major brought Cleo's hand to his mouth and she stared up at him, lips moist, as if awaiting his kiss, Leslie felt the champagne curdle. His stomach roiled, rushing up into his throat. Good God, he was about to be sick! He stumbled for the door and stood beside the balustrade, sucking in the air. A moment more and he found Madame Zala at his side.

"You are unwell, my lord," she murmured, hand cool upon his brow. "Allow me to find you a room where you can lie down."

Leslie shook his head, and the landing tilted crazily under his feet. He couldn't cast up his accounts like some green youth fresh from the country. He refused to be drunk when he had to protect Cleo. And how could he be drunk anyway? Surely even he could handle a single glass of champagne.

"I'm fine," he gulped. "I just need a moment to myself."

She withdrew instantly, and he took a deep, fortifying breath. He could do this. He must, for Cleo's sake. Slowly he straightened. The floor obliged him by remaining in its customary place, and fairly steady too. With a nod of satisfaction, he strolled back into the card room.

Only to find that Cleo and Cutter had vanished.

On the terrace outside the first-floor landing, Cleo inhaled the warmth of the summer's evening.

"Better?" Major Cutter asked solicitously beside her.

She nodded. "Much. It was simply too close in there." She glanced hopefully around the little landing and out into the garden she could see below her. There was no sign of Leslie. She had been so sure that the major was correct, that Leslie had only stepped out for a bit of air, being overcome as she was by the heat of the room. But she could see nothing of his lean figure, and there was no other logical reason to linger on the balcony. In the moonlight she could see that the garden was small and overgrown, certainly not the place to take a romantic walk. Besides, even in the warmth of the evening, her bare shoulders were pimpling with gooseflesh.

"We don't have to return immediately," Major Cutter said, moving closer.

Cleo stiffened. "Oh, I'm sure we should. Leslie—that is Lord Hastings—may already be looking for us."

He raised a hand to toy with the curl near her ear. Cleo's pulse began to speed. "I'm sure he can find other amusements," he assured her. "As can we."

He pulled her into his embrace. His mouth descended on hers, warm, wet, and insistent. She squeezed her eyes shut and counted to ten, willing herself to relax. But his tongue forced its way between her lips and she gagged.

He raised his head but did not release her. "What's wrong?" he asked, and she was shocked to hear annoyance in his tone.

"I think you'd better unhand me," Cleo said. "I am not interested in your advances."

To her surprise, his grip only tightened. "Perhaps you don't understand, my dear," he replied. "Lord Hastings has lost interest in you. He practically begged me to take you off his hands. I assure you, I am more than ready to replace him in your affections. Allow me to demonstrate."

He smothered her in another kiss. Cleo wanted to cry out in vexation. Leslie was right—Cutter was a miscreant. As if to prove it, his hand slipped up to cup her breast. Cleo heaved herself back and struck him.

"You," she panted, scrambling out of reach, "are much mistaken. If you insist on taking my virtue, you will not find it easy."

Even in the moonlight she could see the reddening mark of her hand on his cheek. He did not finger it, although it had to sting. Instead, he smiled.

"Go ahead, scream."

Cleo stared at him, her whole body cold. "I could. Leslie would come for me, even if the others refused."

Cutter's smile grew. "I wouldn't count on that. I suspect Lord Hastings isn't feeling quite the thing right now. At least I paid good money to make sure he wouldn't be."

"What have you done to Leslie!" Cleo demanded.

"Nothing permanent," Cutter assured her. "At least it might not be permanent, if you cooperate. If he passes out without me there to protect him, I cannot promise that my compatriots will be kind. I suggest you do exactly as I say so that we can return to him quickly."

Though Cleo now had no doubts he could do something so wicked, she prayed for Leslie's sake that he was lying. "What do you want from me? I won't let you molest me."

"I do not need to. Though the idea has merit." Cleo forced herself not to shiver as he continued. "I merely wish to confirm some information I have about you. I've heard gossip about how you lost your innocence in school."

"That's a lie," Cleo snapped.

"I would be inclined to agree, but there is evidence to support it. It is well known that your sisters cannot stand to be near you. Is it because of the disgrace?"

"Do not judge me by my sisters' actions," she warned him. "They are entirely too busy to bother with me, nothing more."

"A pretty story," he allowed, "but that doesn't explain why only your godmother has been willing to squire you about."

Cleo tossed her head. "And do you truly believe Lady Agnes DeGuis would have a thing to do with me if I were ruined?"

"Her devotion to you is commendable," he agreed. "Unfortunately, it may be that she knows nothing of what happened. I understand your ruin was only known to a select few."

"You *think* you understand a great deal, sir," she informed him. "You understand nothing."

"On the contrary, I know all too well how easily a young girl's head can be turned. I've turned a few myself. But you needn't think I blame you. Jareth Darby's conquests are legendary."

"Jareth Darby?" Cleo knew she had paled. He thought she was the girl who had been compromised in the hayloft that day. She wanted to shout her innocence to the stars, but she could not tell him the truth without betraying Eloise. "I never dallied with Mr. Darby, or anyone else, for that matter," she assured him.

He shook his head. "I'm afraid I have the story from a rather reputable source. I did not believe it, at first, but your behavior of late has been rather convincing."

Her behavior. Her attempts to shock her sisters had confirmed the hideous lie in his warped little mind. "You could not possibly understand," she said, "but I had my reasons for behaving as I did."

"Perhaps," he allowed. "I suppose it does not matter. It would have been easier if you had a dark secret with which to blackmail the Carlisles. Your sister's husband craves entrance to society too much to lose it now. However, just having compromised you here should be sufficient. Particularly as I am so willing to marry you and make it all come out right."

"I will never marry you," Cleo swore.

"Yes, you will," Cutter replied, with confidence so supreme, she could cheerfully have struck him again. "Or I will drag you and your sisters' reputations though the mud. I imagine they will pay a pretty penny to keep me quiet. And I will see that they keep on paying."

He was hideous. She imagined he had planned the same for Eloise, until the rumor and her behavior had made her an easier target. She knew she was blameless. She had to convince Ellie and Annie to refuse him. But she needn't let him know that.

"Your plan is flawless," she said. "Now may we go see whether Lord Hastings is all right?"

He frowned at her, as if not believing she would comply so easily. She tensed, afraid he would attack her again. He took a step toward her, and she brought up her fists, ready to fight if she had to.

Behind him, the door to the house clicked open as loudly as a shot from a rifle. Madame Zala floated onto the balcony.

"Has she agreed?" she murmured, coming close enough to peer at Cleo in the moonlight.

"A minute more," Cutter snapped, and Cleo's fists tightened.

"You do not have a minute," Madame Zala told him. "Hastings is fighting the drug I put in the champagne. He insists on searching the house for Miss Renfield. I cannot hold him off much longer."

Cleo thanked God silently that Leslie was safe. "Let me go to him," she urged them both.

Cutter hesitated for a moment more, then nodded. "But never fear, Miss Renfield. I shall see you tomorrow morning to confirm my undying devotion. And unless you agree to my suit, I will confess a great deal more." He turned to Madame Zala. "Take her."

"Certainly," the woman murmured, reaching out to her. Her touch on Cleo's shoulder was gentle, but Cleo flinched back. Madame Zala's look tightened as she turned. Cleo followed her back into the house.

She hoped to see Leslie right away, but to her frustration, Madame Zala led her not to the card room but to a small sitting room at the front of the house. It was tastefully furnished; in fact, the furnishings were better coordinated and in better shape than the items with which Ellie had furnished the house she'd rented for Cleo and Lady Agnes. Wickedness, apparently, paid well.

"Wait here," Madame Zala advised her.

Cleo would have liked to tell the woman exactly what she thought of her, but that would hardly get her back to Leslie and safely out of the gaming hell. She sank onto a brocaded settee as her hostess slipped from the room. She wasn't sure if she could wait calmly, as this room seemed to demand, for however long it took the woman to locate Leslie, but it was only a few minutes before the door opened again to admit him.

Cleo rose to her feet. His hair was tousled, his

eyes wild, and his cravat was in a shambles. She ran to his outstretched arms and he clasped her to him.

"Are you all right?" he begged against her hair.

For the first time, Cleo felt tears coming. "Oh, Leslie, it was awful! You were right; he is a monster! He plans to ruin me and blackmail Ellie to keep the secret."

Leslie swore under his breath. His hand stroking her hair trembled. "I'll kill him," he raved. "I'll see his craven carcass hung from Tyburn Gallows."

"I would be delighted to assist you," Cleo promised, leaning back to gaze up into his face. Any fear she had felt vanished in his obvious concern. He was ashen, and dark circles rimmed his eyes. She put her head back down and hugged him tightly. "Leslie, it's all right. *I'm* all right. We will not let him win. Please, will you take me home?"

He stared down at her, and the anger seeped out of him, to be replaced by a sadness she could feel. "Oh, Cleo, I'm sorry. I failed you."

"Nonsense! Major Cutter should be the one to apologize. Only a villain would take advantage of gossip. He chose me for his victim because he heard gossip that I had already lost my innocence."

"What?" Leslie's voice turned angry once more. "Who'd have the gall to claim you as less than a lady?"

Cleo had a fairly good idea, but she didn't intend to compound the gossip with any of her own. "Never mind. Suffice it to say that my behavior of late only served to convince him that the gossip was correct. So, you were right, Les. I should be the one to apologize for not believing you."

Leslie's embrace tightened, but unlike Cutter's fierce hold, it didn't frighten her. Indeed, she relished his closeness. "It isn't your fault," he told her sternly.

"You did nothing wrong. Anyone with an ounce of intelligence would know you are a lady."

She hiccoughed a laugh. "Then we are doomed, Les, for Lady Agnes claims my sisters to be dense as doorjambs. We must pray that for once they listen to reason."

"We shall make them listen," Leslie swore. "You will not marry Cutter, Cleo. If you marry anyone, it will be me."

Cleo started. Slowly she lifted her head to meet his gaze, and when she did her heart started racing again. Leslie kept his eyes locked with hers for a few moments, as if allowing her time to refuse him if she wished. She could not move, even to shake her head no or nod yes. He bent and caressed her lips with a kiss.

And it was a caress. It was sweet and gentle and full of promise. Instead of fleeing or gasping against it, she wanted to sink into it, deepen it, prolong it. She leaned against him, and he granted her unspoken desire, pressing her even closer, moving his lips against hers. Small wonder Eloise cried to lose such closeness. Cleo clung to him again, but this time in joy. She'd never felt so alive! Leslie's touch awakened a seed deep inside her. She could feel it growing, budding, blossoming until her desire matched his own. She gave herself over to his touch eagerly, unashamedly, and when he groaned aloud, she laughed against his mouth with delight.

He broke the kiss then, pushing her back from him with a growl. "I'm a wretch. What kind of creature takes advantage of you at your weakest moment?"

"You didn't take advantage of me," she scolded, cuddling against him even as she marveled at the sensations singing through her. "I rather think it's the other way around. You've been drinking. I could taste the champagne."

He shuddered. "Forgive me, Cleo. I should never . . ."

She put up a hand to stop him. "Don't. Don't you dare apologize for the loveliest moment of my life. I've never felt happier! But I promise to wait to hear a formal declaration from you, when you are sober."

Eighteen

Leslie's first thought was to protest that he was quite sober indeed. The shock of losing Cleo in the gaming house should have driven any remaining alcohol from his blood. If he acted drunk now, it was because of the desire singing through his veins. Kissing Cleo had been unlike anything he could have imagined, and he knew he had a rather good imagination, as well as experiences to back it up. He would have liked nothing better than to keep on kissing her. Gazing down at her, he could see that she had never looked lovelier. Her skin was suffused with a rosy glow; her lips were swollen from his kisses. It would have taken little for him to pull her back into his arms, or to try to keep her there. He raked a hand back through his hair.

Cleo giggled, rising as well. "You're only making it worse. Let me." She stood on tiptoe, reaching up to smooth down his hair. With her body so close to his, her hand stroking him, he was nearly undone. He caught her hand between his.

"Cleo, perhaps you are right. Perhaps I am intoxicated. But I meant what I said."

"As did I," she explained. "The champagne was drugged. Believe me, your declaration will mean more when we have put all this behind us."

He could not argue with her in that regard. Together, they descended the stairs to where the footman waited with their cloaks. Leslie had half a mind to lay the fellow out for his knowing smile, but after Cleo's words, he could not be sure of his own abilities. Who could know how the drug might have affected him? He did feel a little unsteady as they settled into his carriage.

"I should never have agreed to this charade," he said as they started off.

Cleo shook her head. "I would have insisted. You only saved us considerable time by agreeing. And do not think I regret a moment of it. I learned a great deal."

"I cannot regret you learned the truth about Cutter," he acknowledged. "But I cannot help but blame myself for how you learned it."

"I wasn't talking about Major Cutter," she informed him with a grin. Leslie felt his face coloring. Why was it only Cleo and Lady Agnes could make him blush as an adult?

She reached across and patted his hand. "Poor Leslie. I've led you a merry dance, haven't I? Never fear. We will muddle through somehow. For now, let's just go home."

She settled back against the squabs. Leslie was just as glad for her silence. He wasn't sure what to say to her. He had had no right to kiss her the way he did, but, like her, he scarcely regretted it. She was sweet and fiery; her kisses melted in his mouth like a spoonful of honey. While he had been lusting after her for days, the depth of his reaction had surprised even him. Obviously his attachment to Cleo had grown beyond mere friendship or even manly ardor. He had not been surprised to hear himself propose.

He knew he would never survive seeing her wed to another.

They were nearly back at the town house when Cleo started. "Oh, no, Mrs. Winston's ball! Leslie, we promised!"

He shook his head. "You are in no condition to attend and neither am I."

"But Lady Agnes's reputation," Cleo protested. "She went out of her way to get you invited. If we do not appear, her word will be suspect. Besides, with what Major Cutter claims to have heard about my reputation, I don't want to hide away as if it were true!"

Leslie sighed. "You have a point. Very well. We'll make a brief appearance. Then you can plead a headache and we'll escape."

The plan agreed upon, Leslie instructed his coachman to make for Curzon Street, where Mrs. Winston had her residence. Luckily, the ball was a tremendous crush, and even though they were well over an hour late, they were able to slip onto the end of the line of people waiting to be received. Cleo had taken a moment to pin an intriguing piece of lace in place across her bosom and shoulders, which he had to own went a long way to taking the shocking delight out of the dress. Leslie had attempted to fix his cravat in the carriage, and if it still looked a bit flat, it was no worse than those worn by other gentlemen who were wilting from the heat of three hundred closely packed bodies and five hundred beeswax candles.

The dancing had already started by the time they reached the ballroom upstairs. He exchanged glances with Cleo, and by the droop of her mouth knew she had no interest in displaying herself so prominently. He managed to find a chair partially obscured by a potted palm, only tripping twice on his way across the room to reach it. Cleo's sigh of relief was audible as she sank onto the embroidered seat.

"I had no idea it would be so warm," she murmured, fanning herself with her hand. "It will be painfully easy to plead a headache. In the meantime, would it be too much to ask for you to fetch me a glass of lemonade?"

Considering what she'd been through that evening, it was the least he could do for her. He bowed, congratulating himself that he only wavered slightly as he straightened. "Your servant, my dear. Back in a moment."

He scanned the room again and located the refreshment table on the far side. He nearly groaned aloud at the number of bejeweled, beribboned people crowding the space between himself and it, but squared his shoulders with a manly hiccough and set off.

Ten minutes later he fetched up against the table with a gasp of relief. He had had to detour around doddering dowagers, dewy debutantes, and dilettante dandies. He'd only trod upon two sets of toes, three hems, and Lady Amathant's pet pug, who never left her side, even at balls. He snatched up a tepid lemonade with victorious glee and turned to run the gauntlet back to Cleo.

Only to find himself facing Eloise Watkin.

She did not smile. Indeed, her face was pale, her jade green eyes wide. "Lord Hastings," she said quickly, "thank goodness I saw you. I have been trying to think what to do all evening. I heard the most distressing gossip about Miss Renfield."

Had the news traveled so quickly? But no, surely no one at the gaming hell would have come to this ball before them. He'd seen no sign of Reddington about, and surely he was one of the few people from the hell Mrs. Winston would allow in her popular event. And Cutter would not have dared show his face before Leslie. If the fellow had any sense, he'd be making for the Continent. Leslie narrowed his eyes.

"I assure you, whatever you've heard is overblown," he informed her.

Her face reddened. "And I assure you, Lord Hastings, that it is not only wrong, but so egregious as to keep her from all polite society for the rest of her life."

Leslie stared at her. "My God, Miss Watkin. What have you heard?"

She dropped her gaze. "I will not repeat it in this crowd. But I do not think it can wait until tomorrow for me to call on Miss Renfield."

"You needn't wait," Leslie informed her, sluggish mind trying to grasp what he was hearing. "She sits behind that palm across the room. Though talking to her here will not solve your concern for the crowd."

"No, it won't. And we must fight this story, sir, and quickly, or all is lost." She lowered her voice, leaning closer. Her scent was heady with rose and lemon, stronger than the drink in his hand or the drug in his blood. "We must talk in private, without delay. There is a room just down the corridor, a library. If you slip out now, I shall fetch Miss Renfield and join you in a few moments. That should keep tongues from wagging."

Leslie nodded, and she straightened. He handed her the lemonade. "If you'll take this to Miss Renfield, Miss Watkin," he said aloud, for the benefit of any who might be listening, "I'd be greatly in your debt. I must get some fresh air."

He turned and sauntered toward the door, rather

pleased with himself that he only bumped the wall once in the process.

Cleo sat behind her potted palm, hands folded in her lap. The chair was far too hard for her to relax, but she could not have lounged even if it had been a feather bed. Her body still tingled from Leslie's touch; her mind still hummed with the wonder of it. She did not understand the reaction, but she could not doubt its potency. She had thoroughly enjoyed his kiss. Once she thwarted Major Cutter, she would be only too happy to do something about Leslie.

She could not wait until he returned and she could appear before her hostess and plead a headache. No one would doubt her. The noise in the room was strident, the heat oppressive. She wanted only the silence of her room in which to ponder the events of the evening. She looked up expectantly as someone ducked behind the palm.

Then clambered to her feet when she saw it was Eloise.

The girl held out a lemonade. "I am sorry to keep appearing before you like this, Cleo. Lord Hastings asked me to bring this so that we might talk."

Cleo crossed her arms over her chest. "I wouldn't take food or drink from you, for it would very likely be as poisoned as your speech."

Eloise blanched. "What are you talking about? I thought we cried truce."

"So did I until I heard how you had betrayed me."

"I betrayed you? What have I done to betray you?"

"Only spread malicious gossip about me." Cleo shook her head. "Did you think I would forget your threat?"

"I should have known you'd blame me for that

awful gossip," Eloise cried. "You've heard it then, haven't you?"

"I know you told Major Cutter that I was the one in the hayloft with Jareth Darby."

The glass fell from Eloise's fingers, crashing to the polished wood to splinter into a thousand pieces. "Don't say that here!" she cried, heedless of the yellow liquid that seeped onto the floor.

"Why not? I'm tired of lies. What good have they done? They have only served to land me in the soup. And I do not see that your life has been easier for them."

"You expect me to tell everyone about . . . that?" Her tone was incredulous.

"Perhaps you should. Look at yourself, Eloise! You can trust no one. You spend your days in fear that the truth will out. Is that why you told Major Cutter a version of it?"

"No," Eloise insisted, shaking her head. "You are wrong."

"Or was it jealousy?" Cleo persisted. "When you saw he was taking an interest in me, you were willing to tell him anything to drive him away. Well, you lost, Eloise. Major Cutter is as big a liar as you are."

Eloise shook her head again, her eyes tearing. "You are wrong. It is you who lies. Major Cutter cared for me, just as Jareth Darby cared. You drove both of them away. I tried to help you. I sent Lord Hastings to the library so that I could help."

"You leave Leslie alone!" Hands balled at her side, Cleo took a step toward her. Eloise held her ground.

"Oh, Leslie, is it?" she cried. "Is it not enough that you've stolen Major Cutter's regard? You cannot stand to see me happy, and I've never understood why. Well, you may keep Major Cutter, but I will not allow you to poison Lord Hastings against me as well. He has treated me with respect. He might even come to care for me."

"You don't stand a chance," Cleo informed her icily. "We are already engaged."

Eloise glared at her through her tears. "Why should I believe you? And even if it is true, how do I know he was not trapped into an engagement with you after your shocking behavior at Almack's? Your Leslie is no different from any other man. I could have him eating out of my hand anytime I choose. If you want proof, be in the library in ten minutes' time." Dashing away her tears, she flounced back into the thick of the ballroom and was immediately swallowed by the crowd.

Cleo sank onto the chair. Eloise's reasoning was as convoluted as ever. But she had to be lying about the gossip. No one knew of the liaison in the hayloft except herself, Eloise, and Miss Martingale. Even Marlys, to whom she'd poured out her concerns, only knew that something bad had happened. Eloise was clearly the gossip and just as clearly was intent on denying it. And now she thought to trap Leslie in the process.

Cleo snorted. Leslie would see through her in a minute. He was far too intelligent to play Eloise's game. But then, she had thought herself intelligent and she had fallen into Major Cutter's trap. All Eloise had to do was to be found alone in the same room with Leslie and he could be accused of seduction. He was a particularly easy target after his censure by Lady Jersey. Once again her behavior was threatening someone with ruin!

With a groan, she pushed herself out of the chair. It looked as if Leslie needed rescuing, and she was the only one who could do it. If she could just find

Mrs. Winston in this crowd, she could learn where the library was and bring an ally along too.

Leslie found the library empty, though someone had thoughtfully lit the wall sconces so that the gilt lettering on the many books gleamed in the golden glow. He wandered around, perusing the titles on the shelves, noting that Mrs. Winston had more knick-knacks than novels. He couldn't remember the last time he'd seen so many pug-faced dogs and blue enameled vases. He grimaced at a particularly ugly chow with a green lacquered cap. He was contemplating the state of mind of a person who would buy all seventeen volumes of *The Fall of the Roman Empire* and stack them under an equally interesting volume called *On the Prevention of Conception in the Modern Female*, when Eloise slid through the door to join him.

He turned expectantly, then frowned when he saw she was alone. Her color was high as she hurried to his side. "Oh, Lord Hastings," she said breathlessly, "she wouldn't come with me. She thinks I spread that distressing gossip."

Leslie eyed her. Had Cleo and the girl developed a rivalry? Eloise was certainly pretty enough, even behind her painted finery, to warrant some good old-fashioned envy, though not, he thought, from Cleo. "And did you, Miss Watkin?" he asked, raising a brow.

Her high color waned, as if he had sapped her blood. "Of course not. You must believe me, Lord Hastings." He watched as she swallowed.

Something wasn't right, but he still was not clear-headed enough to determine what. "I would like to believe you, my dear. Perhaps if you told me what this gossip was all about."

If anything, she turned even more pale. "Perhaps I can explain myself. Give me a moment to catch my breath. I nearly ran all the way here."

He thought perhaps she would sit upon one of the armchairs that were scattered about the room or the sofa by the grate, but instead she paced, swinging her arms as if she were trying to keep herself alert. Her hips, swinging in an even more interesting manner, were not as alluring as Cleo's, although he did enjoy the view. He waited while she strolled about, but when time stretched and still she had said nothing, he cocked his head.

"You *are* the culprit, aren't you?" he asked.

She halted, rounding on him. "I am not! If you understood the magnitude of this rumor, you would know that *I* of all people would say nothing about it. To my mind, it is a subject best left unspoken."

"So why is someone speaking it about Cleo?" he pressed.

She shook her head. "I cannot understand how it got so turned around. Cleo should be the heroine of the piece, not the victim." When Leslie continued to eye her, she sighed, shoulders sagging. "I suppose there is nothing for it. But Lord Hastings, you must promise me never to reveal what I tell you to a soul."

Leslie bowed. "You have my word, madam."

That seemed to satisfy her, for she seated herself at last, motioning him to do likewise.

"We must hurry," she said, "for I do not know how long we have before we are interrupted."

He wondered who she thought would be dying to visit the library, but he supposed the ballroom was so crowded it was possible that any number of Mrs.

Winston's guests might be seeking a cooler refuge. As he sat on the chair opposite her, she began.

"I think you know that Cleo and I attended the same school."

Leslie nodded. "In Somerset, I believe."

"Yes. It is an endowed school, kept on a corner of the Darby estate. The Earl of Wenworth provides the upkeep. At the time we were there, one of his sons, Jareth Darby, was in residence, having been sent down from London for the summer."

Leslie knew of Jareth Darby, although the charming rake had been on the Continent for the last few years, fleeing a militant husband, it was rumored.

"I think I begin to see," he said. "Darby trifled with one of the girls, was that it?"

She nodded, color fading once again. "He was quite handsome and he could be quite convincing. Or so I have been told. He claimed to have fallen in love with one of our classmates and she allowed him . . . certain liberties with her person, but before he could take her up on the offer, she became frightened. He was attempting to console her when Cleo found them in the hayloft. You know how she likes horses."

"She did," Leslie agreed. "She seems to have lost her taste for the stables."

"I would imagine they remind her too much of that day. She must have thought our classmate under attack, for she came after Mr. Darby with a pitchfork. He fled, leaving the girl to shoulder the blame. She tried to convince Cleo not to tell our headmistress, Miss Martingale, but Cleo was determined that justice be done." She shook her head. "She was far more innocent than the rest of us. We knew who Miss Martingale would favor. The whole event was quickly hushed up lest any damage be done to the school or its benefactors. Miss Martingale never even let the girl tell her father. Any letters sent were destroyed."

"That's ghoulish," Leslie declared, rising. "The poor girl sounds as if she did what she did out of innocence. She deserved someone to care for her."

Eloise rose as well, and Leslie was surprised to see tears pooling in her eyes. "Yes," she said softly. "She does."

Leslie stared at her. His brain informed him that something momentous had just happened, but the thoughts slipped away before he could grasp them. His attempts must have shown on his face, for she gasped suddenly. To his alarm, her eyelids fluttered, then closed, and her body crumpled. He caught her easily and swung her limp body up into his arms. Staggering slightly, for she was not nearly as light as Cleo, he managed to deposit her on the sofa. He went down on one knee beside her and took her hand, rubbing her wrist.

"Miss Watkin? Can you hear me?"

She moaned, the other hand fluttering to her brow. Leslie rubbed harder.

"That's it, my dear. Wake up."

Her eyes slid open, and a smile slowly spread. "Why, Lord Hastings, you saved me." She slid her arm up around his neck, her lashes drifting lower. "You should be rewarded," she murmured, pursing her lips.

"On the contrary," Mrs. Winston said from the doorway. "He should be shot, the libertine."

Leslie groaned, climbing to his feet. "Mrs. Winston, this is not what it seems, I assure you," he started. Then he caught his breath. Standing at her side was Cleo. Her face was ashen, her eyes huge. He felt as if he'd been stabbed through the heart.

Eloise sat up, adjusting her décolletage as if it had

been disturbed by his hand. "Oh dear, it appears we have been caught, Lord Hastings," she said sorrowfully, offering him her hand to help her rise. When he ignored it, she got up herself. "Do not be concerned. I promise I do not expect you to offer for me."

Leslie swallowed. Cleo bit her lip.

"I think your father may have something to say in the matter, Miss Watkin," Mrs. Winston replied with a sniff. "I expect you to call on him in the morning, Lord Hastings, after such a shocking display. And I shall have a few words with Lady Agnes as well. Godson or not, you will have earned her wrath, I have no doubt. She will likely cut all ties with you after this sorry episode. Come, Miss Watkin, Miss Renfield."

"Cleo," Leslie started, moving toward her. She did not move, but Mrs. Winston put an arm protectively around her shoulders.

"Come no closer, sirrah. I would be remiss in my duties if I allowed Miss Renfield to associate any further with you this evening."

Leslie drew himself up to his full height and affixed her with a glare that would have made Chas Prestwick proud. "Miss Renfield, madam, is my fiancée. As such, I have an obligation to see her home."

"Don't worry, Mrs. Winston," Cleo put in as their hostess squared her shoulders as if to do battle. "I know I can trust myself to Lord Hastings's care."

Leslie sagged with relief, but Mrs. Winston's grip only tightened, even though her tone to Cleo was kind. "I appreciate your loyalty, dear girl, but I am afraid that is out of the question. I have no doubt your family will insist you call off this engagement.

I shall have my carriage brought around to take you home."

Leslie wanted to fight, but he knew Cleo must be nearly done in. He could not put her through more.

"It's all right, Cleo," he said. "I know Mrs. Winston has your best interests at heart. I'll see you tomorrow."

Eloise sucked in a breath. "What about me, my lord?"

Cleo was watching him. Mrs. Winston was glaring at him. Eloise sniffed back a tear. Leslie offered her a short bow.

"It would appear, Miss Watkin," he said, "that I will be speaking to your father in the morning."

Nineteen

Cleo thought she had been through entirely enough for one night. Mrs. Winston had insisted on sending her home immediately, and given Leslie's capitulation, she could not argue. She refused to think about what would happen should he be unable to appease Eloise's father. It was daunting enough to think that she would have to explain the situation to her godmother.

Of course, she had not counted on Ellie and Annie being present.

Mr. Cowls warned her the moment she stepped into the town house. "A shame you could not have stayed later at the ball, Miss Cleo," he murmured as he removed her cloak with palsied hands. "Your sisters have been closeted in the drawing room with her ladyship this past hour, and none too happily by the sound of it."

Cleo would have liked nothing better than to retire to her room, but she could not let her godmother be so abused. Thanking Cowls, she hurried up the stairs.

Her sisters were indeed agitated. Ellie was pacing, the crack of her brocaded skirts audible as she turned. Annie was perched on a chair, hands worrying before her chocolate-colored evening dress. Lady Agnes sat on the sofa with arms folded and lips compressed.

Even Hector looked tense—his feathers were ruffled and he shuffled back and forth on his perch, head jerking one way, then another.

"What's happened?" Cleo demanded from the doorway.

Ellie came to an abrupt halt. "Why didn't you tell us about Jareth Darby?"

"We are your sisters," Annie added with a sniff. "We deserved to hear it first."

Cleo took a deep breath. "You heard the gossip. It isn't true."

"I told you!" Lady Agnes all but crowed. She jumped to her feet and glared at Ellie over Annie's head. "I knew my Cleo wouldn't have been so foolish."

As Ellie returned Lady Agnes's glare and Annie stared in obvious confusion, Cleo grimaced. "Oh, your Cleo can be quite foolish," she assured her godmother. "But we shall discuss that in a moment. For now, let me promise you that the story is nothing but a spider's web, and as easily destroyed."

Annie slumped in relief. Ellie did not resume her pacing, but her face was still tight. "Your word," she told Cleo, "will mean little when compared to your behavior of late."

"So I have heard," Cleo replied with a sigh. "And there is more, but perhaps you should sit to hear it."

Ellie did not move.

"Cutter," Lady Agnes guessed. "What happened? Is he a villain or your fiancé?"

"He intends to be both," Cleo said as Ellie stiffened. "He forced a kiss from me at a gaming hell."

Annie gasped, falling back against her seat as if in a faint. Ellie blanched. Lady Agnes had fire in her eye.

"He seems to have the idea," Cleo continued doggedly, "that by threatening to ruin me, he can get money from Ellie's husband."

"Mr. Carlisle would never . . ." Ellie started heatedly, then she slumped. Annie rose to go to her side.

"Position is very important to Mr. Carlisle," she explained, patting Ellie's shoulder. "He thought he might be elevated by marrying Ellie, given our famous connection with the DeGuises."

"Ha!" Lady Agnes barked. "I wager he felt cheated when he learned the only Renfield I favor is Cleo."

Ellie raised her head, eyes proud. "I did not need your support to win a rich husband, madam. I do not need it to keep him."

"Of course not," Annie agreed soothingly. "Besides, there is always Lord Stephenson."

"Your husband," Lady Agnes replied, "is a rackety rakehell. Mr. Carlisle may be a wizard at business, but he obviously knows nothing about people."

Neither Ellie nor Annie answered her, but Cleo thought she understood. "So, Mr. Carlisle helped Annie to marry Lord Stephenson in hopes of gaining entrance to society. But when Lord Stephenson proved a scapegrace, he set his sights on me and my marriage."

"After how he supported you," Ellie snapped, "it is the least you could do."

"But how could Major Cutter know?" Annie asked with a frown.

"He applied to Mr. Carlisle for a loan," Lady Agnes supplied. When they all looked at her, she shrugged. "I had the fellow investigated the moment he showed an interest in Cleo, something either of you should have thought to do if you'd had your eyes on anything but a title."

"I sincerely doubt Mr. Carlisle would confide in him," Ellie said with a sniff.

"I am certain he didn't. But Cutter no doubt learned enough to make him curious. He's a clever villain, I'll give him that. Very good at taking little bits of information and building a full picture. I imagine that's how he got promoted so many times. Pity his last commander did not live long enough to tell the tale."

Ellie sighed. "Whatever the case, we are too late. Mr. Carlisle will not allow his name to be connected with scandal. Cleo will have to marry the scoundrel to save us all."

"No," Cleo said. "Cleo will not."

Annie's hand fell away from her sister's shoulder as Ellie drew herself up again. "Do not be ridiculous. Your irredeemable behavior caused this problem. You are the only one who can solve it."

"No," Cleo repeated, striding forward to confront her sister even though she had to look up to do so. "Your determination to please Mr. Carlisle caused this problem, Electra. Between your prodding and my concern over this story about Jareth Darby, I have lied and postured and generally made a mess of things. No more. Your control of me stops here."

"The law thinks otherwise," Ellie replied, her eyes flashing. "Mr. Carlisle is your guardian. You must do what he says, and I have no doubt he will tell you to marry Cutter."

"I won't do it. He cannot bodily carry me to the church. He cannot force my hand to the marriage lines. I will not lie or pretend because of you again, Ellie. It is finished."

"But what shall we do?" Annie asked plaintively. "There will be a scandal."

"Very likely," Lady Agnes agreed. "But Cleo is

right. Better to weather the scandal once than to put yourselves in the control of a monster."

"You do not know how Mr. Carlisle thinks," Ellie protested. "You cannot know how important this is to him."

Cleo laid a hand on her sister's shoulder. "Tell him the truth for once, Ellie. It is amazing how free you will feel."

Ellie shook her head, but Cleo thought she saw tears in those angry eyes. She turned and crossed purposely to the parrot's cage. Hector regarded her with obvious suspicion.

"No more lies, Ellie," Cleo promised. "We will weather this as a family should—together." She sprang the latch on the cage and flung open the door. Darting past her, Hector leaped into the air. His emerald wings spread and he climbed to the ceiling. He flew as free as her conscience, circling the room twice before coming to a rest at Lady Agnes's feet.

"Clever Hector!" he crowed. "Clever Cleo! Clever, clever girl!"

Leslie was nearly as exhausted as Cleo when he fell into bed fully dressed. Unfortunately, as he lay sprawled on top of the covers, he found it impossible to go to sleep. The last of the drug was seeping out of his system, leaving him tense and not a little frustrated by the course of the evening's events.

He still wanted to get his hands on Cutter. One good punch to the chin should put the fellow under, though he rather fancied breaking his nose and bloodying his lip first. Then perhaps he'd request several of his father's men to stuff the villain in a sack and drop him in the deepest part of the Channel. Of course, that might ruin the fishing for some time.

Much as he'd like to vent his anger, the important thing was to keep Cleo safe. He had rather hoped marriage to him would achieve that. It shouldn't be a hardship; they were good friends, and after tonight he could not doubt that they would be compatible in other ways as well. She had enjoyed his kiss as much as he had. She had admitted it, but even if she had not told him, he could have guessed it from the way she'd kissed him in return. Just the memory of it was enough to set him burning on the covers. It would seem that Cleo wanted him as much as he wanted her. But thanks to the evening's events, he could do nothing about it.

He shuddered. He had been outmanipulated. He, Leslie Petersborough, who had managed any number of manipulators through the course of his life. He should have seen it coming. He could only blame the drug and his concern for Cleo for not guessing Eloise's intent. While he was certain that she had spoken some version of the truth in her tale of woe, there had been no reason for her to faint or offer him her lips for a kiss. It was as if she knew she would shortly have an audience. He'd been put in a position of having to offer for her. But no one could force him to marry her.

The best thing he could do would be to take a page out of Jareth Darby's book and flee for the Continent. With hostilities over between Britain and France for the moment, he ought to have a high time in Paris. Let Eloise catch some other titled fellow in her net of lies. He didn't need to subject himself to the disagreeable task of speaking to her father. He'd leave tonight, before anyone was wiser. Cleo was always prime for a lark. It wouldn't take her long to pack.

He jerked upright, staring into the darkening room.

How had Cleo gotten into the picture? He could scarcely run off to Paris with her. Lady Agnes would disown him, if godmothers were allowed to do so. Her sisters would send mercenaries after his hide. Besides, Cleo deserved a great deal more than to spend the rest of her life running from an enemy.

So what should he do about her? He ran a hand back through his hair. He couldn't leave her alone to bear the social repercussions of tonight's act. Besides, she still had the gossip to contend with. Someone was intent on making it appear that she had lost her virginity. Any man who believed the rumors would think he was getting damaged goods. She'd never make a decent marriage. Worse, there'd be those who would be only too happy to offer her an opportunity to profit from her loss. She could easily end up like Madame Zala, running some gaming establishment or working in a house of prostitution. He'd like to hope her sisters would save her before that happened, but they hadn't particularly shown themselves as fonts of compassion. And even Lady Agnes would be hard-pressed to remain on the social scene if the Ton thought she had accepted a soiled dove in her household.

The best thing for all was to prove the rumors false, but to do that, he'd have to expose the girl who had been Jareth Darby's accomplice. The girl hardly deserved the shame that would follow. Better would be to expose and discredit the one spreading the gossip. But he was not convinced that it was Eloise Watkin. Yet who else knew of the event or stood to profit if the story were told?

He groaned as the logic chased itself around his head. He should marry Cleo and protect her with his name. But he couldn't marry Cleo when he had compromised Eloise Watkin. If he stayed in England,

Eloise Watkin's father would surely call him out. And if he left, he couldn't take Cleo with him unless she was his wife. But if he took the time to marry her, he'd be caught.

He groaned again. Why did he have to make decisions like these? All he had ever wanted was to have fun. No matter which way he turned, he was faced with responsibilities he had never wanted, duties he would never like. Why not simply run away and let someone else handle the consequences?

Because he was the Marquis of Hastings.

Leslie smiled. He was the Marquis of Hastings, descended from a long line of Petersboroughs bred for the task. Without realizing it, he'd been slipping into the mantle. The last few weeks with Cleo, he'd made any number of decisions, planned any number of activities. Certainly not all of them had gone as he'd hoped, but surely no one was foolproof. Look how many schemes Chas had had to enact to win Anne Fairchild's hand. He'd done far better than that. Of course, he had Cleo.

Cleo inspired him. She had a way of looking at him that made him feel the cleverest of mortals. With her beside him, he had indeed regained the joie de vive that he'd lost when his father had died. With her beside him, he could accomplish anything.

He shook his head. Why hadn't he seen it before? Cleo brought out the best in him. She made him think, challenged him to live according to his principles. Dash it all, he hadn't really believed he had principles until Cleo had awoken them. Small wonder he'd fallen in love with her.

And he was certainly in love, he could see that. More, he could feel it. Cleo was curled around his heart, protecting it, cherishing it, nourishing it. He'd be a fool to let her go. He'd be a greater fool to lose her over this misunderstanding with Eloise.

It was time he took matters into his own hands, long past time he showed himself as the new Marquis of Hastings. He settled back against the pillows with a satisfied smile.

Tomorrow would be an interesting day.

Twenty

Leslie stood stiffly in the silent entry of the Watkin town house while the imposing butler made his ponderous way up the polished oak stair with Leslie's card on a silver tray. The liveried footmen with their white-powered wigs stood equally stiffly on either side of the door, eyes resolutely ahead, mouths in a grim line of authority. Even the woman in the portrait over the stairs stood stiffly, aristocratic nose in the air. It was all so very formal, and so unlike Eloise, that Leslie began to wonder whether he'd blundered into the wrong house.

The ormolu clock on the side table had ticked off twelve long minutes before the butler returned to his side. "Lord Watkin will see you now, my lord," he intoned. "If you will follow me."

He turned and made his stately way back up the stairs. Swallowing, Leslie followed.

He was ushered into a paneled study, the sound of his footsteps lost in the thick Turkish carpet. A small, spare gentleman turned from the single window to regard him with blue eyes sunk in a pale face. He stretched out a hand.

"Lord Hastings, welcome."

Leslie accepted his hand gingerly, quickly releasing it. "Thank you, Lord Watkin, but you may want to withdraw the welcome when you hear what I have to say. I trust your daughter has apprised you of last night's events?"

He frowned, reaching into the pocket of his plain brown vest to pull out a simple watch and snapped it open. "We have approximately eighteen minutes before my daughter's chaperone brings me her daily report. Shall we wait or would you like to elaborate?"

Leslie would have preferred to leave right then. This man could not be the father of Eloise Watkin, though Leslie was certain this was the address Mrs. Winston had given him the night before. Of course, she had been rather gleeful about it, so perhaps the old bird was having him on. No, she had been all too glad at the idea of him being leg-shackled. He shook his head. "I would prefer to speak to you immediately," he told the baron. "You'll pardon my assumption. I naturally thought you'd be expecting me." He couldn't help barking out a laugh. "Actually, I thought you'd be after me with a horsewhip if I didn't show up."

"I see," the man replied, frown deepening. "I take it, sir, that you have compromised my daughter."

Leslie stood straighter. "Through no intention of my own, I assure you."

"And I suppose you're here to offer for her like a gentleman," he mused, though Leslie thought he saw a glint of emotion behind the cold blue eyes.

"Actually, no," Leslie replied. "I'm here to tell you that your daughter is quickly convincing the Ton that she is a conniving tart and I refuse to have her."

Baron Watkin stared at him. Leslie waited for him to call him out, call him a liar, or at least call him names. Instead, he turned and strode for the door, yanking it open. "Bryerton," he yelled into the corridor. "Fetch me my daughter." Then he slammed the door shut and strode back to his place by the window. He motioned gracefully to a chair.

"Will you have a seat, Lord Hastings?" he asked, as if inviting him to tea. "This might take a few minutes, as I am uncertain what activities my daughter's chaperone has her engaged in at this hour."

Leslie wanted to sink into the chair nearest him, but something about his host's mercurial demeanor advised him it would be best to stay on his feet and keep his wits about him. Unfortunately, he wasn't sure how to handle this latest development. He hardly wanted to discuss the matter before Eloise, but he couldn't very well forbid her father to allow her in the room.

He did not have long to worry, however, for there was a polite tap on the door. At Lord Watkin's bark to enter, a large, heavyset woman in black bombazine scuttled in. Leslie recognized her from the night he'd first been reintroduced to Cleo at Almack's.

"You wanted to see me about Miss Eloise, my lord?" she asked, with a curtsy so hurried, it set both her chins to quivering.

Lord Watkin frowned. "No, Miss Tidwell. I distinctly asked to see my daughter."

She paled, starting to tremble, and Leslie was suddenly reminded of a dish of blanc mange. "But you have impressed upon me the importance of your time," she all but pleaded. "We are never to disturb you except by appointment. Eloise knows she is not allowed to trouble you."

Something in her tone arrested Leslie. A memory tugged. Last night, Eloise had said the girl who had been wronged had not been allowed to contact her father. Could Eloise herself be that girl? If so, she was in just as serious a position as Cleo.

"Correct," Lord Watkin was saying. "Your atten-

tion to detail is laudable. However, this gentleman"—
he waved a hand at Leslie—"tells me that my daughter is a conniving tart, and I think she should be given the opportunity to defend herself."

"Actually," Leslie put in as Eloise's chaperone puffed herself up like a hot-air balloon, "I said that the Ton thinks your daughter is a conniving tart. I personally think she's quite delightful."

Lord Watkin inclined his head at the correction. Miss Tidwell glared at him. Her eyes were dark and entirely too close together. Leslie felt as if she'd leveled a pair of dueling pistols at him.

"How dare you, sir!" she blustered. "I will not have my Eloise maligned in this way."

"Pity," Leslie replied, flicking a nonexistent piece of lint off his navy jacket. "You should have thought of that before you let her out of your sight at all those events."

She sputtered, but Lord Watkin cut her off with an imperious wave.

"How many times have you seen my daughter without a chaperone, Lord Hastings?" he asked.

At the sound of his name, she paled, and he wondered why. Had Eloise mentioned last night to her? Had she been about to brief his lordship? Yet surely something as significant as a threat to Eloise's reputation warranted more than a dutiful morning report. Leslie forced his thoughts back to the question Lord Watkin had asked.

"Three times before last night," he replied after a moment's thought. "And one of those times, I'm ashamed to say, she called on me at home. I, of course, immediately sent her off, for her own protection."

"Lies!" Miss Tidwell cried, her face turning even

whiter. "Who do you think you are to impugn a faithful retainer who has given years of good service?"

"That will be all, Tidwell," Lord Watkin said quietly. "Send me my daughter. I shall have more to say to you later."

She looked ready to fight, but another glance at his lordship's set face must have convinced her of the futility. She gave a curt nod and hurried back to the door. When it closed behind her, Lord Watkin sighed.

"Raising a daughter is not easy," he said, but more to himself than to him, Leslie thought. "I never did appreciate social nuances the way her mother did, and certainly not the way your father did."

Leslie's head came up. "You knew my father?"

"I was one of his men." The words were said with a melancholy pride, as for a fond event from days gone by. Leslie had heard the tone all too often in connection with his father since his death. "Traveling abroad so frequently, I felt it best that Eloise be sent to boarding school. I suspect I became accustomed to other people looking out for her."

There was a hesitant scratch at the door, as if a hand had touched it and been hastily withdrawn.

"Come in," Lord Watkin called gently.

Eloise entered, and Leslie found himself staring. Gone were the blackened lashes, the rouged cheeks, the clinging gowns. Her face was fresh and clean, her white muslin gown plain and simply cut. She was far lovelier than he had ever seen her, eagerness in every line as she curtsied.

"You wanted to see me, Father?" she breathed.

"Do you know this gentleman, Eloise?" her father asked, nodding toward Leslie.

She must not have realized he was in the room,

for she started, then paled. "Lord Hastings," she murmured, dropping her gaze.

"Miss Watkin," he replied with a bow. "I was surprised you had not told your father about our problem last evening."

She kept her eyes on the floor. "I am seldom given the opportunity to speak to my father." The words were not blaming, merely a statement of fact. Still Lord Watkin winced visibly.

"An oversight on my part, I assure you," he put in, causing her to gaze up at him in wonder. "Would you care to explain what happened?"

She bit her lip, glancing between him and Leslie. "It was nothing, Father. I told Lord Hastings he did not have to call today."

She looked so contrite that Leslie could not doubt her sincerity. He would have liked to put her whole manner down to artifice, but something told him that his theory was correct. And just as surely, he knew she was not the gossip trying to harm Cleo's reputation.

"If you will allow me, my lord," he said smoothly. "I believe there has been a mistake. Gossip led me to think that your daughter had manipulated me into a compromising situation last night. However, I begin to see that we were both victims." He bowed again, more deeply this time. "I must beg your forgiveness, Miss Watkin. I see now that you have tried to befriend me all along."

Her lower lip trembled, but she held her head high. "Thank you, Lord Hastings. I understand all too well how easy it is to be swayed by gossip."

"I knew you would understand," Leslie told her carefully. "So I must ask you to help me stop the gossip that is being spread. Who told you the story you told me last night?"

She paled, swallowing, but kept her eyes forward. "I . . . I'm sure I heard it from a girl at school."

Her father leaned forward, eyes narrowing, and Leslie feared he had given her away. He tried another tact. "Yes, I believe you mentioned that last night. Stupid of me to forget. But you had heard it again recently, in connection with Miss Renfield's name."

She nodded, relaxing a little. "Yes. Major Cutter told me."

Cutter? His flare of anger must have shown on his face, for she flinched away. Cutter could very well have spread lies, but it would profit him far more if he knew the story to be true. Someone else had told him, someone he could believe. But who?

"Does that answer your questions, Lord Hastings?" her father put in.

Leslie nodded. "Yes, thank you, my lord. And thank you, Miss Watkin. You have been very helpful."

"Thank you, Lord Hastings," she murmured. "And please give my regards to Miss Renfield. Tell her I am sorry for the way I behaved last night. She knows me far better than most. I think she will understand."

As Leslie nodded, her father spoke up. "It sounds as if we have a great deal of catching up to do. Will you excuse us, Lord Hastings? That is, if you have nothing more to discuss with me?"

Leslie bowed. "Nothing I can say can be more important than your charming daughter, sir. Miss Watkin, I bid you good day."

She smiled at him then, and he returned the smile, leaving the room far more free than when he had arrived.

Cleo had thought she would feel free in the morning. After seeing her sisters out the door and explain-

ing to Lady Agnes the situation between Leslie and
Eloise Watkin, she had retired and dropped immediately into an exhausted sleep. While she had awoken
surprisingly refreshed, she could not seem to occupy
her mind. She tried reading, writing to her friends
still at school, and working on embroidering a pillowcase for her trousseau. None of them took her
mind off Leslie, particularly the last. She was ready
to give it up and go for a ride when Mr. Cowls
knocked at her door.

"Miss Rutherford is here to see you, Miss Cleo,"
he murmured. "She is waiting in the drawing room."

Cleo put aside the pillowcase and hurried down
the corridor. She found Marlys gazing out the windows, face tight, arms wrapped around her yellow-
sprigged muslin dress as if the summer day somehow
chilled her.

"You've heard the news then," Cleo guessed, moving to join her.

Marlys watched her approach. "That you are to
marry Lord Hastings? Yes. The announcement was in
the paper this morning."

Cleo pulled up short. "Oh, that."

"Yes, that," Marlys said with a laugh. "Is there
something else of greater import that has happened
to you?"

"Countless," Cleo replied, but she moved to sit on
the sofa and patted the space beside her. "The last
few days have seemed endless, Marlys. Please sit
down and talk to me."

"I cannot," the girl replied, remaining by the window. From downstairs, Cleo heard the faint sound of
a knocker. "I promised Mother I would only wish
you happy. She does not approve of Lord Hastings,
or you, I am sad to say."

Cleo made a face. "Fie on her! Surely you have better sense, Marlys."

She shrugged, moving from the window at last. "Surely you will let Major Cutter go now with your engagement announced."

"I assure you, I have no desire to speak to him ever again," Cleo told her vehemently.

Marlys obviously did not take her meaning, for she smiled. "I am very glad to hear that. There are plenty of other girls itching for a chance at him, you know."

"Then they lack the sense they were born with," Cleo informed her. "Major Cutter is no prize."

Marlys's smile faded. "Why do you say that?"

Before Cleo could answer, Mr. Cowls poked his head into the room. "Major Cutter is here to see you, miss," he wheezed with a frown. "He's in the sitting room with her ladyship."

Cleo rose slowly from the sofa. She had forgotten that Cutter intended to show up this morning to offer for her. "Wait for me, Marlys," she said as she moved into the corridor. "I have a great deal to tell you, and your mother would want you to hear it."

Marlys paled, but Cleo did not stop. She went resolutely down the stairs, head high. She forced herself to remember that any moment Leslie would come for her. Her heart should be full of hope. She wanted only to see Leslie, to hold Leslie, to be held by Leslie. Just inside the sitting room door, however, she could only stop. Major Cutter rose from his seat beside Lady Agnes.

"I will not marry you," Cleo blurted out.

Cutter snapped her a bow, but he could not hide his gloating look. "Your servant, Miss Renfield."

"He says he's come to offer for you," Lady Agnes put in with a great deal more glee than Cleo felt was called for. "Tell him your feelings on the matter."

"I wouldn't want him if he was dipped in chocolate and studded with almonds," Cleo informed her, head high.

He smiled condescendingly. "I can, of course, understand your contempt of me. My behavior last night was unconscionable. I can only say in my defense that I was misled."

"By your own desires, my lad," Lady Agnes declared. "Don't you dare imply that my Cleo would flaunt herself at you."

Cleo waited for him to protest, but he shook his head with apparent sorrow. "No, Miss Renfield tried to tell me the truth. I refused to listen. I was so sure that damnable gossip was true."

"Hell and damnation," Hector said obligingly from where he was perched on the mantel.

Cutter started, and Cleo hid a grin.

"Never mind him," Lady Agnes said with an imperious wave. "What about this gossip? Who's talking behind my Cleo's back?"

Cleo was certain she knew exactly who, but she refused to name her. Major Cutter shook his head.

"A very good friend of Miss Renfield's, who revealed the information to me in strictest confidence, and rather tearfully too, I might add."

Cleo rolled her eyes, imagining the scene Eloise must have enacted. She would have been pathetic in her false loyalty. Small wonder the major had been convinced enough of the story's truth to try to trap Cleo.

"She was rather convincing," Major Cutter continued. "And I fear she will convince others. The safest thing for all is if Cleo marries me, and quickly, before Miss Rutherford can spread the tale further."

"Miss Rutherford?" Cleo cried. "Marlys Rutherford told you that story?"

He nodded. "And you know others will believe her, particularly when it becomes known that you were alone with me at a gaming hell."

Cleo's mind whirled. Marlys? How could Marlys have even known? Had she been listening outside the door that day when Cleo had told Miss Martingale? Had she been listening the day Eloise Watkin had called? But even if she had known, how could she have betrayed Cleo? She could not believe the girl had been so overcome with jealousy that she would jeopardize their friendship. There was only one way to find out. Cleo whirled, intent on returning upstairs to her friend, only to find Marlys in the corridor behind her.

"It *was* you!" Cleo declared.

Marlys put up her head. "I told you the Season is a battle. You use your beauty as a weapon. You cannot blame me for using the weapons I possess."

"What, lies and gossip?" Cleo demanded.

"No," Marlys snapped, "intelligence and cunning. Something happened in the hayloft that day. If you would not speak of it, I certainly had a right to learn the truth another way. How else could I compete against Eloise Watkin?"

"You see what I mean?" Major Cutter asked, coming to the door. Marlys took a step back from him. "She is well respected, Cleo. You must marry me if you wish to save your family from dishonor."

"No, that was not my intent!" Marlys protested. When neither Cleo nor Cutter responded, she turned and darted for the door.

Cleo could not stop her. She would never have thought Marlys could be so unfeeling. Now she wondered how many other things the girl had told her had been wrong or been designed to warp her thinking. Indeed, it very much looked as if she had been misjudging Eloise Watkin all along.

"You see how it is," Cutter pressed as Marlys left the door open behind her. "You have no choice but to marry me."

Cleo sighed, suddenly very tired. "Yes, Major Cutter, I have. Tell your lies to whomever you please. I am done with you, sirrah."

Cutter barked a laugh. "Your family will see it otherwise." He turned to look at Lady Agnes. "Surely you understand the wisdom of my proposal, madam."

"Poppycock!" Lady Agnes declared.

"Clever girl!" Hector shouted, spreading his wings and fluttering to the carpet.

"My sentiments exactly," Leslie said from the doorway.

Twenty-One

Cutter stared at him. Just so the villain would have no doubt where her loyalty lay, Cleo stepped back beside Leslie and crossed her arms over her chest.

"You will not protect her, Hastings," Cutter threatened. "You know the truth of what she is."

"I certainly do," Leslie replied. "She is a cozening little sprout, and I would like nothing better than to be her husband, if she'll have me."

Cleo threw her arms about him and felt his encircle her. His embrace felt so warm, so safe, so right, that she was amazed she had never realized before how much she loved him. "Oh, Leslie, of course I'll have you!"

Leslie grinned down at her, then raised his head long enough to glare at Cutter. "You heard the lady, you dastard. You cannot touch her as the Marchioness of Hastings. Now, take yourself off before I do what I've wanted to do for days and break your blasted nose."

Cutter's jaw was tense, but Hector sprang for him, hissing. The major swept out of the house as hurriedly as Marlys had. Only he slammed the door behind him.

Lady Agnes cackled and Hector shrieked. Leslie ignored them both. "Are you certain, Sprout? You said I had to ask you again when I was sober, and I swear to you the only drug in my body this morning is my desire to kiss you."

"I am certain," Cleo replied. "But are you free to ask? What happened with Eloise?"

"We agreed to part friends. She wasn't the one spreading the gossip, by the way." He glanced at Lady Agnes, who was watching them with as great an interest as was the parrot. "If we might have a moment alone, Godmother? Your bird has a notoriously big mouth."

"I wasn't the one who taught him to swear," Lady Agnes replied, but she called to Hector and he scurried after her out of the room. Leslie returned his gaze to Cleo, and kept his arms about her, to her great satisfaction.

"I think I understand about Eloise now," he said. "She told me a little of the story last night. She was the girl in the hayloft, wasn't she, not you?"

Cleo nodded. "Yes. I promised Miss Martingale, our head mistress, never to tell."

"Miss Martingale was wrong, I think. Eloise became the victim because of her silence. She was never allowed to tell her father. She has lived with the fear that the world will find out and censure her."

"I think I begin to understand as well. She wants to be loved. That's why she behaves the way she does, Leslie. She's trying to get someone, anyone, to prove that he loves her, even when she's not convinced anyone can. Oh, the poor dear! I've been awful to her."

"You've both been through a great deal," Leslie said softly, moving a hand to stroke her curls. "What I wouldn't give to find out who started this dastardly gossip."

"Marlys Rutherford," Cleo told him. "She admitted it just now. I would not have thought it of her. But perhaps she's hurting as much as we are. I'm learning nothing good can come from hiding your feelings." She gazed up at him again, noting that his dear half smile was in evidence. "I don't want to hide my feelings, Les. I'm not sure I could hide them. I love you."

Leslie looked at her as if he doubted he'd heard her correctly. She tried to give him a little shake, but he was much too solid for her. "Oh, don't you see, Leslie, it's been you all along? It simply took Major Cutter's disagreeable proposal to shock me into realizing it."

He gazed at her a moment more, then he swooped her up into his arms, turning her in a circle that only made her dizzy. When she laughed, he kissed her so deeply that she was very nearly breathless by the time he finished.

Leslie could not believe his luck. She loved him. It was more than he could have hoped. His heart swelled in his chest. "Cleo Renfield," he declared, "I love you. You are impertinent, incorrigible, and completely irredeemable."

"Quite right," she replied, snuggling brazenly against him in a way that assured him of her devotion. He wanted nothing more than to carry her farther into the house and kiss her until they both were senseless. But perhaps they already were. All he knew was that he would not rest until she was his. He turned with her still in his arms and started for the door.

There was a sound from behind, and Mr. Cowls made his way past them to open the door, as if he generally assisted gentlemen in carrying his mistress's goddaughter from the house.

"If I may be of assistance, Lord Hastings?" he murmured with a smile.

Leslie grinned. The old fox had finally used his title. Perhaps that was because he finally deserved it. Cleo giggled as he swept her down the steps. Behind them came a gasp, and turning, they beheld Lady Agnes at the door.

"Leslie Petersborough!" Her voice rang in the street. "Where do you think you're going with my goddaughter?"

"Gretna Green," Leslie replied with a grin. Cleo squealed in delight. Lady Agnes cackled with glee.

"Electra and Andromeda will be beside themselves," she predicted. "Mr. Cowls, fetch me my carriage. I want to see their faces when I tell them."

"I wish I could join you," Leslie commiserated as Cleo hugged him happily. "Unfortunately, Cleo has a distressing tendency to get the two of us into trouble. I thought that since she has agreed she loves me, I'd better not let her out of my arms until we're safely married."

And he didn't, and then not for a very long time afterward.

Dear Reader,

I hope you enjoyed the story of Cleo and Leslie. Leslie has been waiting a long time for his story, ever since the publication of my first Regency romance, *The Unflappable Miss Fairchild,* in 1998. Leslie was the lovable sidekick in that book, which tells the story of how his friend, the infamous Chas Prestwick, met his lady love. Leslie was so lovable, in fact, that other readers have consistently begged for him to have a book of his own.

Eloise Watkin may not be as lovable but I'd like to see her have a happy ending. Look for her in my August 2002 book from Zebra Regency. I promise to give Jareth Darby his long overdue comeuppance.

Some of the other characters in *The Irredeemable Miss Renfield* have also appeared in other novels. Lady Agnes first began arguing for me in *The Marquis's Kiss,* which tells of the romance between her nephew Thomas and the Original Margaret Munroe. The ball at Almack's where Cleo and Leslie first get reintroduced is also featured in *The Incomparable Miss Compton,* where you learn who Lord Malcolm Breckonridge finally chose for a bride. Finally, Leslie's father, the dapper Harold Petersborough, Marquis of Hastings, was featured in a number of my books, including *The Unflappable Miss Fairchild* ("pluck to the backbone, that's my girl"), *The Blue-*

stocking on His Knee (he never did recruit Kevin Whattling), and "The June Bride Conspiracy" in *His Blushing Bride* (yes, he ended up catching and keeping The Skull). I hated to see him go, but it was time for Leslie to shoulder the responsibilities of the marquisate. Rest easy, old friend, things are in good hands.

I love to hear from readers, and, as the publication of this story attests, I listen! Feel free to write to me care of Kensington or via e-mail at regina@reginascott.com. My web page is at www.reginascott.com. And please look for my next book, *Lord Borin's Secret Love,* coming in May 2002 from Zebra Regency.

God bless!
Regina Scott

More Zebra Regency Romances

The Queen of
Romance

Cassie Edwards

BOOK YOUR PLACE ON OUR WEBSITE AND MAKE THE READING CONNECTION!

We've created a customized website just for our very special readers, where you can get the inside scoop on everything that's going on with Zebra, Pinnacle and Kensington books.

When you come online, you'll have the exciting opportunity to:

- View covers of upcoming books

- Read sample chapters

- Learn about our future publishing schedule (listed by publication month *and author*)

- Find out when your favorite authors will be visiting a city near you

- Search for and order backlist books from our online catalog

- Check out author bios and background information

- Send e-mail to your favorite authors

- Meet the Kensington staff online

- Join us in weekly chats with authors, readers and other guests

- Get writing guidelines

- AND MUCH MORE!

**Visit our website at
http://www.kensingtonbooks.com**